KWIK KRIMES

KWIK KRIMES

EDITED BY OTTO PENZLER

Printed in the United States of America.

Published by Thomas & Mercer
PO Box 400818
Las Vegas, NV 89140

ISBN-13: 9781612183008
ISBN-10: 161218300X
Library of Congress Control Number: 2013900001

For Ian Kern

With thanks for making this book better.
And for the amazing job you
do every day.

Contents

INTRODUCTION

It doesn't take very long to commit a crime. A bullet will travel the distance between the shooter and the victim in a very small fraction of a second. The sudden stroke of a knife doesn't take much longer. Bank robbers—those who aren't complete imbeciles—know that there is a two-minute rule: from the time they start a robbery, the maximum time they have to take what they came for and get away before the police arrive is 120 seconds flat.

It takes longer to tell the story of a crime. Mystery novels generally run about three hundred pages, though many are much longer and quite a few are noticeably less than that.

The good ones are complex. Not only is the crime described, but there is often analysis of how it was done, why, where, and when. The perpetrators are usually described, briefly as to physical appearance, and in greater depth as to psychological makeup, particularly in recent years when detective stories became less a puzzle to determine *who* did it but more an examination of *why* the crime was done. Other major characters are also introduced to the reader: the victim, the detective (professional, private, or amateur), and the other players who serve the valuable function of throwing readers off the path to a final understanding of exactly what happened and why.

The great Golden Age writer of "impossible crime" stories, John Dickson Carr, maintained that the short story was the proper form of the mystery story—that the crime and its solution could easily be presented in twenty or thirty pages, and the rest was just padding.

So how long must a novel be to be called a novel? Too short and it's called a novella. Too long and it's called a bore and it doesn't get published, the occasional exceptions aside.

And how long must a short story be to tell the story it wants to tell? I have commissioned many stories over the years for a variety of anthologies and other publishing projects. Authors customarily have three questions: How long do you want it, when do you want it, and how much are you paying? The answers to the latter two questions have various answers, but to the first I usually suggest a "normal" length of twenty to thirty pages. Actually, being a smart mouth, what I usually say is, "Start the story, tell the story, and when you've finished telling it, stop writing."

As you already know, this collection is different from other anthologies. As the series editor of the annual *Best American Mystery Stories of the Year*, I have had brought to my attention over the past several years that a lot of interesting fiction is being published in various e-zines—electronic magazines with material available exclusively online.

Without the normal constraints of a printed book, which can be neither too long nor too short, the editors of these innovative sites have the freedom to run stories of any length at all. Many are very, very short, and would almost always be unsuitable for traditional print magazines or books. Some of these stories, I further learned, show remarkable creativity on the part of the authors who produce them.

It seemed a good idea, then, to collect a lot of these nasty little tales and assemble them in a book. It is tempting to draw the analogy of a meal made of tapas, lots of little dishes of wonderful variety, rather than a single giant portion of one dish, however delicious it may be.

This compilation went a little further than plucking the best short-short stories off the Internet, however. I thought it would be fascinating to see what authors could conjure if given the specific assignment of producing a mystery, crime, or suspense story of no more than one thousand words.

The range of style, plot, tone, voice, sensibility, and characters assembled here will astonish the reader. I didn't think it possible to have this kind of variety, given the extraordinary restriction of so few words in which to tell a complete story, but here is the evidence that I was wrong.

Most of the stories, not surprisingly, are criminal adventures rather than detective tales because, let's face it, it is hard to hide clues and have enough reasonable suspects in a total of about four pages. However, having said that, I must prepare you for some remarkable revelations in these pages that will turn your expectations upside down. Be prepared, too, to be at the edge of your seat as these hugely talented writers create the kind of suspense that a less accomplished practitioner would need ten times as many pages to concoct.

Please indulge me for a second while I express my gratitude to Ian Kern and Nat Sobel, both of whom who did a lot of reading and made so many excellent recommendations of stories for this collection.

Otto Penzler
New York
December 2012

LAMBS OF GOD

Patricia Abbott

The first time Kyle Murmer's mother tried to kill him, he was nine. But he couldn't remember a day when he didn't worry about it. At night he asked God to smite her, but he had no hope this would happen, and it did not.

"Let me see your teeth."

Her personal supply of dental tools twinkled fiercely in the transparent case on the top medicine chest shelf. Her left hand held his chin as the right one forced his mouth open.

"People not much older than you have lost all their teeth."

The desire to bite down on her fingers was nearly overpowering.

On the days when she got up early enough for a frenzied completion of household chores, she hadn't taken her medication. On good mornings, the ones when the perphenazine made her sleep late, his father fixed them a bowl of cereal and they tiptoed out of the house, sharing an embarrassed smile.

She was waiting for him when he came home from school in October of fourth grade. Hair curled, makeup applied perfectly, neatly dressed in a khaki skirt and white blouse, she wrapped panty hose around his neck. It happened with such speed, he wondered if she'd practiced it on the back of a kitchen chair.

"Where have you been?"

Her nails were inches from his face, and beads of spit, scented with dental wash, shot into his eyes. He wasn't surprised. His life so far seemed exactly like a place where such things happened. A place where mothers might practice lassoing kids.

"At school."

"Liar," she said, dragging him around the kitchen by his neck. "The devil has you in his grip."

"I *was* at school," he repeated, trying to wait out this bad stretch.

That's what his father always called it—a bad stretch. Kyle and his father were always waiting for the other shoe to fall—another phrase his dad used a lot.

"They called and said you weren't there. Said your desk was empty, no coat on your hook."

"That was on Monday." His mouth was so dry, his voice scratched it.

Her eyes looked like the dead blooms on an African violet, and a sort of eggy smell began to radiate from her mouth.

"You forgot to call the attendance line, and they called here. On Monday," he repeated.

Her grip on the panty hose loosened. Then she was sitting at the table, collapsed and sobbing. "Don't tell your father. I wanted to lift you up to God." She raised her arms, and he tried hard not to flinch.

But he did tell his father; how could he not?

"Let me see your neck." His father ran a light finger over the bruises. "Your mother means well, but she gets confused. Must've been a hormonal thing. Maybe the thought of having another kid just broke her. Probably flushed her meds."

Another kid—no one had told Kyle. In fact, he understood none of what his father had said but knew he'd have to be even more careful.

His father also told Kyle he'd found signs she tried to kill the baby.

At the Church of the Living God, even birth-control devices were forbidden—an impediment to the holy duty of women to bear as many children as possible. Children were the lambs of God. Abortion would mean expulsion.

When Kyle was sixteen, his mother attacked him while he slept. Her fists were hammers on his head. In her pocket was a small knife. She tried to carve Aramaic words into his forehead.

"The devil will flee once you're marked." She'd flattened a crumpled piece of paper with the proper marks on his bedside table. A flashlight shone on it.

His mother was jailed for several weeks, and he went to school with two strange marks on his forehead. Nobody asked about them. Such things were not unheard of at his school.

Kyle began college in Ann Arbor and never came home if he could help it.

"I have to work at the library over the break," he told them. "I need to study for finals—I'm helping out at my church." The last was a lie. He'd given God a chance and been turned down.

"Kyle." It was his sister, Jolene, whispering on the phone. "Mom thinks I'm having sex. I don't—I don't even know what having sex means."

Lambs of God didn't need such information. Information led to experimentation, ruin.

"I'm locked in my room. She's looking for a way in."

He borrowed a car and drove home. His mother was in the garage, looking through his father's tools.

"Kyle," she said. "Can you help me find something to jimmy a lock? I hate to use a blowtorch. The wood's oak. Maybe we can remove it with a screwdriver."

Her eyes were fixed and dull, dead moths again. "Jolene doesn't understand I'm trying to lift her up to God." She looked at him closely. "Like I did with you." She smiled beatifically.

He put out his hand, and she gave him the blowtorch. He used it without hesitation, watching her cheap acrylic blouse go up in a flash, her face melt away. Her screams seemed inconsequential coming from a black hole as they did.

She was cast alive into a lake of fire burning with brimstone.

He didn't try to deny it when the police arrived, didn't try to run or hide. He'd heard about Judgment Day often enough to recognize it when it came.

THIS STORY WAS FIRST PUBLISHED IN *SPINETINGLER*.

Patricia Abbott is the author of the e-book Monkey Justice *(Snubnose Press) and co-editor of the anthology* Discount Noir *(Untreed Reads). More than one hundred of her stories have appeared in print and online outlets. She won a Derringer Award in 2009 for her flash story "My Hero" and has had three stories included in Ed Gorman's yearly crime-fiction anthologies. She lives outside Detroit.*

THE DAY AFTER TOMORROW

Richard Aleas

It wasn't the rain, Jack knew, that would keep them from going into town. Mother would say that was why, and Father would nod behind his newspaper, and Celia would believe it because she was only seven and believed anything you told her. But the rain had nothing to do with it.

Jack got up from the table and went to the window. Buckets of the stuff were being flung against the glass. The waterspout on the side of the roof was pouring like a faucet. Dark clouds made everything gray.

But rain doesn't last forever, not even a storm like this one. By the day after tomorrow, it would be gone. Then they'd roll the tent out again and bring the elephants and horses out of the traveling cages they were cooped up in. They'd string the high wire and hook the trapezes and lay the nets and set the harnesses. And then Kenny would take his place behind the barred window of the ticket booth, and he'd thumb off tickets one by one to each kid who showed up with three dollar bills in his fist.

Would he wonder why Jack didn't show up? Oh, probably not. After the scene Mother had made—in front of everyone, in front of everyone!—he'd probably be glad not to see Jack in the crowd.

Jack kicked the wall, as hard as he could.

They'd promised. He'd x-ed off the days on the calendar they'd given him for Christmas, had watched as the crisscross of ink grew, snaking from one week into the next, toward the last day of the month. The last day before the tents were tucked away into the monster hauler that would follow slowly as the performers' vans lumbered onto the highway and out of town. It was all Jack had asked for, for Christmas. It was what they'd said he'd get.

Jack closed his bedroom door and hung a metal coat hanger on the inside knob. It'd clatter if anyone turned the knob.

He opened the closet and knelt inside, in front of his toy chest.

Mother had screamed. That's how Jack had known she was there. He hadn't seen her; he'd been looking at the green and blue woman inked into the flesh of Kenny's arm. The woman had moved as Kenny drew, her upraised arm waving from side to side.

And then the scream. Were there words, or just the sound of it? There were words later, many words, words for Kenny that Jack had never heard his mother use and words for Jack, too, shouted as she pulled him out through the flap of the tent and stood him in the sunlight, surrounded by kids from school, and rubbed at the ballpoint ink Kenny had put onto his arm.

That night it had started to rain.

Jack unpacked the top layer of toys and pawed through the folded sweaters underneath. He pulled out the box he found there.

It was a flat box that said *Brunckhorst's* on it. The picture was of green leaves, and the box had a minty smell to it. Jack had no idea what had come in it originally.

Before opening the box, Jack turned his left arm palm up. Kenny's half-completed drawing was still there in ghost-lines on the red surface, rubbed raw by Mother's scrubcloth.

Comet will take that off, she'd said.

Celia had stood in the doorway watching, three fingers in her mouth and her eyes showing that she wasn't sure if she was seeing something bad or something good.

Where had Father been? In the living room behind his newspaper. He's your son, he'd said. Jack had heard the pages turning while the chlorine scoured his skin.

His arm was still raw, but it didn't hurt very much anymore. And under the pink, still visible if you looked hard, he could see the faint lines of blue, the half-finished woman with her upraised arm.

The Brunckhorst's box was packed with Kleenex, which Jack carefully placed next to him on the floor. He took out the knife that lay underneath, held it by its heavy handle the way Kenny had showed him when they'd cut the tent's binding cords together.

The day after tomorrow.

The rain will stop, Jack thought, and I will go to the circus.

The pseudonym of an American mystery writer and editor, Richard Aleas was nominated for both the Edgar Allan Poe Award and the Shamus Award for his first novel, Little Girl Lost, *and won the Shamus for his second,* Songs of Innocence, *which was described by the* Washington Post *as "devastating...an instant classic." The author lives in New York City.*

HANSEL, GRETEL, AND THE WITCH

Gary Alexander

The station manager called the witch into his office. He couldn't procrastinate any longer. "We, uh, have some scheduling issues."

"*Cauldron Cookery* isn't doing well?"

The station manager realized the witch's black cape and peaked black cap was only a costume. The wart on her nose, too. So why did she seem so natural in the role?

"*Cauldron Cookery* isn't doing terribly as far as niche cooking shows go, but your ratings are flat."

"You're canceling me," the witch snarled.

The station manager flinched, then lied. "No, no. Not canceling. You'll tape your last segment tomorrow and go on hiatus."

"Hiatus. Yeah, right. Tell me what I did wrong."

"Well, some of your dishes do have ingredients that are hard to find."

"For instance?"

"Eye of newt."

"I explained that you can substitute cilantro. Who's bumping me?"

"We're expanding Hansel and Gretel to a full hour."

"Oh, please! Their *Gingerbread Magic* is mind-numbing."

"Their popularity is growing. The kids will be hosting *Sugar 'n' Spice*, too. Tomorrow we'll do a pilot episode. They'll be making confectionery delights from around the world. Cupcakes are hot. They'll do a lot of cupcakes."

The station manager flinched again as the witch stormed out and slammed the door. She passed the set where Hansel and Gretel were preparing for a taping.

"How are you kiddies?" she asked sweetly.

"Good, ma'am," they answered in unison.

"What's for today?"

"A gingerbread roof," Hansel said. "For last week's gingerbread house."

"With glazed roofing and wafer shutters," Gretel said.

Hansel's and Gretel's real names were Chip and Susie. They were cherubic and adorable, him in lederhosen, a budding Hitler Youth type, and her in a ruffled peasant dress. They made the witch sick. And weren't there child-labor laws?

"Oh, that sounds positively wonderful. You do so many delightful things with gingerbread."

The witch went home and phoned Phil, her fifth ex-husband. "I need your help."

Phil carried a torch for her the size of the Statue of Liberty's. "Anything, Mary Lou."

"My career's in shambles," she wailed. "You're my knight in shining armor. Come over now."

Phil was also a major-appliance repairman, having learned the trade in the state penitentiary.

"But that's 220 voltage," Phil said at Mary Lou's condo. "You're asking me to booby-trap the stove and electrocute them?"

"They booby-trapped my career," she cried. "I have an image problem. Will you do it?"

"Okay, but how do you expect me to turn your TV kitchen into a death trap?"

"The range tops are in the front counter, closest to the camera. The oven is built into a side wall. It's part of the set, too, so the rear is completely concealed. I cook on the stovetops, and they bake their stupid gingerbread monstrosities in the oven."

"How do you get me into the station?"

Mary Lou presented a yellow-toothed grin. "How'd you like to be in showbiz?"

Next morning, Mary Lou introduced Phil to the station manager. "My new assistant."

The station manager gulped.

On the set Phil said, "Mary Lou, the cameras make me nervous. I have mug-shot flashbacks."

"You'll be fine. How long will it take?"

"Not long. I know that model oven. They've had recalls for bad junction blocks. Behind the fake wall, I remove a screw from one, lay it there like it worked loose and fell out, and rest a hot wire on the range chassis. Turn the oven on and touch any metal part, like the handle. Zap!"

"Do it when the stagehands go on break. I have to tape first so the little darlings will have all the time they need for their precious masterpieces."

Mary Lou tied an apron on Phil. "I'm making my famous Sorceress Stew. Dice and chop and peel, my galley slave."

The crew went out for coffee before they rolled tape, giving Phil and his screwdriver plenty of time.

He was uncomfortable during *Cauldron Cookery* and spilled a bowl of diced carrots on the floor as he tried to dump them into the bubbling kettle. Everybody had a chuckle.

The witch mugged for the camera, cackling and saying, "The man's all thumbs. I dearly hope neither of them land in my stew."

Phil dropped and broke a dish.

"Wet hands," he said.

"That's the third," Mary Lou said. "Relax."

"Easy for you to say."

Hansel and Gretel appeared as Mary Lou and Phil sat at a table offstage, eating her stew.

Gretel opened the oven, peered inside, and shut it.

"Nothing happened," Mary Lou whispered.

Phil said, "It's gotta be turned on."

The witch smiled. "Ah, Gretel just set it to preheat."

The station manager rushed up to Phil and Mary Lou. "I have fantastic news! The station owner watched the taping in the control room. He loved you two together. You had him in stitches. He's giving *Cauldron Cookery* a better slot and a full hour."

After he was gone, Mary Lou whispered to Phil, "Quick, fix what you did after I turn the oven off."

"I can't," Phil said. "There's no time."

She went into the kitchen to turn the oven off and slipped on diced carrots and dishware shards. Instinctively she grabbed what she could on the way down—the oven handle.

The station lights flickered.

❧

Gary Alexander has written thirteen novels, including Loot, *fourth in the series featuring Buster Hightower, which will appear in 2013.* Disappeared, *the first, has been optioned to Universal Pictures. He has written more than 150 short stories and sold travel articles to six major dailies.* Dragon Lady, *his Vietnam War novel, is being published by Istoria Books.*

PREPARATIONS

Tasha Alexander

Precision was essential. There was nothing more important in a lady's life during the London season. Every gown, every piece of jewelry, every hair on her head must be perfect or disaster could strike. Disaster in the form of no marriage proposal. Disaster in the form of forced retreat to the country or, worse, to Egypt, where Shepherd's Hotel might provide a groom willing to overlook failure in England in exchange for an adequate bank account. Gwendolyn Banks had suffered no such indignities. She had attended to every detail of her appearance, took care to be charming, but not too charming, danced like a dream, and had paid rapt attention to every word from her suitors. Her debut was a smashing success, culminating with her engagement and marriage to a gentleman of fortune and, perhaps more important, heir to the Duke of Highgate.

After marriage Gwendolyn did not allow her standards to slack. Perfection was her daily goal. She would not be one of those women who grew matronly too soon, and her husband's friends frequently commented to her how lucky he was. She would bestow upon them a smile, demure and flirty at the same time, but never let her eyes linger for a moment too long. Gwendolyn was an ideal wife. Or so they thought at first.

On this particular day, she took extra care dressing. Her finest lingerie, purchased in Paris during her honeymoon trip, covered the bruises down her back, black-and-blue, purple, and green changed for silk and Burano lace. Her maid laced her prettiest corset so tightly she could hardly breathe, but Gwendolyn welcomed the feeling of a pain she could control. She had debated the choice of gown for hours the previous night when, unable to sleep, she had flung dress after dress onto the floor after rejecting them. Red was too obvious. Blue too placid. Rose was right, a pink of the palest shade, the embodiment of innocence and sweet beauty.

Gwendolyn stepped into her slim silk shoes. She went through boxes of kid gloves before she found a pair in just the right shade of cream, the leather so thin they could not be worn again. They would come to pieces when removed, which seemed fitting to Gwendolyn, who turned her attention to her jewelry box. The suite of diamonds from her mother-in-law would be too flashy for a garden party. The rubies were too obvious a choice with rose. She slung long ropes of pearls, a gift from her parents on her eighteenth birthday, two weeks before her wedding, over her head and studied her reflection.

Elegant and refined. She clipped on the matching earrings and held out her arm so that her maid could fasten an intricate bracelet around her wrist. Her hat was the only easy choice that day. Its brim was wider than Gwendolyn's shoulders, and its crown was covered with an enormous mass of ostrich feathers. The hatpins were next. She would need three to hold the monstrous creation in place. She first chose two relatively plain ivory ones and then her very favorite, a swirl of gold and precious stones handmade in Florence that was long enough to go through both the hat and the pile of hair on top of her head.

Hat firmly in place and gloves pulled on, Gwendolyn descended the stairs to her husband, who ushered her into their waiting carriage. They made a striking couple and were both much in demand from the moment they stepped into the party, but Gwendolyn knew what the gossips said, that in private she was frigid and icy, denying her husband affection. They speculated there might never be an heir to the Dukedom of Highgate. Yet Gwendolyn was so lovely and so kind and so gracious in every other capacity that they adored her nonetheless. She smiled, knowing she would not have to tolerate the overcrowded crush of the garden for long, and knowing that today, unlike so many other days, she would not object to being removed to a more private environ.

It happened as it always did. He paid little attention to her at first beyond the usual family duties, but circled back to her when he had grown tired of his friends and their wives. He pulled her aside and complimented her appearance. He took notice of every carefully chosen detail and reprimanded her for any perceived flaws. There were always flaws, and because of them, he would be forced to take her to a hidden copse, or a small room, or a back staircase where they would not be disturbed, and he would remind her that his son deserved a better wife. He would cajole her for a bit, then his hands would begin to wander and grope. He would raise her skirts. He would cover her mouth, though she had long ago learned not to scream. When he finished, he would bend her forward and strike her eight times with the walking stick he carried. The bruises it left would have to be hidden. Until they faded, her bedroom door would have to remain locked. This time, especially.

Gwendolyn made no sound as he beat her and braced herself for what she knew would come next. He took her in his arms and kissed her, rocking back and forth, imploring her to be a better wife. Today she did something she never had before. She kissed him back, and while he reacted with delight to this, she reached up, pulling the long Florentine pin from her hat. She flung one arm tight around his grizzled neck, bringing him closer, and felt for his ear. The pin went in with ease at first, but required more pressure as it went deeper. Gwendolyn had no difficulty finding the necessary strength. Her father-in-law crumpled to the ground.

Gwendolyn returned her pin to her hat, smoothed her skirts, and returned to the party, the picture of wifely perfection.

Highgate had a new duke.

Tasha Alexander attended the University of Notre Dame, where she signed on as an English major (with a concentration in medieval studies) in order to have a legitimate excuse for spending all her time reading. Her work has been nominated for numerous awards and has been translated into more than a dozen languages. She and her husband, novelist Andrew Grant, divide their time between Chicago and the United Kingdom.

THUNDER AT THE HORIZON

Charles Ardai

In the alley behind the Wigwam Club, Dolores bent low to shield her cigarette from the night breezes. It took two matches to get it lit. She hadn't bothered to put on a robe before stepping outside. None of the girls ever did. It would smear your war paint and crush your feathers, and anyway the nights were plenty warm. It was one good thing about Arizona. The only good thing.

She took a long drag on the cigarette and turned when she heard the fire-exit door open behind her.

"Your third break tonight, doll. You think I pay you to come out here and smoke?" Roman came forward, thumbing open the button on his suit jacket.

"The boys needed some cooling-down time. So did I."

"The *boys* are our customers. We don't want them cooled down. We want them hotted up."

"So why don't you take your clothes off and dance for them, Roman, if you want to make them happy so bad? Maybe you'd like it when they grabbed your ass."

He was within touching distance now, and he laid a meaty palm against her cheek, patting gently. "The mouth on you," he said quietly. "I don't let anybody talk to me like that."

Dolores let out a stream of smoke out of the corner of her mouth. She didn't bother to cover her breasts, and he didn't bother to look at them. It was nothing for either of them, just the product they sold to keep the dollars coming in.

The door opened again. The man who staggered through it was Roman's size—six foot plus—but thinner and younger and much less sober. He put up one arm to steady himself against the brick wall of the club.

"Where'd you go to," he said, his words slurred and thick. "You're s'posed to…to…dance." This boy was no more than twenty, and Dolores's bare breasts were not nothing to him. He stared fixedly at them as he spoke.

"You see, doll?" Roman said, and swatted her on the rear. "Your public awaits."

She took another drag on her cigarette, thought seriously about quitting, but not for long. The end of the month was just two days away, and with it would come an envelope, a neat white envelope with nothing written on the outside, slipped under her door by her landlord. The envelope would contain a request for eleven hundred forty-three dollars and eighty cents, her rent for this month and last, plus interest. She didn't have it, and she wouldn't have it if she danced here two more nights. But she'd be closer to having it than if she didn't.

She looked up at Roman looming over her, a leer spread across his swarthy face, and then over at the boy by the door, the fly of his jeans unbuttoned, the bulge beneath straining at the fabric. One day. One day she'd do more than quit. She thought about the outfit she was wearing: the paint and headdress of a warrior. For an instant she imagined herself astride a palomino, gun barrel in hand, like the Indian brave whose costume she wore. She imagined chasing these two men down on the open desert plains, riding hard behind them till they dropped to their knees and begged, exhausted, for her mercy.

Or, hell, forget the horse and war paint. The modern equivalent would do fine: a semiautomatic pistol in the front seat of her Pontiac. She pictured herself having a smoke and waiting for them to show their faces at the door. Then, *one, two*—a bullet for each.

One day. But first she had rent to pay.

"All right, big boy," she said, dropping her cigarette in the dirt and grinding it beneath her bare heel. She pressed her palm to the crotch of the boy's jeans as she passed. "Let's give you what you came to see."

◆◆

Charles Ardai has received the Edgar Allan Poe Award and the Shamus Award for his crime fiction, as well as recognition as founder and editor of the Hard Case Crime line of novels, whose authors have included Stephen King, Mickey Spillane, Ed McBain, Lawrence Block, and Donald E. Westlake. He is also a writer and consulting producer on the TV series Haven.

FORTUNE

Erik Arneson

"You always smell like french fries, Putter. I can't take it anymore."

"Give me a few minutes, Nat. I'll shower."

"It doesn't matter if you shower, baby. It's in your pores or something. When you get out of the shower, you smell like Axe-scented french fries. Not an improvement."

"I'll scrub, I'll do, I'll...what do they call it...I'll...exfornicate."

A grin from Natalie. "Exfoliate. Look, I love you. I just can't stand the odor right now. Take a few days off, you'll smell great again. Call me."

With that, she was gone.

Putter's buddy Eli had come up with the idea to steal barrels of used cooking oil from restaurants. And Putter had to admit it was good money despite the fact it made him stink and he didn't understand why people wanted to buy the stuff. Something about biodiesel fuel. Eli said even jets can use it. Crazy shit.

But if the side effect was not getting any from his girl? No money was worth that.

Although...it was nearly eleven o'clock on Sunday night, and in rural Lebanon County, Pennsylvania, that meant the restaurants were all closed. Maybe one last big score before he found a no-stink way to earn some cash.

Putter grabbed his cell and dialed. "Eli? Hey, it's me…"

It turned out to be a great night, a dozen barrels from seven restaurants—all full and all with oil clean enough to earn serious cash. Probably a couple thousand bucks total.

"Fortune's just a day away," Eli said as they lifted the final barrel into the plain white box truck, a beast of a vehicle that he originally bought for what turned out to be a remarkably unsuccessful attempt at a legitimate moving business.

With his battery-powered lantern, Putter climbed into the back where his job was to make sure none of the barrels tipped over. Eli lowered the door but left it unlatched, always did, so Putter wouldn't spaz.

Minutes later Putter heard what sounded like a police siren. Eli pulled the truck to a stop on the side of the road.

Slamming his fist on the metal wall behind Eli's head, Putter yelled, "What the hell? That a cop?"

Eli yelled back, "Don't panic! I'll handle this."

Putter panicked.

He had done time once, just a few months but long enough to know he couldn't handle going back.

"Shit, shit, shit," he muttered. "Shit."

He turned off the lantern and tried not to make any noise.

Officer Bill Evans approached the driver's side door. "License and registration, please."

"Of course, Officer. I have them right here." Evans could tell the driver was struggling to keep his voice calm.

"What's in the back of the truck?"

"It's…it's empty." The driver handed him the documents.

"Stay here," Evans said.

Walking back to his patrol car, Evans knew he had one for the chief county detective. Apparently some yahoos had been stealing used cooking oil from restaurants. Local police departments had been notified earlier in the week to look out for an unmarked delivery truck, probably smelling like french fries. This truck reeked.

A rhythmic noise from inside the truck caught Evans's attention. He pounded on the backdoor, yelling, "Police! Who's there?"

Sudden silence. Putter realized he had been oblivious to his own foot tap-tap-tapping on the floor. His body tensed. "Shit," he whispered.

The cop banged on the door again.

"I'm opening this door! Whoever's inside, I want to see your hands in the air!"

Putter said to himself, "I can't go back. I can't…"

He knew he had to run for it, at least give himself a chance to escape. He crouched in the dark, ready to sprint.

As soon as the door started rolling up, Putter ran forward. His knee hit one barrel, and then he lost his balance and slammed headfirst into another. Dizzy, he fell to the floor as the second barrel tipped over, spilling fifty-five gallons of used cooking oil all over him.

"Ah, fuck me," Putter said, losing consciousness. "I'm never getting laid again."

◆◆

THIS STORY WAS FIRST PUBLISHED IN *SHOTGUN HONEY*.

Erik Arneson lives in Pennsylvania with his wife, Elizabeth. His stories have appeared in Needle: A Magazine of Noir, Mary Higgins

Clark Mystery Magazine, *and the charity anthology* Off the Record 2: At the Movies, *in addition to the websites* Shotgun Honey, Near to the Knuckle, *and* Out of the Gutter. *He blogs at ErikArneson.com and tweets @erikarneson.*

ONE PERSON'S CLUTTER

Albert Ashforth

Detective Steve Stewart watched Eric Swanson's reaction closely as the morgue attendant silently drew back the sheet covering Peg Falkner's lifeless body. Swanson went pale, nodded, and then turned away. Sometimes people asked to ID a murder victim keel over. In Stewart's experience those are often your murderers, and all that remains is to nail down a confession.

But Swanson, though shaken, remained upright. After he'd signed the form, Stewart offered to drive him back to One Person's Clutter, Swanson's downtown memorabilia shop.

"Peg and I'd decided to marry," Swanson said as he unlocked the rear door. Inside, he ran his fingers through his thinning blond hair. He was a gangly six-one, not a bad-looking guy.

When he saw Stewart frowning at the magazines and comics piled all over the shop's back room, he smiled. "Comics, pulp magazines. When they're old, they can be worth very big bucks, hundreds of thousands sometimes."

Peg Falkner's body had been discovered the previous evening in a quiet suburb. She'd been walking her dog when she was attacked for no discernible reason by a thug who'd throttled her with a pair of pantyhose.

"Your fiancée was very attractive—"

Stewart was interrupted in midsentence by the jingle of the shop's bell, which caused Swanson to leap to his feet. "I'm expecting someone, an important collector."

The collector, a heavyset guy who'd arrived in a limo that he'd double-parked, was shouting loudly about "the detectives" as Stewart was about to leave.

Stewart turned. "I'm a detective. What's the beef?"

"No beef!" the man said impatiently. "Something else!"

Standing behind the counter, Swanson pointed his finger toward his head, indicating this collector was slightly balmy.

"Also I want actions! Actions!" the man announced. "Now!"

Leaving Swanson to his eccentric collector, Stewart decided to visit the small engineering firm where Peg had worked.

"She was a conscientious employee and a dutiful daughter," her boss said. "After her father died, she moved back with her mother. But then her mother died just two months ago."

A colleague said Peg had recently broken up with her boyfriend, but she hadn't known the guy's name.

It was already dark when Stewart parked his car down the block from Peg Falkner's home, a nicely maintained split-level.

As he approached, Stewart saw a man sitting in the cab of a battered Dodge pickup truck parked in the shadows. He flashed his badge and told the guy to climb out and take the position.

"You got a permit for this?" Stewart asked as he removed a 9 mm Beretta from the guy's pocket.

"My name's Marcus Desmond. And yeah, I have a permit." Desmond was beetle-browed, broad-shouldered, and was wearing a black leather jacket and a baseball cap turned backward. "The woman who lived in that house there, with the yellow tape in front?"

"What about her?"

"She was murdered yesterday. She was a...friend."

"Do tell." More likely, Stewart thought, this was a murderer returning to the scene and maybe intending to knock off a witness who'd seen too much.

The way Stewart now figured, Peg gave this Desmond the gate after she'd met Swanson. Desmond didn't have Swanson's looks or style—and, quite likely, any means of support.

Stewart thought the sight of a picture of Peg or even a familiar article of clothing might trigger an emotional meltdown or possibly a confession. "Let's go inside," he said.

After a tour of the first floor, Desmond said, "She wanted to sell the house, but she had to get rid of the junk in the basement first. Her father was a clutterbug, someone who could never throw anything away."

Stewart pointed the way downstairs.

In the basement, he saw Desmond hadn't exaggerated. There were toys, clothing, tools, and furniture, all dating back to Peg's father's youth. The basement was so packed he had to turn sideways to move through it.

With a handkerchief over his face to keep from choking on the dust, Stewart thanked his lucky stars that his wife was a neatness freak.

"I was going to help her," Desmond said.

"Help her how?"

"With my pickup truck. We planned to haul everything out to the city dump. Peg wanted a clean basement. She hated to come down here."

Stewart shoved aside a metal bed in the front room. "What's the sense of keeping this junk?"

Desmond shrugged. "Beats me."

The really old stuff was located at the front of the cellar, and Stewart saw someone had been in there recently.

Whoever it was had pushed aside a Schwinn bicycle and a Flexible Flyer sled in order to get behind an old wooden chest where an ancient mattress was lying on top of some cardboard cartons.

Pushing aside the mattress, Stewart saw yellow newspapers and *National Geographics* from the 1930s.

And underneath the papers and magazines Stewart saw something else: the cartons contained hundreds of Depression-era comic books, all in seemingly fine condition.

What clinched it for Stewart was the sight of Batman on the cover of *Detective Comics* and Superman on the cover of *Action Comics*. Stewart remembered the collector in Swanson's shop shouting about "detectives" and "actions"—and he was undoubtedly referring to these comics. Swanson had said comic books were valued at very big bucks.

The name of Swanson's shop was One Person's Clutter. Stewart recalled a TV show on which people brought in stuff like comic books from junk-filled basements and attics, and an expert had declared, "One person's clutter is another's bread and butter!"

"The stuff here is worth a damned fortune!" Stewart announced.

"You kiddin' me?" Desmond said.

Swanson had already concealed the comics, which Peg didn't know were valuable, beneath the mattress. But after their breakup, Swanson was desperate. He'd killed Peg, thinking he could later break into the empty house and retrieve the rare comic books.

By the next morning they had Swanson's confession.

<hr>

After serving in the army overseas, Albert Ashforth worked for two newspapers. He is the author of three books and numerous stories and articles. His recently published espionage thriller, The Rendition, *was described by one reviewer as "smoothly written, fast moving and suspenseful." He is a professor at SUNY and lives in New York City.*

FIGHTIN' MAN

N.J. Ayres

Orville Davis was a fightin' man. He'd fight a bug off a bush, a crow from a tree, a shoeshine man for the finishing rag. He'd word-war with a woman pushing a stroller who merely wanted to cross the street in front of him.

Men, now, he'd fight for real—with fists, tire irons, or, once, a Maori club embedded with abalone shell, which still carried the rusty sheen of someone's long-ago blood. The man he clobbered did not die, but the poor thing could be seen months afterward in any of the three taverns in town hoisting drinks with a hand that trembled of its own heartless accord.

Then one day when Orville Davis was holding a garage sale outside his home, the one with the roof fallen in on the back side, he had a vision. It came to him uninvited—cruelly, you might say—when a roof joist leapt out from its rightful place and aimed itself directly at a point behind Orville's right ear while Orville was bent over, laying a flat of blue tarp on the muddy patch of lawn in order to display the boat gear he wanted to sell.

At least that's what the neighbor on his south side said when police came to interview him. Cal Wilton told how he and Orville had been having a discussion over the rightful ownership of the push-type lawn mower rusting between his and Orville's shed and which on this day Orville had sought three dollars for from a passerby. The would-be buyer drove off without a thing after Cal caught a fist heaved by Orville, Orville being such a sour-tempered man. It was as if, Cal said, the heavens had enough of Orville's antics and hurled a punch of hard wind through the neighborhood; just have a look at his own tree branches down and trash cans scattered. Cal believed Orville to be dead, the way his eyes showed fish-belly white in his head when he rolled his neighbor over.

But then Orville rose up with a dopey grin, looked beyond as if into a land of golden poppies gently nodding in the breeze, and said, "Love is the only answer."

All this time his neighbor on the north side, Mrs. Miller, hastened around in her own yard, setting right articles rearranged by gusts. She observed Orville lift a hand to Cal for assistance in rising and saw Cal smack the hand away and then hustle off to his own back door, twice glancing back as if concerned that mean Orville would soon be on his trail.

"I was out again this morning to get my birdhouse, which I didn't see got flung into my hedge," Mrs. Miller said. "That's when I spied Orville there in the rose bushes." She told this to Officer Newton and his female partner Officer Nettle, two names starting with *N* on their badges about which she also made comment, to no reply.

"Did you disturb anything, touch the victim?" Officer Nettle asked.

"All them TV shows, no ma'am, you can be sure I did not. Except to roll his face out the dirt, which any kindhearted person would do."

"Then you did touch the subject," Officer Nettle said.

"Not with his hair like it is, greasy on a good day and way bad now. Alls I did was grab my glove off the top of my faucet over there and turn Orville's face out of the fertilized soil. He was good about them roses, I'll say that."

And what a face it was, as any bystander gathered on the broken sidewalk could see. Cold storage was the place for Orville Davis now, a man left in peace to fight no more.

By the wooded lot behind the houses, a boy of about twelve jumped around slaying the ghosts of men, making cartoon noises with his mouth. Abruptly he would stop and flap his hands as if he'd grabbed hold of a burning bush, then go back to fighting again.

"That's Cal Wilton's son," Mrs. Miller said. "Milton. Orville said don't call him that, might make him grow up stranger than he already is. Milton Wilton. Orville called him Sarge, said he was artistic, helped him make things. Orville was a stinker, all right, but never to that kid. The boy doesn't talk. What's he doing now?" she asked, as though the officers would somehow know.

A figure lay on a slant in a wheelbarrow that young Sarge pushed to a spot in Orville's backyard. Officer Newton told the boy to stay back, but Sarge lifted the figure out, which was near his own height, and set it by a boulder, two rocks on either side to steady the feet. There it stood, a plaster butler figure with a monocle, and arms extended. Mrs. Miller said it formerly held a chalkboard menu at a restaurant's front door in town. "I guess that's something Orville didn't want to sell."

Out of the wagon the child hoisted an army shovel, short but wicked. He posed before the butler to whack the little servant good, though not hard enough to break him. Ponged and pummeled the little man, then slung a final blow with his fist that knocked the good man forward, face down in the squishy mud. Sarge turned full frontal to the audience then, and uttered the first words anyone ever heard from his spit-shiny lips: "My papa done it."

Then he turned and ran with the army shovel into the woods, pinging this skinny tree and that hearty one with the tool until he quickly reversed his path to return and shoot the shovel like a javelin back into the yard. It lodged point first, standing almost at attention in the receptive earth where Officers Newton and Nettle stood by to collect its silent testimony. Sarge marched briskly into the woods, flapping his tender hands.

—◆—

N.J. Ayres is the author of three suspense novels featuring a former Las Vegas stripper now working in a crime lab (the TV program CSI was developed later with a similar character). Ayres is also the author of a poetry book and numerous short stories and was an editor for environmental-engineering documents and a technical publications manager for military-missile and aircraft manuals for twenty years.

BREAK-IN

Eric Beetner

The gun was still warm from the stranger's hand.

Michael stared at the figure face down in the entryway of his house. His eyes moved from the body to the broken lamp he'd used to coldcock the guy.

He tried to remember the last thirty seconds, but it was a black hole.

He could still recall the brief conversation through the door, the stranger knocking after midnight and pretending to have car trouble. Even before he opened the door, Michael thought it strange that someone would wander so far off the highway to make it to his front porch. The pleasure and peril of living far away from town: seclusion.

Michael remembered seeing the gun, the man commanding him to step back, stay quiet. The memory ran out a second before the moment he smashed the man over the head with a marble-based lamp.

Michael set the gun down on the small table by the door where he normally tossed his keys. The man on the floor continued to breathe, and the pool of blood around his head continued to grow.

It was no life-threatening blow. Michael knew the stranger would come around soon.

"Michael?" Amy called from upstairs.

"Stay there." He could hear the whining nighttime cries of Dylan, his two-year-old, and that was sure to wake Kaitie, his four-year-old. "Amy, listen," he said. "Call the police. Tell them someone tried to break in."

"Oh my God." Michael heard her footsteps reach the top of the stairs. She gasped. "Michael!"

"It's okay. Just call them. See how fast they can make it out here."

"Is he…?"

"No, he's not dead. Now, go."

Amy padded away to make the call.

Michael thought about how it might be better if the stranger was dead. The intruder would wake up any second, angry. He was obviously capable of violence whereas Michael had just drawn his first blood on another human. Applied physics professors don't have a reputation for bloodletting.

His eyes drifted to the gun. If the man stood up and attacked, could Michael use deadly force? The lamp had been beyond what he thought himself capable of already, so he didn't know the answer himself.

Dylan's cries intensified. The man on the floor stirred. Michael heard Amy's feet move quickly down the hall to Dylan's room, and the crying soon stopped.

The old farmhouse was easily twenty minutes from town. If the police were anywhere but sitting right by the phone, it could be as much as a half hour before help arrived.

A decision would have to be made before then.

Michael stepped around the body to close the front door. The invader had dropped a small bag, now blocking the threshold. Michael kicked it aside to make room for the door to swing shut. Inside the pack, metal clanked together. Curious, Michael opened the worn black gym satchel.

Duct tape, wire, a hammer, a hunting knife. These were not the supplies of a stick-up, a simple "give me all your money and jewelry" home invasion. This man was prepared to stay.

Michael thought of the children. He felt sick to his stomach. Bikes, a sandbox, a rope swing all decorated the front yard. Advertising that young kids lived here. The house was far enough away from everything, a man could stay for weeks without anyone noticing. Fall semester at the university didn't start for another month.

A chill ran through Michael. The stranger on the floor groaned.

"Amy? Did you talk to the police?"

Her feet padded urgently down the hall. He turned to her. She cradled Dylan in her arms, his head lolling slack, asleep. She whispered. "They said they'd send someone."

He whispered back. "How long?"

"They didn't say."

There was movement from the carpet in the entryway. "Go back to the room. Get Kaitie. Lock the door."

There was panic in Amy's whisper now. "Michael—"

"Just go."

Michael turned back to the stranger, Amy's feet shuffled away above him.

The man rolled, brought a hand to his head and felt the blood, opened his eyes.

Michael reached out. This time, the gun was cold.

This story was first published in *A Twist of Noir.*

Recipient of the Stalker Award for Most Criminally Underrated Author, Eric Beetner is author of The Devil Doesn't Want Me, Dig Two Graves, *and the story collection* A Bouquet of Bullets. *He co-authored (with J.B. Kohl)* One Too Many Blows to the Head *and* Borrowed Trouble. *He wrote two in the acclaimed Fightcard series,* Split Decision *and* A Mouth Full of Blood. *His award-winning short stories appear in more than a dozen anthologies. He blogs at EricBeetner.blogspot.com.*

ONCE UPON A TIME IN THE WOODS

Raymond Benson

The detective was assigned to the case three days into it. The department had already allocated 80 percent of the force to the investigation of the missing twins. It had begun when the parents, who were suspiciously hostile, reported that their children had gone into the woods to play as they did most every day. When they didn't return that evening, the father called the police.

On the second day, the team searched the woodlands; the dogs picked up a promising scent and led them deeper into the forest. The officer in charge called off the search at sunset, and the men resumed the next morning with the detective in the lead. The dogs once again found the trail. At midday the animals directed the party to an isolated, lone cabin to which no path led. While the detective was amazed that there would be a dwelling so deep in the wilderness, he was even more confounded by its appearance and construction. Its red, yellow, blue, and brown colors were very bright, almost syrupy, and the exterior material felt soft to the touch and smelled nice. His first thought was that he wanted to take a bite out of it.

The dogs became frenzied and had to be tied to trees at the area's perimeter. At first the detective thought their noses may have led them to the place because of its pungent, sweet smell rather than by the elusive trail of the missing children.

An elderly blind woman stormed out of the front door and demanded an explanation for the men's presence. When asked for her identity, she said her name was Barbara Yaeger. She was not cooperative. She told them to go away and refused to let the officers inside. Without a warrant, the detective couldn't insist, but they did have a look around the exterior. At the side of the strange house was a large six foot by six foot cage. The detective knew that the horror of its contents would forever haunt him. Inside were the remains of what looked like several human bodies. From the size of the bones, the officer was certain they were mostly of children. The Yaeger woman was immediately placed under arrest and taken to the precinct. The judge quickly gave them the warrant to search the house. The interior was more of the same sickly sweet decorations.

An experienced detective knew when he was in the residence of a mad person.

A fine crystal dust clung to one man's index finger when he touched a sparkling blue lampshade. Before the detective could stop him, the officer had already put his finger to his tongue.

"It's sweet," the rookie said. "Like sugar."

They found more bones in various rooms, but the biggest pile was in the kitchen area. There were a total of thirty-three human bones at the crime scene, although there were no complete skeletons. The Yaeger woman was charged with murder, and the detective believed the DA could and would charge her with cannibalism.

Because the difficult crime scene was immense, the commissioner approved calling in a more sophisticated forensics outfit to process it. The FBI intervened and met the investigative party at the command center set up at the edge of the woodlands. Using a GPS, the detective directed the much larger group to the same area of the woods where the house was, or so he thought.

They couldn't find it. The men searched until nightfall, and there was no indication that the peculiar house ever existed. The detective ordered another search for the following day.

When they got back to the station, the detective and the Feds went to interrogate the suspect and found her cell empty. The flabbergasted sergeant on duty insisted that once Yaeger was locked inside, no one came in or out of the jail all day.

The FBI put out an all-points alert for the woman.

The mystery confounded everyone.

The next day they searched for the house again. The men spent all day in the woods, and the dogs were no help at all. The detective began to question his sanity.

The case grew ice cold after a few weeks. The FBI went back to DC, or wherever it was they came from.

One afternoon on his day off, however, the detective took an excursion into the forest on his own. He followed the usual routes to where he remembered the ghastly dwelling to be.

The man didn't find the sweet abattoir, but he did discover a different abode erected where he thought the previous lodging had stood. This one was made of logs and appeared to be completely normal. The smokestack issued dark puffs. Someone was inside. The detective approached the front door and knocked.

He knocked again.

A woman called, "Who's there?" It wasn't Yaeger, for this lady's voice had a younger, much more pleasant timbre.

"Police, ma'am. May I have a word?"

"Oh, lovely, I've been expecting you. Come in, please! The door's unlocked."

He turned the knob. Sure enough, it opened easily.

The place was a nice, femininely decorated home. The modest kitchen was spic and span, and the detective could swear he smelled soup cooking.

"Ma'am?"

"I'm back here, darling," she called from what the detective assumed was the bedroom.

He cleared his throat. "May I speak to you please?"

"It's all right, sweetheart. Don't be shy. I'm…I'm in bed, and I'm wearing something I think you'll like. Come inside so that I can see you with my baby-blue eyes."

What?

The detective gulped.

What did she say?

"Are you coming or not, big boy? I'm waiting!" The giggle that followed was playful and teasing.

This sort of thing never happened to him.

What kind of vixen awaited him beyond the threshold?

The detective couldn't help himself. The lure was too tempting. He entered.

The last thing the man's brain registered was a violent onslaught of brown fur and glowing red eyes.

And very sharp teeth.

❖

Raymond Benson is the author of twenty-seven published books. His latest series of thrillers are The Black Stiletto *and* The Black Stiletto: Black & White, *with a third installment coming in April 2013. Aside from original works, Raymond is a prolific tie-in writer and was the fourth official—and first American—author to pen authorized James Bond novels. Visit his website at RaymondBenson.com.*

JOB OPENING

John Billheimer

B aker hadn't looked at his 401(k) statement for a year. He'd been afraid to. Then his broker called to tell him his ruined retirement account wouldn't last three years at the rate he was spending.

The easiest solution was to go back to work. But after fifteen years, there was no way to resurrect his old day job as a statistician. His old night job, though, was a different story. He retrieved the shoebox from his bedroom closet and unwrapped the oiled rag that protected the sleek .45 caliber automatic. There'd always be a demand for his old night job.

It would be a lot easier to find night work if Big Bill Ellison were still alive. Big Bill had run the gambling concessions in East Wheeling and had given Baker his start as a contract killer. Big Bill's older son, Jeff, had been engaged to Baker's daughter, Sally. She was on the back of Jeff's motorcycle when a hit-and-run driver turned left in front of them. It took two blocks for their mangled bodies to bounce free.

The police eventually gave up, but Baker haunted the accident intersection for months, making lists of left-turning sedans that fit the scanty witness descriptions. He finally found a Lincoln sedan with a wine-red smear on its muffler that matched the color of Sally's helmet.

Instead of going to the authorities, who had let the sedan's owner back on the roads after two DUI convictions, Baker went to Big Bill Ellison. The two men coaxed a confession from the owner, then force-fed him alcohol until he passed out and drove him and his Lincoln into the Ohio River. And Baker's moonlighting career was born.

Big Bill's son, Little Bill, had inherited his father's gambling operations, but not his intelligence, and had always resented Baker's close relationship with Big Bill. Baker took a deep breath, dialed the phone, and heard the throaty rasp of surprise in Little Bill's voice when he said he was looking for work.

"We didn't part on very good terms. Got a kid doing your old job. Might be he could use some backup this weekend."

"I work alone. You know that."

"I need to be sure your head's still into the work. You want the job or not?"

"I want the job."

"Good. I'll courier the details. Be in our parking lot Friday night at eight. The kid'll find you."

"The kid have a name?"

"No. And neither do you."

The kid was a half hour late pulling his red Mustang into Ellison's parking lot. He was wearing a Pirates baseball cap atop a face pocked with acne scars.

Baker slid into the passenger seat and asked, "How old are you, anyhow?"

"Twenty-four. How old are you?"

"Seventy-five." Baker shaved a few years off his age out of habit.

"You don't look it."

"Neither do you. How long have you been doing this kind of work?"

"Long enough. You don't need to worry about me, old man. I've turned in two of these jobs already. Goddamned if I know why they're sending you along."

After ten minutes, the kid drove into a narrow alley, parked, and pointed up at a lighted warehouse window. "That's our man. He'll come out around nine."

"How do you know he'll be alone?"

"He was alone last night."

"You only watched him one night?"

"My time is valuable."

"So's mine." Baker didn't tell the kid he'd watched for the last three nights. "If he's not alone, we abort."

"No need. We'll just take out his buddies, too." The kid reached inside his Steelers jacket and pulled out a revolver.

Baker held out his hand. "Let me see that."

The kid smiled and handed over the revolver.

Baker spun the cylinder, extracted a bullet, and squinted at it in the dim light. "Hollow points."

"Stops vics dead in their tracks. I carve 'em out myself."

Baker handed the gun back. "No point in both of us sitting here. I'll go across the alley. Hide in that doorway behind the Dumpster. Anything goes wrong, we'll have our man in a crossfire."

"Nothing's going to go wrong."

Baker left the car and vanished in the shadow of the Dumpster.

At ten till nine, a homeless man pushing a shopping cart full of rags and bulging garbage bags came up the alley. He stopped in front of the Mustang and raised a small bottle of Windex spray.

The kid waved him away.

The man started spraying the glass cleaner on the windshield.

The kid raised his hand again. This time his revolver was in it.

The man dropped the spray bottle on the curb and stuck both hands in the air. He backed away from the Mustang and put one hand on the handle of the shopping cart, indicating he was leaving.

The kid nodded and lowered the revolver out of Baker's view.

The homeless man pulled a sawed-off shotgun free of the rags and emptied both barrels into the window of the Mustang.

There was no sign of the kid between the shattered window and the bloody dashboard.

Baker stepped out of the shadows and raised his right hand. "Nice shooting."

The homeless man swung both barrels of the emptied shotgun toward Baker. "You must be the guy that called."

Baker shot him twice in the heart with the .45 concealed in his left pocket. "I'm the guy." Then he exchanged the .45 for the kid's revolver and walked quickly away.

When he was safely removed from the scene, Baker called Little Bill Ellison and told him their target had surprised them and killed the kid before Baker could put him down.

"My God," Ellison said. "How could that happen?"

Baker took the hollow-point bullet he'd palmed from the kid's revolver and rolled it between his thumb and forefinger. "I don't know. It's almost like the man knew we were coming."

—◆—

John Billheimer holds an engineering PhD from Stanford and is the author of the "funny, sometimes touching," Owen Allison mystery series set in his native West Virginia. A new series featuring a mid-western sportswriter with a gambling problem made its debut in September 2012 with the title Field of Schemes. *Visit his website at JohnBillheimer.com.*

THE CHAIR

Peter Blauner

As Arturo Burgos read the computer screen over his daughter's shoulder, he let out a cry of anguish so sharp his wife, Nila, came running into the room.

"*Ai*, Nila." He held his right elbow with his left hand as if he were having a heart attack. "How could this happen?"

On the monitor of the secondhand HP desktop that he'd paid a hundred dollars to have repaired for his daughter to take to the rich people's college in Pennsylvania was a review of his business.

"Arturo Burgos es a fraud," it began. "Most korrup furne-chure-restore en the Bronx. Mi abuela's best dinning roomchar kollaps soon as she sets on it."

The corners of his eyes burned. Twelve years of long hours and earnest labor, trying to make a name for his business on Fordham Road and carry on the family tradition of the finest craftsmanship started by his great-grandfather in Bogota back in the 1920s. Years spent learning the subtle language of wood grains, of coming home smelling of glue and sawdust, of doing jobs at a loss just to build a reputation as an honest tradesman while trying to save enough to help pay for his daughter's school books at this faraway college. All of it threatened by this character assassination in white letters on a navy background.

"Oh, *Papi*, forget about it," his daughter Linda said. "It's the Internet. You can't take it to heart."

The tender admiration with which she looked up at him, brown eyes and the same black pigtails she'd had when she was six, brought him back to sanity. His pride and joy. His heart soared when he thought of how she'd managed to rise above the norm at her mediocre public high school and win a scholarship based on her advanced math skills, but it plummeted when he thought of how he would miss her.

"Let it go," she advised. "Look how many other good reviews you have. Eleven out of twelve give you five stars."

He nodded and kissed her on top of the head. But all through dinner and watching the Yankees that night, doubt and anger plagued him, distracting him even from a ninth inning rally led by Robinson Cano. Although he had just turned fifty himself, this century bewildered him. A flurry of taps on a keyboard and one's honor could be besmirched forever. In a more noble era, such slanders could be answered in a proper duel.

A week later, he insisted his daughter log on again. Three new reviews had appeared. Two lauded his attention to detail and his sense of "old world" courtesy, but there was a new attack.

"Burgos ruind an antque rockin char that ben in my familia for many year! He returnd with crak spindeles! Hes a peasant pretending to be an artis."

A red mist fell over Arturo. The name on the slugline— SBoliver67—was obviously a ruse, but he recognized the pattern of misspellings and the author's birth year. Undoubtedly, this was the work of his old employee Rafael Nunez, that *boracchin* from Cartagena, who had appealed to Arturo as a countryman in asking for a job and then abused his trust by showing up drunk and stealing from the cash register. He'd been badmouthing Arturo in the bars and bodegas of East Tremont for two years since getting fired, but now it was obvious the coward found a way to disseminate his complaints more widely.

Arturo waited until his wife and daughter were asleep and his beloved Yankees had fallen prey to the cruel stratagems of Boston. Then he went back to the keyboard and, using his daughter's password, logged on to the offending website. Nunez had posted a third scurrilous review, and Arturo began to type out a bitter reply, hunting and pecking with two untutored index fingers. But after two sentences, he backspaced furiously. If Rafael had used trickery to get under his skin, he needed to be equal in stealth. Remembering the drunkard's predilection for unvirtuous women, he began imitating the way he'd seen his daughter copy and move blocks of words on the screen, his fingers flexing and prancing across the keys as gracefully as Linda had danced the role of the deceptive contessa at her tenth-grade recital. "*SBoliver67, you are a man of passion…*"

Two detectives came to the house ten days later. Swollen men in dark suits and polished shoes not of the finest quality.

"We need to speak to your daughter," said one as he sat down in a 1907 wing chair with cherrywood legs that Arturo had spent months varnishing.

"She's busy packing," Arturo said, as his wife joined them in the living room.

"We were telling your husband, we need to speak to her about an investigation. A man named Rafael Nunez was stabbed to death near the Grand Concourse two nights ago. He'd arranged to meet a young lady there. The messages to set it up came from your daughter's e-mail account."

"It's not possible." Arturo felt himself grow faint as his wife let out a wail. "My daughter is attending the University of Pennsylvania."

"Not this term." The other detective leaned on a Chippendale dresser that Arturo had refurbished for Linda to take to school.

"She's coming to our squad. And we got a warrant for her hard drive."

Linda had emerged from the bedroom, bleary-eyed from last night's farewell party. "*Que pasa, Papi?*"

The sight of her standing there, in her pigtails and college T-shirt, about to be yanked away from the promise of a bright future, caused Arturo to feel his heart was being yanked from his chest.

"Take me instead," he pleaded.

"Doesn't work like that, sir." The detective who'd been standing put handcuffs on Linda. "Your daughter should've known better. This is the modern world."

"*Mi corazon!*" Arturo waved his arms helplessly.

"That's a nice chair," the detective who'd been sitting said as he rose and looked back. "They don't make them like that anymore."

◄►

Peter Blauner is the author of six novels, including the Edgar Allan Poe Award–winning Slow Motion Riot *and the* New York Times *bestseller* The Intruder. *His most recent book is* Slipping into Darkness. *He lives in Brooklyn with his family.*

SUCKER'S BET

James O. Born

It was probably the puke that woke me up and left me retching and gasping for air. The panic was caused by a confluence of factors like the handcuffs secured behind a heavy gas pipe in the corner of the dim room and the fact that someone had whacked me on the head hard enough to knock me unconscious. That had never happened before, and I didn't like the feeling. My stomach still wanted to empty, and a trickle of dried blood cut across my face like a scar. I could feel it, but there was nothing I could do. Besides, the chicken parm sandwich I'd eaten for lunch that was splashed across my chest was more annoying than the dried blood.

There was nothing to do but gather myself. I wriggled in the hard wooden chair and noticed my issued Beretta and badge sitting on the bare concrete floor of the room. Then I realized it was a storage locker with a few boxes scattered around.

I tried to move my legs but noticed they were duct-taped to the legs of the chair. I thought of the old saying in the detective bureau: duct tape, the kidnapper's best friend for over fifty years.

Next, my thoughts went to who could do this. Maybe if I still worked narcotics, it'd be easier, but three years in crimes/persons made the suspect list tough. All the homicide suspects were in prison or awaiting trial. But it could be anyone else. And there were a lot of suspects. It could even be an old DUI manslaughter defendant from my years in traffic homicide.

The thought made me remember a talk the chief gave me on my first day in uniform. The hulking bald man with a hard face said, "I want you to be nice to people. Go out of your way to help them. Talk to people on the street. But always have a plan to kill them." That was the life of a cop. Chatting one minute and fighting for your life the next.

After a few minutes of worrying about myself, I started to realize how big this could be. Were my kids in jeopardy? My wives? I only spoke to one ex-wife, but I still didn't want anything to happen to the other two. My mind flashed to Maria, the current title-holder. I had to get word to her at least. Tell her to watch out. She'd been a good wife. I'd just gotten bored. I should've learned, but the same patterns emerged after fifteen months or so. Now, nearly three years into my hitch with Maria, I was back to my old habits. I never should have rolled the dice again, but I was a gambler and I had a thing for Latin women.

I could hear voices but didn't want to risk calling out. I might have a slight advantage if my abductors thought I still was unconscious. I struggled and realized I wasn't moving anytime soon. I gazed across the dank space at my gun. I wanted to hold it so bad. Worse than any woman I had ever wanted to hold. I'd turn down a blow job for my gun right this second, and I'd never turned down a BJ in my life. That partially explained the extra marriages.

Where was the last place I remembered being? The club over on the east side of town, checking out the hot college girls cycling through, picking my next target. I liked them young and malleable. Then something flicked on the left side of the car and must have struck me through the open window. That was Cinco

Muertos territory, but I had no beef with the gang. They were small-time dopers.

Maria wouldn't miss me for a while. I'd told her I was working late. It was a simple excuse that always worked as long as I was home by daybreak.

My stomach growled and my head throbbed. At least I wasn't gagged and could breathe freely. That was one of my fears: killed by my faulty sinuses if someone ever shut off air thorough my mouth. Weird, specific concern, but that's how most irrational fears evolved.

There was movement in front of the room, and the metal sliding door rattled. This was it. The riddle would be solved. It was what happened next that scared me. I held my breath as the door slowly rose, making a clattering sound as the wheels turned along the track.

Sunlight flooded the room, answering one of my questions. I could barely make out the human form as it slipped into the room. I turned my head as my eyes adjusted to the light and mumbled, "What the hell is going on?" Then, with more effort, "Who are you?"

There was silence, and then I heard a woman's voice. My hearing was still fuzzy, but the accent caught my attention.

"What?" I called out, desperate to hear the voice again.

"I said I expected you home hours ago."

I blinked out the haze, and my eyes focused. It was my wife, Maria. I felt a surge of joy, then worried she might be held here against her will, too.

I blurted, "Are you all right?"

She smiled. "I must have hit you too hard."

"Hit me? You?"

"Of course it was me. You gave me no choice. You rubbed it in my face, always chasing those young girls. I should've listened to my family and never agreed to marry you."

"But I don't understand." My voice trailed off because I suddenly did understand. Everything.

Maria gave me a wicked smile and said, "I think my uncle's cement mixer will explain it all better than I can."

It was right then that I finally realized marriage was a sucker's bet.

➤⬤

James O. Born is the author of seven novels. He won the Florida Book Award for best novel and the Barry Award for best short story. He has published science fiction as well as crime fiction.

ENTITLED

Rhys Bowen

"Sorry to disturb you, Professor, but I'm just popping down to the village. Is there anything you need?"

Dr. Woodson turned his wheelchair toward the round, comfortable shape of his housekeeper. "No thank you, Mrs. Broad." The words came out as if spoken by a robot, not from Dr. Woodson's very human face.

"Right-o, then. I'll be off. Mr. Jackson should be back from Cambridge any moment." She closed the door almost reverently behind her. He went back to work. The next second he was lost in the world of quantum physics.

He heard the light click of the door handle, though. His remaining senses had become fine-tuned. Including his brain. Still one of the best in the world.

"Jackson?" he asked, not looking up from the screen. He had been waiting impatiently for his secretary's return. There had been a flood of correspondence since the Nobel Prize had been announced.

"Not Jackson," said a voice behind him.

He spun the wheelchair in surprise to see that the intruder had come in through the French windows.

"Mason. My dear old friend." His face managed the ghost of a smile.

"Hello, Woodson," the man said. They were about the same age, but Mason was still in the full bloom of health. He looked down at the shrunken cripple in the chair, his head held steady in a cradle, a great bellows behind the chair making an almost-human sigh as it breathed in and out for him.

"I gather congratulations are in order," Dr. Mason said.

"Thank you. A great honor. I feel quite humbled by it."

"As well you should," Dr. Mason said, his big shape coming between Woodson and the sunlight. "Getting all the credit for years of shared research."

"Of course you deserve some of the credit," Woodson said. "I'm going to make that clear in my speech."

"Some of the credit?" Mason's face was flushed now. "It should have been my prize, Woodson, not yours. You won it with the sympathy vote."

Woodson's clear gaze held the other man's eyes. "Not true, Mason, and you know it. We did the initial research together, but I went on."

"I took a different tack."

"The road less traveled?" Woodson asked. "And that has made all the difference?"

"The difference of a million pounds."

"Oh, so it's the money that comes with the prize that irks you?"

"I need that money, Woodson."

"My own lifestyle is not exactly cheap to maintain," Woodson said. "All these gizmos just to keep me alive."

"To keep you alive," Mason repeated. "It must be terrifying to be so helpless."

Woodson swiveled the chair as Mason circled around him.

"One tug, Woodson," he said. "One pull of the plug and you're gone." His hands reached for the back of the wheelchair.

"Get away from me." Woodson swung the chair to avoid him.

Mason laughed. "I don't think you can run away from me, old chap. I've wanted you dead for years. Now I'm damned if you're going to get that prize."

"I'll sound the alarm for my secretary."

"I happen to know he's not back yet," Mason said. "I've planned this perfectly. Everyone thinks I'm in France. And, as you notice, no fingerprints."

Woodson realized now what had been bothering him. The man wore latex gloves. One gloved hand reached behind the wheelchair.

"So simple. Disconnect computer. Then I pull out the breathing tube and you stop breathing. So long, old chap. Brilliant brain. Such a pity." He gave a violent yank, looked back once, and then slipped out through the French doors.

Woodson fought rising panic. Had to tell someone. Couldn't telephone without his computer. Couldn't open the door. No way to communicate. His eyes scanned the room. Less than a minute. Only his brain to help him, if he worked fast. The robot arm shot from the computer to grab a book. It fell to the floor, then another…

Inspector Hadley looked around the room. Too many books for his taste. The walls were lined with them.

"You don't think it was an accident then?" he asked the young man and the housekeeper who stood together, ashen faced.

"But someone disconnected the computer," the secretary said. "He couldn't do that himself."

"Who found him?"

"I did, sir," Mrs. Broad said.

"And the room looked like this?"

"He was facing the wall," Mrs. Broad said. "There were several books lying on the floor."

"Where are they now?"

"I picked them up," she said.

"What books were they?"

"Nothing special. Just random books."

"Did he often leave books lying on the floor?"

"Oh, no. He was quite meticulous," the housekeeper said. "He always wanted books put away when he was done with them."

"Can you remember which books they were?" the inspector asked.

"I don't know I paid much attention."

"Try to remember, Mrs. Broad," Jackson said.

"Do you think he might have left them as a message?" the inspector asked.

"If they were out, they were out for a reason," Jackson said.

Mrs. Broad scanned the bookcase and pulled out a cookbook. *One-Pot Dishes.*

"A cookbook?" The inspector sounded incredulous.

"And this one."

"His own book, *String Theory*," Jackson said.

"And this."

"*Moby Dick*?"

"And some Russian book."

"*Anna Karenina*? This makes no sense." The inspector shook his head. "They must have fallen during a struggle."

"Oh, and this." Mrs. Broad put *Northanger Abbey* on the table.

"They have nothing in common," the inspector said. "Jane Austen and *String Theory*?"

Jackson stared at them. "What order were they in on the floor?"

The housekeeper thought hard, then arranged them on the table. Jackson wrote down the titles. "Look, sir," he said, excitedly. "He's named his killer."

The inspector read:

Moby Dick
Anna Karenina
String Theory
One-Pot Dishes
Northanger Abbey

"And?" the inspector asked.

"Mason." He pointed to the first letters. "Donald Mason, Dr. Woodson's arch rival. He wanted that Nobel Prize."

⋙

Rhys Bowen is the New York Times *best-selling author of two historical mystery series: the Molly Murphy Mysteries, set in early 1900s New York City, and the lighter Royal Spyness stories, featuring a penniless minor royal in 1930s England. Her books have been nominated for every major mystery award and have won thirteen to date, including Agatha, Anthony, and Macavity Awards. A transplanted Brit, Rhys now divides her time between California and Arizona.*

GET THE CONFESSION

Jay Brandon

It was a small room, and he was a small guy. I didn't have to do anything to make him feel trapped except be in there with him, towering over him. I just had to put a hand on his shoulder and ease him down into the chair at the table, cutting off most of the room without trying.

"You know what to do," Lieutenant Owsley had said to me a minute ago, and I did. Get the confession. Make sure the details were right. Details only someone who'd been in the apartment would know. Owsley had let me skim the initial report, and there were details enough. Pretty little secretary, neat little apartment. Nicely laid out kitchen, lunch for two, cooking things still on the stove, a simple meal. And the bed nicely made in the bedroom only a few feet away. Her lunch date hadn't shown up, apparently. This burglar had. He hadn't expected to find anyone home, and by the time he left no one was. Just the pretty little secretary on the kitchen floor, her neatness spoiled by the pool of blood around her.

"You know her?" Owsley asked.

I shook my head.

"Worked in the building right across the street."

"Maybe I've seen her then." I shrugged.

Owsley had said something else to me too, just before I'd gone into the interview room. "We need this." He'd stretched to whisper in my ear. I'd just nodded. The code was clear: he was sure, intuitively or whatever, this was the guy, but there might not be enough evidence to convict him without a good confession.

He said something else, just before he left. "We'll be down the hall. Out of earshot."

The suspect knew what that meant, too.

We had more modern interview rooms, but this called for old school: scarred metal table, cold metal chair, outdated equipment. I started the interview a little differently, fiddling with the recording equipment and then saying, "Ah, the hell with it." When I turned back to the guy, he knew. We weren't recording this session. I just looked at him for a long minute, watching sweat appear on his balding forehead. He wiped his mouth, looking up at me from the edge of the chair. "You were there," I said. He shook his head. "You think we don't know, just because you wiped the place clean? That shows what a pro you are. You weren't so careful when you hit another apartment in the same building a month ago. And somebody saw you there last week."

That wasn't in the report, but I figured it was the detail most likely to get a reaction, and I was right. His eyes got big as open windows. "I was just there looking at an empty apartment. To rent. Felons gotta live someplace too."

I just let him think about that bad story while I began writing his confession. He looked over my shoulder. "I didn't. I didn't hit her. She hit her head on the countertop." I backtracked in the confession to say she'd slipped, smiling inside. Hit head on the table edge. The burglar wasn't contradicting anything now. I slipped in the perfect details: lavender panties, the gold watch from her jewelry drawer.

Owsley came in to take it from me. Looked at the blank signature line, then at me. I just looked back. The guy was pressed back against the wall now that there were two cops in the room. He'd sign.

Owsley nodded as he read. "Table edge. Good detail. He said countertop, but you're right, it was the table edge. We found blood. Sure you didn't know her? That's funny, because I saw the two of you at lunch one day. Little out-of-the-way Mexican place. I started to come over and say hi, but it looked like you were having a pretty intense discussion."

I sensed people on the other side of the mirrored glass. Started thinking, didn't say anything.

"So I thought of you, especially after I saw the gift she'd bought. It was in the bedroom. Did you not get that far?" His partner came in, handed him a large gift box, kept his eyes on me. Owsley opened it. A robe. Plush. Burgundy. I looked down at it, rubbed the rich texture of the fabric, and saw my initials on the pocket.

"Nice robe," Owsley said. "Must have set her back half a week's pay. A girl trying to hold on to her man, when he was ready to dump her. Or wanting more than he was willing to give her, breaking up his marriage and costing him half his pension."

Owsley sighed. "Or maybe she just loved him and wanted to do something nice for him. The initials weren't enough. Neither was the table set for two. She was expecting somebody, not a burglar. But now we've got enough, I think. Details that weren't in the report. The table edge. The fact the watch was gold. The report doesn't mention either of those."

I was the biggest guy in the room, but there were two of them. Now three, counting the burglar. And we were on DVD. Now that I was paying attention, I could hear the faint hum of the backup system.

Lieutenant Owsley draped the robe over my shoulders. She must've gotten it at a big and tall men's shop, because it hung nicely on my shoulders and fell almost to my ankles.

"Nice fit," Owsley said.

—◆◆—

Jay Brandon is the award-winning author of Fade the Heat, Executive Privilege, *the Chris Sinclair series of legal thrillers, and more than a dozen other novels. His story "A Jury of His Peers" appeared in* The Best American Mystery Stories 2010. *A pair of new novels by Jay have recently been published,* The Jetty *(2012) and* The Real History *(February 2013). Visit him at JayBrandon.com.*

PIECE OF CAKE

R. Thomas Brown

Hap Callahan walked through the saloon doors of Cowboy Coffee, shaking his head at the lassos in the logo. Seemed every place he went these days tried to make you feel like you were at a theme park, not next door to a James Avery in yet another strip mall filling up suburban space and giving the local commuters a place to spend their money.

He eyed the caffeine cowboy who labored under a flimsy hat. "I'll have a cappuccino." He glanced down at the rows of trucked-in sweets. "And that thing with the little marshmallows on top."

"A cappuccino and a lolly, that's eight bucks even."

Hap handed over a ten. Waved off the change. He turned away. Scanned the room. Holding the treat on a stick in front of his face. Dumbest fucking way to meet someone. Ever. In the corner, a jittery little man made eye contact.

Hap walked among the tables and couches, past the bar with saddle seats, and took the chair opposite Pete. "Looks like you've had too much coffee."

"Fuck you. I've been waiting an hour."

Hap checked his watch. A nice Tag he took off a guy who couldn't dodge punches. "Did you remember to set your clock back, asshole?"

Pete shook his head. Not in response, more like a tick. "You got it?"

Two seconds and Hap was already tired of the guy. "Sure. You?"

"Yeah. I got the pics with me."

"Memory too?" Digital pictures could be anywhere. Everywhere. Made his solution attractive to clients.

"Yeah. All of it. It's right here." He tapped his lap.

Hap took a sip. The drinks were always too damned hot. "Pete. I'm gonna tell you something."

Pete shuddered. "Didn't come for a lecture."

"No. But you're gonna listen anyway." A small sip. "Blackmail's a bad deal, Pete. People with enough money to make it worthwhile usually have enough money to make problems go away."

"Is that a threat?"

Hap rolled his eyes. "Just advice. My guess is you got lucky. Took some pics and thought you'd make a quick score." He took another sip.

"So?"

"So. Look at you. You're a mess. The stress. The fear. Better for you if you give it up. Walk away." Hap fiddled with the ball on a stick.

"Yeah? Or what?"

"See, Pete. My client wants to play along. Most of them do. Just want it to go away quietly. I do what I'm paid to do." A long sip. "I'd rather hunt you down. Find you at night. Alone. Or with someone, I don't care. End it all. No more threats, payments, worries."

Pete swallowed before trying to act tough. "Thanks for the advice. Now. The money."

Hap pulled an envelope from his jacket. "This is the spot. The choice. You take the money, and it doesn't go well from here. Give me the stuff. Leave now. No money. No pics. No trouble."

"Money."

Hap sighed. "Your choice. Here ya go."

Pete started to open it.

Hap slapped his hand. "Not in here, moron. Take it out back. Count it there."

"What if it's not all there?"

Hap sat back. "Keep the pics until you count." He spread his arms across the back of the booth. "Come back when you're done."

Pete furrowed his eyebrows. "What if I just run?"

"Then I'll get to do things my way. Either way, I win."

Pete stood and left out the back. Hap took another drink and twirled the frosted ball on a stick. "Weird shit."

A man sat across from him. Handed him an envelope. "Thanks, Hap. Finding the guy made this a lot easier."

Hap nodded. "Always does. Anonymity makes people brave. Being found makes them stupid." He finished his drink and set it down before a sound like a car backfiring rang out from behind the mall. Hap grinned and placed the envelope in his jacket pocket.

"You'll bring the pics by the office?"

"As soon as I make sure he didn't have any copies anywhere else."

"Thanks again, Hap. You really are the best." The man left the shop.

Hap took a bite of the ball. "Piece of cake."

THIS STORY WAS FIRST PUBLISHED IN *SHOTGUN HONEY*.

R. Thomas Brown writes crime fiction set in Texas. His novel, Hill Country, *was published by Snubnose Press in 2012. You can find his thoughts on fiction and other matters, as well as information on his short fiction and upcoming novels, at RThomasBrown.blogspot.com.*

THUG CITY

Ken Bruen

Their latest gig was as follows: drive at a slow speed through pedestrian areas beside, preferably, an older person, chuck a bottle of dirty water on the poor bastard, rev the engine, and then speed off, leaving the old codger on the brink of coronary.

Oh, the fun.

The rush.

The bravado.

The duo: dumb-ass so-called students of engineering at NUIG, all of nineteen years apiece, named

Dolan

Brady.

Way too fucking cool for first names. Dolan was almost a good-looking kid, if he had had an ounce of feeling, a trainee psycho who got the rush from others' pain. Brady was just the apprentice moron, attached to any ship that provided color and beer money. Their latest wheeze was a plastic bag of red paint, handled delicately, to be lobbed at some prize suspect. The anticipation had them respectively hard.

The Red Letter Night had arrived, and they'd prepared, like *dude*, get seriously wasted first. That they spoke in quasi-American hip-hop only added to their irritating ration. Eight

Red Bull—yup, *Red* Bull, the irony! A bottle of cheap vodka—
the working stiff's cocaine—and a few spliffs, and they were
good to

"Roll."

And they did.

Dillon was sixty-five, a little stooped from an old gunshot
wound in his lower back; that sucker still reared up. Ten years in
a European jail had tamed his wilder excesses—that is, his hair-
trigger temper. Tamed, as in rationed.

Sparingly.

He had hung on to a combat jacket from those wild days on
the Ormeau Road, and *phew*, cruising down the falls, bullets to
backside, oblivious to all but The Cause.

Walking.

Now, slow to slowest as he remembered his dead mates.
Returning to Galway he wanted only some peace, some aged
Jameson maybe, and three pints of the black, stretched over four
hours.

Stretched over the meager euros they called a *pension*. Those
walks, he'd think…

"One good jolt afore I go, to rock one more glorious time."

He'd reached the top of Eyre Square, his daily ritual, one more
kilometer before he headed for the pub and half-arsed ease.

The car was turning by the Meryck Hotel, about two minutes
from him. Dolan was getting angry. Not a single person in sight. Jesus!

Everybody hanging with some other fucking body. Brady
said,

"Ah shite, the paint is leaking. We got to get rid of it."

Dolan saw the hunched man, shouted,

"An old fuck. Look, see the bollocks in the combat jacket?
Move, for Christ's sake, before he crosses the road."

They moved.

An old woman in her fragile eighties got off the Salt Hill bus, on the blind side of the car. Dolan roared,

"Sling it."

The bag sailing high, suspended for one glorious moment, then exploding over the lady, like a prayer gone so badly wrong. Covering like a spectrum of blood, her frail small body, a tiny cry as she collapsed in a coronary cloud.

The car desperately vying for balance, nigh losing it, then righted but straightened, then roaring off.

Dillon, momentarily stunned, then recovering, his eyes fixed on the license plate—old habit. He bent down, tended to the lady, his mind already in the cold place. A flick, a light, the years-old spark about to turn.

Burn.

To burning.

A blaze when the ambulance came. Told the guard who arrived:

Saw nothing.

Know nothing.

Thought:

The Sig.

Daily primed, like an exercise in hope.

Did go to the pub, had only the Jameson, two doubles, no Guinness, no bloated feeling required.

Just sleekness and fire.

How many places could two idiots hide? Found them close to one in the morning. A flat off the canal, top floor, the sound of Thin Lizzy bouncing off the water. The dead car parked sloppily outside. Dead from the moment he focused on the number plate.

He stormed in, put a bullet in the sound system, killing Phil Lynott mid *Whiskey in the Jar*. Still moving, lashed Dolan across his face with the butt of the Sig, whirled, put a hard kick to Brady's knee. As the duo

Moaned

Groaned

On the floor.

He took a Miller, drained half, said,

"Guys, here's the deal."

They stared at him, stared at the gun. He said,

"The old lady isn't going to make it, so one of you isn't going to make it."

He paused.

Everybody loves a dramatic interval, then,

"I'm going to…as you *dudes* say…*waste*…one of you."

Let them digest that, finished the brew, said,

"So, you guys choose, or…I'll kill you both."

Dolan looked at Brady, thought,

"Never liked this eejit."

Brady thought,

"Uh-oh."

⧫

Ken Bruen received a PhD in metaphysics, taught English in Africa, Japan, Southeast Asia, and South America, then became a crime novelist. His Jack Taylor series has had worldwide acclaim, and his novels have been nominated for numerous awards, including an Edgar Allan Poe Award for The Guards. *His novels* Blitz *and* London Boulevard *have served as the basis for feature films. His most recent Jack Taylor novel is* Headstone.

WHAT YOU WISH FOR

C.E. Lawrence

"Make a wish," said the genie.

Marie crossed her arms. "I don't think so."

"Oh, come on." He beamed genially. "You dragged me out of the bottle—you might as well use your wish."

He was big and blubbery, rotund and round-faced, just like the illustrations from her childhood copy of *Aladdin and the Lamp*. His skin was the color of polished brass. He wore loose-fitting yellow silk pants, a tiny vest barely covered his fleshy chest, and a wide, multicolored belt was wound around his enormous belly. His head was completely bald, the skin smooth as river stone.

Marie frowned. "Don't I get three wishes?"

The genie shook his head, the enormous gold hoops hanging from his earlobes tinkling like tiny bells. "We've been hit by the recession, too. We've downsized to one wish."

Rain pelted the cabin's roof, fast and furious, like the sound of popcorn popping. Marie shivered and buttoned her sweater. She wished she had never ventured into her grandmother's attic. With her grandmother gone to her bridge club, there was little else to do on this dreary rainy afternoon. Like all teenagers, she was easily bored, and today she was feeling especially restless. Sarah

McGinty had bullied her again at school, teasing Marie about her lumpy thighs and unfashionable clothing.

Marie looked down at the shards of crimson glass at her feet. She hadn't seen the ornate red bottle with its heavy glass stopper until it was too late. While digging through a pile of old clothes, she had knocked it off the dusty bookshelf, watching helplessly as it splintered to pieces on the wooden floor. She sat on a dusty old steamer trunk, brushing away the cobwebs at her feet.

The genie sat down beside her. He smelled of sandalwood and sawdust. "So what's your wish?"

"How did you end up stuck in a bottle?"

He looked down at his hands, which were immaculately manicured, the nails shiny with just a touch of clear polish. "I lost a bet."

"With who?"

"Another genie. Look," he said, "I haven't got all day. I have to find a new master before sunrise, or I'll lose my powers."

"Why can't I be your new master?"

"I need someone with experience. Otherwise terrible things could happen."

"Like what?"

He glanced out the dusty window at the rain drumming down on the roof. "Have you heard of the bubonic plague?"

A clap of thunder rattled the loose windowpane, startling her. "You mean—"

"That was started by a nasty little German peasant who stumbled on a really powerful genie living in his hayloft. Apparently his neighbor owed him money, and things got out of hand."

He brushed the attic dust from his silk trousers. "Do you want your wish or not?"

She studied him, eyes narrowed. "Whatever I wish for isn't going to go horribly wrong?"

His fleshy face fell. "Why would it?"

She chewed on the side of her index finger. "I can't think of anything."

"What do you want more than anything else?"

She shivered as the gold band around his upper arm grazed her shoulder. An idea began to form in her mind. "Can you kill someone?"

He looked alarmed, his chocolate-brown eyes wide.

"You have to do whatever I say, right?" she said.

"Well, yes, but—"

"I want you to kill Sarah McGinty."

"Who's she?"

"The meanest girl in school."

"I don't recommend—"

Marie felt the hot wind of power rise up her neck, and with it a reckless fearlessness. "I want you to *kill* Sarah McGinty!"

The genie sighed. "If you insist."

A smile crept across Marie's face as she heard the front door slam—her grandmother had returned. Marie dashed downstairs to greet her, deciding to keep her encounter with the genie to herself.

The next day at school Sarah McGinty was much nicer to her. She invited Marie to sit with her at lunch and, after school, offered her a ride home in her snappy red vintage Mustang. Everyone knew that Sarah McGinty loved that car more than anything in the world. She washed it once a week and wouldn't allow any food or drink in it, for fear of stains on the leather upholstery. The car had buttery leather bucket seats, whitewall tires, and the thought of the whole school seeing Marie riding in it was irresistible to her. She began to have second thoughts about her wish.

The rain had dried up, and a lemony sun cast a soft glow on Sarah's summer-wheat hair as they headed toward the railroad crossing on Bridge Lane. Sarah chatted about a former boyfriend and why she was so "over him" since he had been dropped from the football team.

As the car rumbled up the incline toward the tracks, the engine suddenly sputtered, rattled, and died. The car slid forward a couple of feet and stopped right in the middle of the tracks, just as the warning bells clanged their alert that a train was approaching. The white-and-red striped gates on either side of them closed, cutting them off from the road. They were trapped on the tracks.

Panic shot through Marie's stomach, sour and hot. "We have to get out!" she cried as Sarah McGinty tried vainly to start the Mustang's engine.

"I'm—not—leaving—my—car—behind," Sarah muttered, sweat beading on her pretty forehead as she turned the keys in the ignition. Marie reached for the door handle, but Sarah was faster. "Neither are you!"

Marie heard the click of the driver's side switch that locked all the doors. "Please! Let me go!" she screamed, her veins flooding with terror at the sight of the oncoming freight train, black smoke pouring from its chimney.

As the train bore down on them, the harsh sound of its whistle flooding her ears, she knew that her first instinct in the attic had been right.

Her last thought as the metal beast barreled into the little car was how pretty Sarah's yellow hair looked in the early evening light.

—◆◆—

Carole Bugge, writing as C.E. Lawrence, is the author of nine published novels, award-winning plays, musicals, poetry, and short fiction. A two-time Pushcart Prize nominee, her fourth Lee Campbell thriller is Silent Slaughter. *Titan Press in the United Kingdom has recently reissued her first Sherlock Holmes novel,* The Star of India. *Visit her website at CELawrence.com.*

WHERE'S DAD?

Peter Cannon

"Where's Dad?"

That was the question running through the mind of fifteen-year-old Jim Neyland as he lay awake in the room he was sharing with his forty-year-old father at London's Claridge's Hotel that summer of 1967. Dad didn't say where he was going when he said good-bye around eight o'clock the last night of the Neylands' stay in London, only that he was meeting "some friends." Dad also hadn't said when he'd be back, but the luminous clock showed it was now well past midnight, and Jim was getting worried.

This was the first vacation Jim and his twelve-year-old twin sisters had taken with their father alone since their parents separated the summer before. Where was Mom? Mom was spending much of the summer at Lake Tahoe, at a place called Glenbrook, getting divorced. Why Dad and Mom were getting divorced was unclear to Jim, but according to Mom, it had something to do with Dad being a poor communicator, among a host of other faults she took care to share with her son, who in many respects, she noted, took after his father.

In contrast to Mom, Dad didn't talk about the reasons for their divorce. Maybe the topic was painful for Dad because of his own unpleasant experiences as a child. The marriage between Dad's father, who was of Irish Catholic descent, and Dad's mother, who was of Protestant English descent, had lasted ten mostly unhappy years. Jim knew just a few details—in particular, that Dad's father, who had a drinking problem that only got worse, died at age fifty-nine in the hospital, where he was being treated for kidney stones, the year before Jim was born. Jim's robustly healthy grandmother, who turned seventy-three earlier that summer, never spoke of her ex-husband, despite enjoying the occasional tipple.

In the aftermath of the separation, Dad had nothing bad to say about Mom. In fact, he soon had reason to be grateful to her. While Dad was pretty fit (he'd boxed in college), his appendix ruptured the following spring. After he got out of the hospital, Mom let him stay in the guest room at her house outside Boston, what had once been his house too, while he recovered. No one else at that point was prepared to look after him.

During his convalescence, Dad sold Mom on the idea of his taking the children on an extended tour of Ireland and England while she did her time in Nevada. (Although Dad scarcely ever mentioned his parents, he was fond of their ancestral homelands.) Joining them for part of the Irish leg of the trip was a pretty, if proper, Englishwoman named Fiona. Jim and his sisters learned that Dad had met Fiona through mutual friends while Fiona was in the States on holiday earlier that year. Jim's sisters weren't too pleased about sharing hotel rooms with Fiona while Jim got to bunk with Dad. At least you could give Dad credit for not losing any time seeking a replacement for Mom. Perhaps Dad was staying out late with Fiona, but Jim sensed that Fiona and Dad hadn't hit it off that well during their Irish tour, and Jim and his sisters had seen her only once in London, near the beginning of their week there. Still, maybe the "friends" Dad said he was meeting was in fact just the Englishwoman, whom he was making one last effort to woo.

The hours passed. Jim must have drowsed. Then sometime before dawn Dad returned. In the half-light, as Dad entered the bathroom, Jim noticed Dad rubbing his hand. Over breakfast, before they left for Heathrow to catch a plane home to Boston, Jim thought the fingers on Dad's right hand looked a little red and swollen.

One night, about a year after Jim and his sisters returned safely home to Massachusetts, the subject of their trip with Dad came up between Jim and his mother. They were alone in the kitchen; his sisters were in bed.

"Dad stayed out really late that last night in London. I don't know why," Jim said.

"Didn't he tell you?" Mom said.

"No."

"Your father was robbed."

"What?"

"He was in some bar."

"Wasn't anyone with him?"

"I gather he had company, but she left early. He was drunk."

"And?"

"Someone picked his pocket. They took his wallet, with your passports and airline tickets in it."

"Then how…"

"He was sober enough to realize the people who ran the bar, the people he'd been talking to, had set him up. He offered them a deal. They could keep his money if they gave him back the passports and plane tickets."

"And if they didn't give him back the tickets?"

"He threatened to kill one of them. Then he slugged one of them hard enough to show he meant business."

"Then what happened?"

"They gave him what he wanted."

"Say, Mom, how do you know all this?"

"Because your father called me collect at Glenbrook that night from London. He was lucky I was near a phone. It took a while, but I was able to wire him the money to pay the hotel bill and get you and your sisters to the airport."

In the decades that followed, Jim never did raise the matter with Dad, who eventually did find a replacement for Mom, a woman more tolerant of his shortcomings who, even now, looks after him in his declining days. Old age is perhaps more difficult for him than it might be because Dad chose to ignore the diabetes he was diagnosed with in his fifties and told no one about until, in his seventies, the severity of his symptoms forced the issue and belated treatment. Jim has never asked Dad why he decided to pretend he didn't have the disease because, like Dad, Jim prefers not to discuss unpleasant family matters.

Peter Cannon is a senior reviews editor at Publishers Weekly, *where he assigns and edits the mystery reviews. He's also the author of* Pulptime, *a Sherlock Holmes pastiche. His short fiction has appeared in such anthologies as* The Resurrected Holmes, The Confidential Casebook of Sherlock Holmes, *and* 100 Crooked Little Crime Stories. *He and his wife live with their three children in New York City.*

THEY'LL CALL ME WHISTLIN' PETE

Chuck Caruso

My ma weren't even goin' to take me to see it when they hanged my pa. But I put up one hell of a fit about that and set her straight. Somebody hangs your kin, I told her, you go and watch them doin' it. My sister, Charlotte, didn't want to go, but she's only eight so Ma left Sis with old Widow Atwell while her and me went down there to see the hangin'. I reckon I'm growed up enough to see a man swing when it happens. I turned eleven last October.

Early in the morning that day I hitched our horses to the wagon, and me and Ma rode near twenty miles down to Perseverance where they held the trial and were doin' the execution. Ma said we'd just go down for the noon hangin' and travel home by nightfall, but I stashed a bundle with some things under the seat anyways.

Perseverance is a pretty big town with a newspaper and a sheriff's office and all. Pa had been sittin' in the one-room jail there for a week since they got the verdict passed on him. Guilty of murder as charged. Pa claimed he'd been dead drunk in the back room of some whorehouse when the deed was done, but he never could explain how an ax from our barn and his hat with his name in it got out to the Reed ranch all by themselves the same night somebody kilt both Mr. and Mrs. Reed.

At his trial, they said Pa done them murders to rob the Reeds. Besides their everlasting souls, a few other things went missing from their house, like some coins and banknotes, a gold watch, and a gun belt with an old Colt pistol in it. Mr. Reed's ivory dentures went missin' too, but that got shrugged off as what they called a "minor peculiarity." Dead men don't need to chew much anyways.

They were a nice old couple, the Reeds, and folks said neither of them would hurt a fly. Course they never seen the whuppin' old Mr. Reed give me and my friend Butch when he caught us stealin' an apple pie off the windowsill of his wife's kitchen.

Everybody was real broke up about the Reeds gettin' done for by my no-good drunk of a pa. It was true enough that Pa got ornery and mean when he'd been hittin' the whiskey bottle. Ma and I both had scars enough to show for that. Last time he laid into me, he even busted out some of my teeth, including one of the new big ones in front. I'd only had the damn thing for three years. After that I whistled when I talked and kids made fun of me. I told Butch that someday when I'm a famous outlaw they'll call me Whistlin' Pete on the wanted posters. We had a good laugh about that, him and me, but I was mostly serious. I am going to be an outlaw some day. You just wait and see if I ain't.

When Ma and I got to Perseverance on hangin' day, we found lots of folks crowded in the town square where they'd put up the gallows. You'd a thought it was the Fourth of July the way most of them were drinkin' and hollerin'. It was almost catchin' how they was carryin' on like it was some sort of holiday. I pert near found myself smilin' along with them as we pushed through so's we could stand near the front.

Me and Ma held hands at the foot of the gallows while the deputies made Pa walk up them pine steps and stand there facin' the crowd. Pa said sorry to me and Ma when he saw us. It was a familiar enough word on his lips, so I recognized it right off even though we couldn't hear the sound of the actual word above the hootin' of the crowd. Ma wiped her eyes with a hanky from her sleeve, but I didn't spill no tears myself. I'd heard that lie comin' from him too many times before to believe it now, and I was done with cryin' anyways.

Pa's eyes searched ours in the last moments before they pulled the burlap sack down over his face and looped the noose over his head. I don't know what he mighta been lookin' for, but he sure as hell didn't see it in my eyes. Ma turned away weepin', but I watched to the finish. When the trap fell, he dropped down and his neck snapped. He didn't kick or nothing, just became dead weight swayin' on a line. The crowd hushed then, and I could hear the sound of the hemp rope whisperin' against the crossbeam.

Back at the wagon I grabbed my bundle of things and told Ma I had to go check on somethin'. Most days she would have peppered me with questions, but she just nodded and climbed up on the wagon, seemin' real sad on account of Pa. I kissed her on the cheek and run off. I don't know how long she waited there before she figured out I wasn't never comin' back.

I didn't really have nothin' to check on except the time of the next coach out of there. Down at the depot, I paid for a ticket as far as Fort Boise and waited around for the stagecoach to come through at one thirty. A pretty lady showed me how to tell time on my gold watch. I told her it was an inheritance from my dearly departed grandfather. I felt good leavin'. I had some cash and an old Colt pistol in my bag, and I was hopeful that if I did good for myself I'd find a dentist who could fix these dentures I was carryin' so they'd fit me proper. Otherwise, well, I guess they'd still just have to call me Whistlin' Pete.

Chuck Caruso teaches American literature at Marylhurst University near Portland, Oregon, where he lives with his wife, Petra, and their two cattle dogs. Recently his Western noir tales have been published online at The Flash Fiction Offensive, Shotgun Honey, Fires on the Plain, *and* The Western Online. *An assistant editor for* Dark Discoveries *magazine, Chuck also moonlights at Portland indie bookstore Murder by the Book.*

THE BUNNY

William E. Chambers

She appeared in a pink bunny costume every day for one week straight.

I take the L train from Bedford Avenue in Williamsburg, Brooklyn, to the last stop—Eighth Avenue in Manhattan—and walk several blocks downtown to my job tending bar in a gay/straight pub in Greenwich Village. Thank God—if He exists—that I miss the madness of subway rush hours. I leave home at three thirty p.m. and start setting up at about four fifteen for the opening five o'clock happy-hour rush. The Bunny is usually on the platform when I arrive at Eighth Avenue, and then she scoots up the steps throwing backward glances toward me as I follow. But she always trots uptown as opposed to my Lower Manhattan direction. I once called out "Excuse me, miss—" but she either didn't hear me or pretended not to, which is just as well since this figure in pink was arousing instincts within me better left dormant.

I always close up between one and four a.m. depending on the crowd. The big Swede who owns this pub called Thor's Hammer backs up his bartenders' judgments. He trusts that neither I nor the busty young woman who replaces me on my days off will pull out early as long as the drinks—and tips—keep flowing. Common sense, right?

But there are weeknights where it doesn't pay to stay open past one. So this Monday, having stood alone for more than an hour past midnight, I dimmed the lights and began upending the stools across the bar. That's when the Bunny walked in. She had pink whiskers painted lips to cheeks and big green eyes. My heart leaped like a happy unborn in the womb. I fought the excitement back from my voice but couldn't control the shock on my face I guess because she smiled coyly when I asked, "Can I help you?"

"Surprised, aren't you?"

"Yes." I nodded, noting the colorful straw Easter egg basket in her left hand. "And delighted."

"I'm delighted too, Mr. Ketchum."

"Ketchum…" Blood rushed to my face. "My name's Wally…"

The Bunny flipped the top of the basket open and withdrew a small revolver. "My sister Florence—"

"Sister?"

"…was beaten and strangled in the Pennsylvania mountains by persons unknown, but she confided in me beforehand that after her divorce and drug rehab and several years surviving lonely and depressed in rural seclusion she began an affair with one Wally Ketchum. Because she lived in a cabin in the woods, no witnesses ever saw this costume-fetish-obsessed lover she described to me as a bartender, handyman, and—in time discovered—borderline sadist. I offered to send her money to leave him, but she was too frightened. I couldn't prove anything from the collect pay-phone calls she made to me, and local police just drew blanks. But as a successful California businesswoman, I had the wherewithal to hire the best PI in the state who tracked down a Horace Ketchum, Wally, who had done heavy time for brutal rape in Delaware. Your prison picture matched Florence's description perfectly, and my gumshoe had no problem locating your latest whereabouts."

"Gumshoe." I slapped her hand so hard the little pistol flew over the bar and plunked to the floorboards. Grabbing her throat I marched to the main switch, doused the lights, and said, "Melodramatic aren't you?"

The perpetual glow of the red exit sign above our heads revealed her lips twisted in an oddly cynical smile rather than the fright I expected to see on her face. This was disappointing since alarm heightens pleasure. So I squeezed a little tighter to alter that damn expression but was surprised to be greeted with a short laugh. Enraged by her audacity, I drew my right fist back, warning, "When I'm done you'll think your sister's ordeal was sheer ecstasy—"

An explosion erupted in my groin, and nausea swept me from stomach to tongue. Electric shocks surged through my left wrist and fingers, and my numbed hand fell from her throat. A sharp cramp shot along my Achilles tendon, and then her forehead struck my nose and I felt my legs being swooped upward. My head slammed to the tiled floor so hard I saw her and her double until I blinked the flashbulb bursts out of my eyes. While my sight was off, my hearing wasn't, and she stated clearly, "Jujitsu, Ketchum—one of my many accomplishments."

I managed to grunt, "Please—don't kill me…"

"Never intended to. That's why I let you take the weapon so easily." She grinned. "Not even loaded."

"Then…what…"

"What are Bunnies famous for?"

"Uh…"

"Humping." She sniggered. "Now let me turn you over."

I was too weak to stop her from rolling me onto my stomach, then kneeling on my spine. She placed her hands under my chin and drew me upward like a human bow. The first jerk of her palms sent fire up my spinal cord. The second triggered an explosion between my ears. Then I felt nothing. She climbed off me, walked around the bar, and fetched the fallen gun. Upon returning she said, "This was carefully thought out, Ketchum. Rather than see you in jail, I imprisoned you in diapers—life sentence at that. Total paralysis waist down. No more sex life. No more beatings of women. And what will you tell police after I notify 9-1-1 on my throwaway cell of your *collapse*—attacked by a woman in a rabbit outfit? Or allude to me as Florence's sister and implicate yourself in her unsolved murder? You don't even know my name or the color of my hair and eyes—contact lenses work wonders. Plus my alibi's been carefully arranged."

She dropped her gun in the basket, headed toward the front door, turned before stepping into the street, wiggled her cotton-tailed butt, and chuckled. "I know. Tell them you were *really* humped by a bunny…"

❦

William E. Chambers, Mystery Writers of America's executive vice president, 2000–02, is the author of the novels Death Toll, The Redemption Factor, *and* The Tormentress. *His short stories have appeared in major mystery magazines and anthologies in the United Sates and England. "If I Quench Thee…," a story of murder through racism, is required reading in London's and Scotland's middle schools.*

THE BANYAN TREE

Joe Clifford

Retreating inside his hoodie, Ricky sprinted into the midnight squall across the empty preserve lot to the car parked beneath the big tree. He pounded on the window. The large man behind the wheel looked over lazily, taking another slow drag on his cigarette, making Ricky wait in the pouring rain a moment longer before finally unlocking the door.

"Fuck, Wade," Ricky said, climbing in front, "I'm drenched now."

Wade cuffed the back of Ricky's head, knocking him forward. "It's Miami. What you want me to do about it?"

Ricky rubbed the back of his skull, mumbling incoherent soft consonants.

Reaching under his seat, Wade retrieved a brown paper bag and held it out. Ricky tried to grab it, but Wade pulled his hand back.

"Not so fast," Wade said. "You know why I'm bailing you out with this?"

"Because I promised to pay you back twice as much?"

"It's not a loan," said Wade. "I'm giving it to you."

"I don't need any favors because I'm Big Rick's kid."

"Wrong. That's exactly what you do need. Your father did right by me—and a lot of other people around here. He deserves better than a drug addict son who's about to land his ass in Metro if he doesn't fly straight." Wade pinched his smoke and took a hard pull.

"Got an extra cigarette?"

"No. It's a bad habit. You got enough of those." Wade shoved the bag hard into Ricky's gut like he was handing off a football.

Ricky doubled over.

"You've forgotten how to take a handoff."

Ricky righted himself and narrowed his eyes. He started to open the bag, but Wade jabbed a hand and cinched it shut.

"Don't worry. It's all there." Wade gestured out the windshield at the big tree they were parked beneath. "You know what kind that is?"

Ricky studied the tree, which looked like it had five trunks, limbs all knotted, gnarled and intertwined, roots anchored in the earth like arthritic alien leg bones. He shrugged.

"Maybe you shouldn't have dropped out of school," Wade said. "It's called a banyan tree. Banyan trees don't grow from the ground like other trees. They start high in the nest of a palm when a bird shits a seed into a frond. When the banyan starts to sprout, it chokes the palm to death as it slithers its own roots down into the soil." Wade stubbed his cigarette in the ashtray. "See, you can focus on one or the other. The violent birth, or the resiliency to rise above origins." He turned to Ricky. "Me? I see a survivor. You dig what I'm saying?"

Ricky giggled.

"What's so goddamn funny?"

"Nothing, man. Just, you know, Wade Wojcik. The Miami City Muscle. Getting all sentimental about a tree."

"You get older, kid, you start seeing things differently." Wade grabbed Ricky by the shoulder. "I was with your father the night you were born, and I seen how proud he was when you started playing ball, before you started fucking your life up with this wannabe gangster shit."

"Well, he ain't around anymore, is he?"

"Listen, you little shit. Your father could've gone to the cops, could've bought himself a little witness protection farm in Kansas, but he didn't. You know why? Because he's a stand-up guy who didn't make excuses. That's what I'm trying to tell you. No matter how screwed up your beginnings, you stake your claim, you dig in and don't let nobody take nothing from you." Wade leaned over, eyes earnest. "All any father wants is for his son to have a better life than him. It's why I'm giving you this money. You pay back your debt. You make this right, however you have to. Then you get your ass back to school, back on the team—"

A loud knock on the driver's side glass stopped Wade's speech. He turned. Out in the rain, a kid Ricky's age stood blank-faced, hands at his side. "What the—"

Ricky pulled the gun from his waistband, firing two shots into Wade's gut. Wade looked down dumbly, trying to stuff the holes leaking bloody intestine. He stared at Ricky and opened his mouth, but only bright red frothed out. Ricky pulled the trigger again, and Wade slumped against the steering wheel, a dead man's gaze fixed on the gun.

Ricky slid over and unlocked the door, and the kid outside jumped in back.

"Holy fuck!" the kid said gleefully. "That was some cold-ass shit!"

"What took you so long?" Ricky snapped.

"Lot of big trees in this park." The kid leaned forward, tentatively peering over the seat. "Is he…?"

"What the fuck you think? Yeah, he's fucking dead." Ricky tried to look tough. "You got the pipe?"

The kid in back fumbled through his pockets, passing pipe and lighter over the console. Ricky tossed him the paper bag full of money. "Stick that in your pocket."

"I thought you were only capping him if he didn't loan you the green?"

"Wasn't a loan. Said he was giving it to me."

"I don't understand," the kid said. "Why'd you shoot him then?"

Ricky dropped a rock in the bowl, sparked the glass. He inhaled deeply, blowing out a thick cloud. "Because while you were beating your meat, I was stuck listening to a goddamn history lesson on trees." The smoke hit, and Ricky felt right.

"Trees? What about 'em?"

Ricky stared through the rain at the ugly banyan tree. He didn't see anything special. There were a million overgrown weeds just like it in these swamps.

"Who the fuck knows," he said. "But I'm on to better things. I popped a cap in Wade Wojcik. When word gets out, I won't just be Big Rick's son anymore.

"They'll know I'm a player in this game for life."

THIS STORY WAS FIRST PUBLISHED IN *NEAR TO THE KNUCKLE*.

Joe Clifford is editor of The Flash Fiction Offensive, *and the producer of* Lip Service West, *a "gritty, real, raw" reading series in Oakland, California. He is the author of three books:* Choice Cuts, Wake the Undertaker *(Snubnose Press), and* Junkie Love *(Vagabondage Press). Much of Joe's writing can be found at JoeClifford.com.*

ACKNOWLEDGMENTS

Christopher Coake

This work—the most significant I've ever attempted—could not have been possible without assistance from many. Please indulge me as I offer my deepest and most abiding thanks to:

Margaret, my wife. You were this story's subject, its reason for being. I think, by its end, you understood me at last.

Paul, who since childhood has been my closest friend. What can I say that I haven't already said? If you never knew me before, you know me now.

My father, who, in so many ways, has been my inspiration. You taught me—in no uncertain terms—that each day in this world we must earn our manhood anew.

Lisie. Here's to the future. Our future.

My children, Melinda and Greg, for your obedience. I have raised you to see only what you must.

Thanks as well to:

The tall, silent man at 437 Wakefield, standing in his yard at two thirty yesterday morning, whose eyes could not penetrate the shadows. To you, sir, I am eternally grateful.

His dog, unchained, who exchanged silence for half a scone.

Ms. Anne LeChance, for Dostoyevsky.

The high-pressure system that stalled last week over the East Coast, causing three days of rain in this city, the rain that softened the ground.

Betsy, my seventh-grade crush, for laughing, laughing.

The Pep-Me-Up, for serving me coffee and a snack at 10:01, even though the sign said CLOSED.

Officer Jim Pope, CPD, for believing.

The admins and message-board community of LastGasp. com, for their most excellent advice.

My mother, for her absence.

All those who have hurt me, for my convictions.

And finally, thanks to the silence, which has lasted.

—◆—

Christopher Coake is the author of You Came Back *(2012) as well as the collection of short stories* We're in Trouble *(2005), which won the PEN/Robert Bingham Fellowship. Coake was listed among "Granta's Best of Young American Novelists" in 2007. His stories have been published in several literary journals and anthologized in* Best American Mystery Stories 2004 *and* Best American Noir of the Century. *He is a professor of English at the University of Nevada.*

THE TERMINAL

Reed Farrel Coleman

Although his window faced a brick wall and the bed was as welcoming as a butcher's block, his dreary little room at the Terminal Hotel was a step up from most of the shitholes he'd crashed in over the years. Rough living and life on the run teaches you how to compartmentalize physical discomfort, and he'd been an apt pupil. The sheer drabness of the joint had its upside. When he was awake, he wanted to be elsewhere.

Given its rich (and by rich I mean pathetic) history, you didn't need an imagination to figure out why they called the place the Terminal Hotel. Unlike the old Half Moon, the place where Murder Inc.'s notorious Abe "Kid Twist" Reles was helped out the window while being guarded by a squad of New York's Finest, death at the Terminal tended to be anonymous and inglorious. Over the decades, it had been the last stop for Drano-drinking housewives, crack whores, and cirrhotic old alkies on a good-bye bender. But like the deaths themselves, the name of the hotel had more mundane origins. It was right across the street from the Stillwell Avenue Terminal in Coney Island: the last stop for several subway lines. Last stops. He knew a little something about last stops.

"They was lookin' for you again, Doc. They out there waitin' for you," the deskman said, fishing for a five-spot. "They know you're here."

Doc. He repeated the name to himself as he put five bucks on the counter. He had a given name too, but that felt more like a pulled tooth in a jar on a dentist's shelf than a part of him.

He stepped out of the Terminal and stood on the corner of Mermaid and Stillwell. It was damp, the ocean breezes cutting ragged little holes right through him. Weather reports were useless this close to the water. Living in Coney had taught him that there was more to the local climate than the heat of the sun, the pull of the moon, or the direction of the wind.

He walked away from the Terminal, past Nathan's, over the boardwalk, onto the beach. He knew they were there behind him. That was okay. She was safe. He was old. He was tired of running. Still, he got the shakes. The salt smell of the sea was nearly overwhelming, but the clank and rumble of subway wheels blending with the swoosh and retreat of the waves relaxed him. He liked it here. He liked how Coney displayed its decay like a badge of honor. It didn't try to hide the scars where pieces of its once-glorious self had been cut off. Stillwell Avenue West was like a showroom of abandonment, the empty buildings wearing their disuse like bankrupted nobility in frayed and fancy suits. He had come to the edge of the sea with the other last dinosaurs: the looming and impotent Parachute Jump, the Wonder Wheel, Nathan's, the Cyclone.

He stared out at the caravan of container ships queuing up to enter the mouth of New York Harbor. He tried imagining what this odd slice of Brooklyn—then populated only by rabbits and local Indians—had looked like to Dutch sailors as they laid their eyes on the New World for the first time. Could they, he wondered, have imagined what this tiny peninsula would become? As he turned to his left to look at Brighton Beach and the Rockaways beyond, he heard their soft footsteps in the sand. He held his ground.

"Hey, Doc." It was Johnny Rosetti and two of his boys. *Boys!* They were the size of the damned Parachute Jump and didn't look nearly as impotent.

"Hey, yourself, Johnny Rosetti."

"Where is she?"

He smiled at Johnny and realized he didn't smile much anymore. "I don't know, and I wouldn't tell you if I did."

"You know, Doc, for some reason I believe you."

"I never lied to you before."

"She used you, Doc. She made a fool of you, old man."

"That may be."

"Was she worth it?"

"I thought she was, but I guess I'm about to find out, huh?"

"I guess you are. I guess you are, Doc. Do us both a favor, old man, and turn around, face the other way. Okay?"

Doc turned his back to the ocean and beheld the amusement park's moth-eaten splendor. From where he stood, in the first light of morning, it still looked a grand place. At that distance, it all seemed in working order. Even the Parachute Jump appeared ready to shine again. From Doc's place in the sand, he thought, you might be able to fool yourself that the sunfaded, blue-finned Astroland rocket atop Gregory and Paul's food stand might fire up its engines and blast off. You had to get much closer to see the truth of it, the rust and folly of the place. So Doc walked ahead.

"Where the fuck is he going, boss?" One of Rosetti's boys asked.

"Fuck if I know," Rosetti answered. "Doc, cut it out. Stop. This isn't going to help you," he called after him.

Doc didn't answer. He didn't stop. He didn't turn back. With each step forward, the truth of the place became more evident. He found a strange comfort in its truth. The truth was that the Parachute Jump was a useless steel carcass and that the Astroland rocket would never fly. Coney Island's truth was its fate, and its fate was Doc's fate, everyone's fate: in the end, we all fall down. In the end, we all have reservations at the Terminal Hotel.

He heard the first shot, but not its echo.

＞＜

Called "a hard-boiled poet" by NPR's Maureen Corrigan and "the noir poet laureate" in the Huffington Post*, Reed Farrel Coleman has published fifteen novels. He is a three-time recipient of the Shamus Award for Best PI Novel, a two-time Edgar Allan Poe Award nominee, and he has won the Macavity, Barry, and Anthony Awards. He is a founding member of Mystery Writers of America University and an adjunct professor of English at Hofstra University. He lives with his family on Long Island.*

THE ANT WHO CARRIED STONES

David Corbett

The woman, on her knees, pressed her lips against the man's rough palm. "I swear, all I've told you, every word—"

"Run through it again." He took back his hand. "All of it."

She didn't dare look at his face. "I haven't lied."

"A thief too proud to lie."

"I didn't steal—"

He got up, kicked his chair backward. It clattered across the bare floor. "I said tell me what happened. Again."

She clenched her hands beneath her chin, steadying them. "My cousin, Marisa—we live in Boca del Monte—she told me all I had to do was carry a suitcase to Panama. I lost my job at the hotel. My daughter, Rosela, she cries herself to sleep—"

"Leave your daughter out of it."

"'People do it every day,' Marisa said. Yes, some get stopped at the airport, the suitcases ripped apart, the money found stitched up inside. But the amounts are legal, just under 78,000 quetzales. No one gets arrested. 'That's why they call us ants, because the amounts are small.'"

"Small to who?"

"Please, I know I made a mistake—"

"A *mistake*?" He snagged the chair, slammed it against the floor. "Talk!"

"Marisa and I delivered our suitcases to a house in Zona 18. They said come back the next day. We did, with maybe twenty others, sitting on the floor in an empty room like this but bigger. Eventually they came and gave us back our suitcases, drove us to the airport. A man named Lorenzo met us there."

"Count yourself lucky you're not him right now."

"It's not his fault."

"You're protecting him?"

"No. I—"

"No means yes. He was in on it."

"There was nothing to be in on, I just…" Her voice trailed off.

"Come on." He snapped his fingers.

"We boarded our plane. Despite what Marisa said, despite the amounts, I was terrified. The police are so corrupt, there's no telling—"

"Getting ahead of yourself, no?"

"Once the plane took off, the others relaxed. I couldn't. Marisa tried to calm me, holding my hand, praying with me—"

"You talked about how you'd get away with it."

"No! Listen to me, she had nothing…It was my stupidity. Mine alone."

She glanced toward the window. Sunlight flared through slatted blinds.

"You landed at La Aurora."

"Lorenzo told us, stay together. But the terminal's so crowded, like fighting a river swollen from rain."

"Screw the crowd. You snuck off."

"I saw a counter, selling blouses. The embroidery, so beautiful. I thought: Rosela would love something like this. My beautiful girl, she's so brave, I've given her so little—"

"I said leave her out of it."

"I didn't even realize I'd stopped walking."

"You thought, Oh, look what I could buy with all this money."

"No. It was a blouse, a simple blouse!"

She put her hand to her face and quietly wept. He let her go for a moment, then another fingersnap.

"The others—they were where?"

"I looked, but there was just this sea of people." She wiped her face. "Suddenly, these policemen appeared."

"Yes, your corrupt police."

"They said they were with the Policia Nacional and ordered me to give them the suitcase."

"Naturally, you obeyed."

"I told you. I fought. They tried to grab it from me. I held on with both hands. I was afraid to call out. What if I just got the others in trouble as well? Try to imagine what I felt. I've never done this, never done anything like it. I'm a simple, silly woman from a poor town. I've never even been in an airport—"

"Yes, yes. These corrupt cops, phony police, whatever, they went for the suitcase."

"One of them slapped me across the face."

He chuckled. "Surely you've been struck before."

She flushed from shame. "I was stunned. I didn't—"

"And they snatched the money."

"They vanished into the crowd. I tried to get my bearings, running one direction, then back, looking for Lorenzo, Marisa."

He turned his head and spat. "You got in a cab."

"I had only a little money, not enough to get back to Guatemala. I didn't know what else to do."

"Who did you call?"

"No one. Who could I—"

"You knew the name of the hotel where the others went."

"I didn't have my suitcase! I was so scared. I needed time to think."

He dug something from his pocket. She dared a glance. The hand she'd kissed now held a pistol.

"Perhaps there's some truth in your story. The river makes noise because it carries stones. But you lost a lot of money."

"Marisa will tell you—"

"She washes her hands of you. Called you a scared, stupid fool."

"Lorenzo—"

"He thinks you went running to the first cop you saw."

"That's a lie! I was confused, scared, I swear—"

"It doesn't matter now." He thumbed back the hammer. "What matters is the money. And the money is gone."

Feeling the gun barrel nestle in her hair, she shut her eyes tight, praying: Lamb of God, who takes away…

He didn't fire. Her terror broke, like a fever, dissolving into clarity, and she could feel, however slightly, that now he was the one trembling.

"I'm not a thief," she said. "You're not a killer. And yet here we are, two stones in the river."

"Stop talking."

"I understand now. Do what you must. I forgive you. Please forgive me."

"Listen to you."

"Whatever happens, you'll go to the airport. You won't be able to help yourself. You'll look for the counter, the one with the blouses. And you'll find it."

"That proves nothing."

"One blouse in particular, with dragonflies and sunflowers and lace. You'll buy it. Tell them to wrap it. Rosela Melendez, Boca del Monte."

"Stop saying her name."

"She's the reason I'm here. Just as you are here because of me."

Finally, she looked up into his face.

—◆—

David Corbett is the author of four novels: The Devil's Redhead, Done for a Dime, Blood of Paradise, *and* Do They Know I'm Running, *as well as the story collection* Killing Yourself to Survive. *His textbook on craft,* The Art of Character, *was published in January 2013.*

WATCH THE SKIES

Bill Crider

Yardley Gardner hasn't been out of his house at night since he was abducted by that UFO five or six years back. He claims he was abducted, anyway. He's never said what the UFO aliens did to him, except that it was so awful that he couldn't describe it to us and that his body cavities were sore for days afterward. Anyway, he won't leave his house at all after dark anymore. Has storm shutters on all the windows and cranks them closed at sundown every day. Got three locks on every door. *Hear no aliens, see no aliens.* He comes out in the daytime, though, to talk to folks. He loves to gossip. The latest thing he's told anybody who'll listen is that Bertha Nance has killed her husband.

"Buried him in the backyard," he told me one day.

Yardley has sort of a dent in the middle of his forehead where his cousin hit him with a shovel when they were kids. Bertha's husband, Harve, claims Yardley's been a total loon ever since. Those two never did get along, always spatting. Most folks think it was the aliens that pushed Yardley over the line, but it could've been the knock on the head, too.

"I believe Bertha said Harve was in Texarkana, visiting his cousin," I told Yard.

Yard had come up to me and started jabbering in the parking lot at Walmart where anybody passing by could hear him. The mayor and police chief and everybody else goes to Walmart, but Yard doesn't know enough to keep his trap shut in public. That was okay by me.

"That's what she'd like us to believe," Yard said. "Truth is, old Harve's out there in her backyard, right under that new flowerbed."

"How do you know that?"

"Where else would she put him?"

I could think of a few places, but I didn't think it would be wise to tell Yardley.

"You never liked Harve," I said. "You ought to be glad he's gone off to see his cousin."

"Son of a bitch killed my dog," Yardley said.

The Nances were Yardley's neighbors. The dog had been digging in Harve's yard and killing his chickens. Harve ran over it one day. He said it was an accident, that the dog had run out to chase his car and got hit. Nothing he could do about it. Yardley didn't believe it. Nobody did, but nobody could prove any different.

"Didn't treat Bertha worth a damn, either," Yardley said.

That was true. Harve was a tight man with a dollar, and he had a mouth on him. He never hit Bertha, far as I know, but he'd cussed her out many a time.

"That's why she killed him," Yardley said. "I heard the gunshot one night."

If he heard it, it would've had to be right under one of those sealed-tight windows, but somebody could've fired off a gun there.

"You can't hear anything, the way you're shut up in that house of yours."

"I got good reason for that."

"Maybe it was aliens you heard," I said, "come to get Harve."

"Ha ha. You're a real comedian." He was trying to show he wasn't bothered, but I could tell he was. He had to lash out at me to make up for it. "You're glad Harve's dead. I know about you two. You probably helped her kill him."

"You told the police that yet?"

"I will, by God. I'll tell 'em today."

"Don't forget the part about the flowerbed," I said as he stalked off across the parking lot.

The police dug up Bertha's new flowerbed the next day. A bunch of us wanted to watch, but they wouldn't let us get real close. They didn't find Harve, of course. They apologized to Bertha, and she told them that she was worried about Harve.

"He usually calls me when he goes to visit his cousin," she said, "but I haven't heard from him."

Leo Goolsby's the police chief. He asked her if she thought something might've happened to Harve.

"I don't know," she said. "He said he was going to stop by Yardley's and apologize about that dog of his before he left. I haven't seen him since."

Leo said he'd stop by and ask Yardley about Harve. We bystanders trooped along behind him. Yardley said he didn't know what Leo was talking about. Leo was about to leave when he noticed that there was a freshly dug patch of ground back of Yardley's house. Maybe somebody called his attention to it. Anyway, they dug it up, and there was old Harve, taking a dirt nap.

Yardley started yelling and said the UFO aliens must've killed Harve and planted the body there after they'd experimented on it.

Leo said, "Sure, sure," and they carried Yardley off to jail. He yelled all the way.

"Yardley'll get off on an insanity plea," Bertha told me that night. "They'll send him to some state hospital or other."

"He'll be happy there just as long as they keep him all closed up at night," I said.

"I thought Leo wasn't going to notice that pile of dirt," Bertha said. "Lord knows it was so big I thought a blind man could see it."

"Luckily somebody called his attention to it."

Bertha smiled and went over to a window to look outside. "You think we'll be bothered by any aliens tonight?"

"Watch the skies," I said.

She turned to me. "We have better things to do."

"You got that right," I said.

Bill Crider won the Anthony Award for best first mystery novel in 1987 for Too Late to Die. *His story "Cranked" was nominated for the Edgar Allan Poe Award. His latest novel is* Murder of a Beauty Shop Queen *(St. Martin's Press). See his home page at BillCrider. com and his peculiar blog at BillCrider.blogspot.com.*

A FOOLPROOF PLAN

Bruce DeSilva

"What'll it be, hon?"

"Just coffee."

"Just coffee?"

"That's what I said."

"You're takin' up a whole booth during breakfast rush, and you just want coffee?"

"Yeah."

She crossed her arms and glared.

"We got banana pancakes today."

"La de fuckin' da."

"Can I tempt you?"

"No."

"Could you maybe move to the counter, then?"

"Just bring the fuckin' coffee, Doris. And ask Vito to drop by my table."

"You're here to see Vito?"

"I gotta say it again?"

She lurched away, clubfoot dragging behind. Two minutes later she returned and placed a ceramic cup in front of him.

"Sit tight. Vito says he'll just be a minute."

As she turned away, he placed his hand on the coffee cup.

"Hey, Doris! This ain't hot."

"Sorry. Let me bring you some from a fresh pot."

So she did.

"Okay now?"

He touched the cup and felt the heat. "Yeah, it is."

"Ain't you gonna try it?"

"I don't drink coffee."

"Then why do you care if it's hot?"

"I'm still payin' for it, ain't I?"

She smirked and hobbled off.

A couple of minutes later, Vito dropped into the seat across from him.

"Help you with somethin', Bobo?"

"Yeah. Two pieces of pie."

"Apple or blueberry?"

"One of each. Mikey don't like blueberry."

"How many times I gotta tell ya? No names."

"Sorry. I forgot."

"Want fries with that?" Vito asked.

"For both of 'em, yeah."

"One box apiece?"

"Way more'n we need."

"See me out back in five."

Bobo spent five minutes watching the rain dent the puddles in the parking lot. Then he trudged out the diner's front door and circled around back.

Vito stood between an overflowing Dumpster and his Mercury Grand Marquis, a model he favored because of the oversize trunk. When he spotted Bobo, he popped the trunk and rummaged through the boxes stacked inside. He chose two and handed them to Bobo.

"Apple for you, blueberry for your bud. Seven fifty, total. I'm throwin' in the fries for free. Don't open the boxes, asshole. Somebody might see."

"I need to know what I'm buyin', Vito."

"Taurus .38 Special for you. Cylinder holds five rounds. Ruger semiauto for your pal. Magazine holds ten .22 longs."

"Better iron than we need. Only using 'em once."

"It's what I got, Bobo. Take it or leave it."

"Serial numbers filed off?"

"Fuck, no. These babies are brand new. Went missing from a gun shop in Worcester last month. Get caught with 'em, just say you bought 'em off some guy at a gun show. Ain't nobody can prove different."

"Gotcha," Bobo said. He peeled the seven fifty from a roll of damp bills.

Mikey was watching bondage porn on his laptop when Bobo shouldered through the door to their Federal Hill flat.

"Get the pieces?"

"What the fuck you think I'm carryin' here?"

"We still a go for tomorrow?"

"Lemme check with Sheila while I take a shit." He slid the phone from his pants pocket, unbuckled his belt, and hustled to the bathroom.

"Jesus! Shut the fuckin' door and open the window, will ya, Bobo?"

Ten minutes later, Bobo exited the bathroom, slumped beside Mikey on the fake-leather sofa, and saw that his roommate had put the video on pause.

"We still good?" Mikey asked.

"Still good."

"Tell me again how it's gonna go down."

"At two thirty p.m., we hotwire two SUVs at Union Station, drive to Honey Dew Donuts on Allens Avenue, and watch for a lime-green Isuzu box truck with Finnerty Shipping on the door panels."

"Why would he use Allens Avenue?"

"Sheila says the driver don't like the downtown Providence exit. Too much traffic. He always gets off on Thurbers and takes Allens going north."

"Okay."

"Soon as we see it, we pull outta the lot, box it in, jump out, and order the driver to get outta the truck."

"And if he don't?"

"He will when I shove my piece in his face."

"You sure he's gonna be alone?"

"Sheila says yeah."

"And then?"

"We leave the SUVs in the street, jump in the truck, and drive to Grasso's warehouse. His boys open the door for us, and we pull right in. Grasso hands us the cash, and we're gone. Whole thing shouldn't take more'n ten minutes."

"And he's paying us how much?"

"Twenty cents on the dollar. A hundred HP Pavilion laptops, seven hundred ninety-nine dollars retail, makes our cut just under sixteen grand."

"Sounds foolproof," Mikey said.

Just after three p.m., the partners slipped on ski masks, gunned it out of the Honey Dew lot, and forced the box truck to a halt. Bobo rapped his revolver on driver's side window, ordered him out, and slipped behind the wheel. Mikey confiscated the driver's cell phone, stomped on it , and climbed into the passenger seat.

Bobo cranked the ignition, bulldozed Mikey's SUV out of the way, and roared down the street. Five minutes later, they pulled into Grasso's warehouse, the overhead door creaking shut behind them.

Bobo and Mikey jumped down from the truck and slapped high fives with two of Grasso's boys. Grasso stepped out of his office and strolled over.

"Any trouble?" he asked.

"Smooth as a teenage pussy," Bobo said. "Give us our cut and we'll be on our way."

"First show me what I'm buying."

Bobo reached into the truck and slid the key from the ignition. He unlocked the rear door and rolled it up.

"Aw, shit!" he said.

"What?" Mikey said. He peered into the back and saw nothing but a load of folding metal chairs.

Grasso's boys drew semiautos from their waistbands. Bobo's piece of apple pie was stuck in his pocket. Mikey had left his slice of blueberry in the truck.

"Boss?" one of Grasso's boys said.

The boss rubbed his chin, thinking it over.

"Load their bodies in the back and dump the rig in the parking lot at Green Airport."

—◆—

Bruce DeSilva is the author of the hard-boiled Mulligan crime novels. The first, Rogue Island, *won the Edgar Allan Poe and Macavity Awards. The second,* Cliff Walk, *was recently published to rave reviews, including starred reviews in* Publishers Weekly *and* Booklist. *Previously he worked as a senior editor at the Associated Press.*

A TREE IN TEXAS

Jo Dereske

For Archie

He woke up under a tree in Texas.

A palm tree, actually, outside a baby-blue building, which, from James's position, appeared to be a cruise ship on stilts. It had a curved prow and porthole windows and balconies like those underwater images of the *Titanic*. A group of gray-haired people lined the railing, pointing at him.

He gave a halfhearted wave—au revoir—hoping for something better next time he opened his eyes. His head pulsed; his stomach roiled.

James struggled to remember. Music festival, that's right. Austin. Reams of people. Too much to drink, no shit. But then what?

"Jimmy?" The voice sounded familiar.

"Grandma?" he asked, opening his eyes as he recalled his grandmother was dead.

"No, honey. It's me, Lily."

It was them, the gray-haired people from the railing. Five, no, six of them, standing in a circle gazing down at him, all wearing lime-green T-shirts that read, CROQUET AT LA MIRAGE—IT'S REAL!

"Lily?" Who was Lily?

She blinked big eyes behind glasses, looking worried, like *somebody's* grandmother, which was probably why James complained like a child, "My head hurts."

"Of course it does, dear," she soothed, "after all that liquor. We were worried about you."

The others, three women, two men, gravely nodded.

"Where am I?" James sat up, wincing.

"Just you sit quiet for a minute," the woman named Lily said. "Georgia, where's that coffee?"

A thick mug was pushed at James, and he gingerly drank the black brew while the women clucked and a man with a walker intoned, "Good for what ails you."

James absorbed his surroundings. More palm trees, a second baby-blue building behind the first. "How'd I get here?"

"This is La Mirage, and you asked for a ride," Lily told him. "To see the Gulf."

"My wallet…"

Glances were exchanged. Murmuring. Lily's face pinked. She appeared embarrassed. "Did you leave it in Dolly's condo?"

"Who's Dolly?"

More glances. Meaningful. Then, as if a group decision had been reached, "C'mon. We'll show you."

They led him to an outside elevator. "Dolly's on third," Lily explained, and all seven of them piled into the elevator, jostling like tourists on an excursion.

"We met last night?" he asked, still fuzzed. "All of us?"

"Mm-hmm," Georgia confirmed. "At the Palomino Bistro."

James had been high when he'd entered the Palomino. A vague image of old people yucking it up in the corner, louder than anybody.

On the third floor, a passing elderly man shook his head. "The Croquet Club rides again, I see."

Georgia giggled, "High-ho, Silver. Away!"

Everybody was old. "Is this a retirement home?" James asked.

"A *community*," Lily amended primly.

Nobody answered Dolly's door. "She doesn't lock," Lily said. "Go on in and find your wallet."

"Check the bedroom," one of the men advised, and the women tittered.

James hesitated, but they shoved him inside and crowded the open doorway, watching.

It was a studio, and he spotted a lime-green T-shirt draped across a chair, gray hair, then her bare leg sticking unnaturally from beneath a flowered coverlet. "Holy shit."

They pressed inside, slamming the door. James heard their stage-whisper voices.

"Is she?"

"She is."

"Poor Dolly."

"Is that a bruise on her neck? Better call the cops."

And lastly, "Oh, Jimmy, what did you do?"

"Nothing," he squeaked in panic. "I don't even know who she is."

"You knew Dolly last night, for sure," Walker-Man said sternly.

"You're joking. Not me. She's old."

Tut-tutting from the women.

"I mean, too old for *me*," James tried to amend. Too late.

"Did you hurt Dolly?" Georgia asked.

"Call the cops," Walker-Man repeated.

"No. Listen," James tried. "It wasn't me. I swear to God." Sweat slid down his pits. "I didn't do anything to her."

"You got reasons to be scared of the cops, young man?"

"No." But he'd paused, and they tensed. "Just a few outstanding tickets, that's all."

James couldn't look at the body. He hadn't seen Dolly's face, but he knew he hadn't…he *couldn't* have. A few drugs, a little light-fingeredness, maybe, but not…*this.*

The stares and silence continued too long. His heart ratcheted. If he could just make it out the door…

"Jimmy, honey," Lily finally said. "I believe you." The others grumbled and shifted.

"Dolly was a wild one." Lily shook her head. "And old people die. But you understand we have to call the police, don't you?"

He nodded.

She sighed. "I think I should take you to the bus station."

"Now?" he croaked, hopeful.

James sat on the floor of Lily's van, watching the fronded tops of palm trees. She hummed from the driver's seat and, when she stopped, warned him, "Stay down. I'll buy your ticket."

"My wallet—" he began.

"Got it right here," she sang out, and the door slammed.

Lily waved from the ramp as his bus pulled away. The driver suddenly braked, and James froze, expecting the cops, but only a flustered older woman scurried aboard.

"Thanks," she told the bus driver and dropped into the seat beside James. "Almost didn't make it."

James nodded, waving one last time to Lily, flooded with gratitude. She *did* look grandmotherly.

"You know Lily?" the woman asked, gazing past him.

"Not really."

"What's that club up to this time?"

"The Croquet Club? I don't play."

She snorted. "Neither do they. They wear those T-shirts—it means they're on an escapade." She shook her head. "Old fools acting like the meanest kids you hated in school. The things I've seen them do. Ugly, just ugly bad tricks."

"Like what?"

"You don't want to know." She shrugged and cozied into her seat. "Shame on me, gossiping. Dolly's one of them, but if she hadn't given me a ride, I'd have missed this bus for sure."

Jo Dereske is the author of eighteen published novels, including the Miss Zukas mystery series, and the Ruby Crane mysteries. She divides her time between Sumas, Washington, and the Bulkley River Valley in northern British Columbia.

AFTER

Tyler Dilts

A fter the flash of terror, after the dull steel head of the hammer strikes again and again, there is darkness.

And there is cold.

And there is emptiness.

Then you, squatting, looking down at the pool of blood on the floor, the tiny islands of bone and brain.

Outside an old woman cries on the porch. You talk to her, say soft things, comforting things.

There are people on the lawn. Inside the yellow line, they have uniforms; outside of it, they don't. The woman sees someone in the crowd, on the other side, a young man in a hat. She starts to raise her arm to point, but you stop her, gently push it back. You call a uniform over, whisper something in her ear, and then she says something into a radio.

The young man in the hat is surrounded by four officers and forced into the back of a police car.

The old woman cries.

In the back of the car, the young man in the hat stares out of the window with nothing in his eyes.

You're in the kitchen. Another woman is there, shorter, darker, in a suit the same dark color as yours. She looks away from the blood and up at you expectantly. You motion for her to join you. When she does, an unvoiced question hanging between you, you nod and you say maybe.

The young man in the hat sits in a small gray room in the pale glare of the fluorescent light. There's a table tucked into the corner. His left arm is resting on it. The hat is gone.

In one of the stalls, a toilet flushes. You run a hand through your hair, then take a travel toothbrush and a small tube of toothpaste out of your pocket. You tuck your tie in between the buttons of your shirt and lean forward while you clean your teeth. When you're done, you spit again into the sink and make a cup out of your hand. You slurp water out of your palm, swish it around for a few seconds, and swallow. Another glance in the mirror, a deep breath, and you're done.

The old woman who was crying on the porch sits at a Formica-topped dining table staring down at an untouched sandwich. She doesn't eat. She is still crying.

Outside the room where the young man waits, the woman from the kitchen speaks to you. Tries to change your mind about something. You don't change it.

You sure? she says.

Yes, you say.

You've both taken off your coats. Your shirts are the same color, too.

In the room it's just you and the young man without the hat.

You speak to him kindly, offer him food, something to drink. He says he is, now that he thinks about it, hungry. You leave but come back quickly with a sandwich and a can of soda. He thanks you.

You talk to him while he eats.

He answers between swallows.

You say something funny, and he lets out a little laugh.

The friendliness is surprising.

In the hall with the woman before you came in, you were serious and composed. Not like this. Not like this at all.

You ask him about baseball, about his hat. You talk about his favorite team. You sound like you know a lot about the game. After a lot of talk about teams and players and games, you're talking about the team at the high school he graduated from and the community college where he's now enrolled.

He doesn't realize you're talking about him now.

You lean forward and talk to him in an understanding and compassionate tone. As you lean back, you grasp the seat of your chair and pull it forward a few inches, so that when you settle against the backrest your face is the same distance from the young man as it was before, but now your knees are closer.

Tell me about Heather, you say.

In the next room, the woman in the same color shirt watches you on a video monitor and smiles a sad smile.

The old woman who was crying on the porch and who didn't eat her sandwich is sitting up in bed, holding her knees to her chest in the dark. She is still crying.

You loved her, didn't you? you say.

The young man nods.

Tell me about her, you say.

He does.

The two of you speak for a long time.

You do the thing with your chair two more times. You're very close to the young man now.

He's sad.

So are you.

You talk about unrequited love. You tell him a story about a girl you loved. How hard it was when she didn't love you back. How sometimes it even made you angry. Angry enough to do something bad.

He looks in your eyes. He begins to weep.

The woman watching the monitor in the next room nods. There it is, she whispers to the empty room.

The old woman in the dark is still crying.

You wrap your arm around the young man's shoulder and lean in even closer, your forehead almost touching his. I understand, you say, I understand. But I need to know about the hammer.

The young man without the hat looks at you, lowers his eyes, and tells you about the hammer.

After his confession, something is different.

There is a receding.

A fading.

And the darkness comes again.

And though I don't understand why, I imagine that the cold does not follow, and that the emptiness, after you, is not quite so empty.

Tyler Dilts is the author of the novels A King of Infinite Space *and* The Pain Scale. *His shorter work has appeared in* The Best American Mystery Stories, *the* Los Angeles Times, *the* Chronicle of Higher Education, *and in numerous other publications. He received his MFA in creative writing from California State University, Long Beach, where he now teaches.*

NEXT RIGHT

Sean Doolittle

In the morning we met Julie for breakfast in the restaurant next door to the motel. She breezed in ten minutes past seven wearing jean shorts with the pockets showing, a low-cut T-shirt, and the cowboy boots she'd bought at a truck stop along the way. She looked almost like someone else's grown daughter until she smiled and slid into the booth. Our girl.

"Look at you," I said. "All ready for the rodeo."

Donna kicked my ankle under the table. Julie poked out her tongue, admiring her own heel. "I think they're drop-dead," she said. "Plus they make me taller."

"You were born taller." I handed her a menu. "Order up, cowgirl."

While she browsed her options, Julie remarked that she liked people in this part of the country. "They just trust you. It's nice."

Donna said, "Just trust you like how?"

"Like this morning I went down the hall for ice," Julie said. "But I left the key card in my room. So I went to the counter and asked for another, and the girl? You know what she did?"

I sipped my coffee. "Gave you another key card?"

"Just asked my room number and handed one over."

Donna laughed. "Why on earth wouldn't she?"

"She wasn't the same girl as last night," Julie said. "She'd never seen me before. I could have been anybody off the street."

"Maybe it was the boots," I said.

Donna bit back a grin.

"Just for that I'm ordering extra everything," Julie said. "I'm completely starved."

"Well, you're getting taller," I said.

We made it to Laramie and found campus by midday. We could see mountains from the stoop of her dorm. Julie clapped and giggled. "Would you look at this place?"

I still couldn't get used to the idea. This kid of ours, who'd tripped over her own feet until she was fourteen, had offers to play volleyball for half a dozen schools, at least four of them closer to home. But the best had come from the University of Wyoming, located in—of all places—Wyoming. To Donna and me, it might as well have been the moon.

We spent the afternoon unpacking the U-Haul and lugging her things up to her room. Then we all traipsed to a local used-car dealership. "I want a pickup truck," Julie said. "With a gun rack!" We settled on a six-year-old Jetta with no rust and decent miles.

An hour before dusk, we stood around hugging and telling our baby girl good-bye. "Only till Thanksgiving," she said. "And Christmas. And I'll call every week." She waved from the parking lot as we pulled away.

Donna made it almost to the edge of town before she broke down sobbing. I pulled over and rubbed her back. "Enough of that," I said. "She'll be fine."

Donna nodded and wiped at her eyes. I dug in the console, handed her a tissue. She honked her nose. Then she took a deep breath and shoved open her door. "Trade places," she said. "I need to drive."

We followed our shadow and watched the prairie roll by until the sun disappeared behind us. The empty U-Haul rattled on our tail in the dark. The Tahoe felt bigger with just the two of us.

We stopped for the night at the same place where we'd started the morning. Donna said she was hungry for junk food and asked if I wanted anything from the gas station nearby. A bag of chips sounded all right. I sat on the bed and watched the news while she was gone.

When she hadn't come back in an hour, I started to worry. Then the door clicked and in she came, reeking of cigarettes, a bulging grocery sack in her arms. She had a look on her face I hadn't seen in years. As far as I knew, she hadn't smoked a cigarette since before Julie was born.

"What's all that?" I said.

She came over and showed me: two laptop computers, two touch-screen smart phones, and a dashboard GPS unit. All used. She pulled them out one after the other, like steaks from the market. I looked at her.

"I asked the girl at the counter for another key card to room 172." She wore a goofy smile. "Know what she did?"

I looked at the pile of loot on the bed and couldn't believe this woman I'd married. Room 172. We were in 124.

I said, "So, no chips?"

When our next-door neighbors sent their kids off to college, Carla picked up her photography again; Roger bought a solid-body Fender and turned the other bedroom into a recording studio. "What empty nest?" he asked me on their patio one evening, grinning like a pirate as he cracked another home-brewed beer.

Over the years I've wondered what Roger and Carla would say if they knew our real story. Donna and I lived pretty fast, once upon a time—we weren't high school sweethearts, like we've always told them; the man who introduced us died alone in prison when Julie was small. As far as Julie knows, she grew up in the suburbs with small-business owners for parents. It would knock that kid right out of her cowboy boots to learn she was born in the back of a getaway car.

"I should feel guilty," Donna said in the morning, somewhere in the Nebraska Sandhills. "They looked like a nice pair." She was still talking about the couple from room 172—at least what she'd seen of them, heading for a late-night dip in the motel pool, just before she'd slipped in and robbed them blind.

I couldn't help smiling. "Well," I said, "At least you got that out of your system."

We drove on toward the sunrise, the empty U-Haul rattling behind us, nowhere to be anytime soon. A sign up ahead said LODGING NEXT RIGHT. She raised her eyebrows at me.

◆

Sean Doolittle is the award-winning author of six novels of crime and suspense, including Lake Country, *his latest. Doolittle's books have been praised by such contemporaries as Dennis Lehane, Laura Lippman, Harlan Coben, Michael Connelly, and Lee Child. His short fiction has appeared in* The Best American Mystery Stories 2002 *and elsewhere. The author lives in western Iowa with his family.*

THE PROFESSIONAL

Brendan DuBois

In the lower Connecticut Valley town of Spencer, Olsen sat in his Crown Victoria sedan, eating a container of boysenberry yogurt, when things around him drastically and spectacularly went to shit. He was on Main Street in a Police Cruisers Only spot, the radio on so he could listen in to the dispatcher's infrequent calls, the latest being that the sole day cruiser suddenly was at the town garage for unexpected repairs.

It was a grand spring day with people milling along the sidewalks, most of them local college students from Massachusetts or Connecticut, spending their parents' hard-invested money. Stores lined both sides of the street, and there was a brown UPS truck making deliveries, a white van near a deli unloading plastic-wrapped food boxes, and a shiny black armored van in a handicapped zone, with a bored-looking guard leaning against the closed doors. The van's paintwork said IRON VAULT PROTECTION SERVICE. Olsen shifted in his seat. The Kevlar vest he wore under his blue blazer, shirt, and tie was stiff, but it was part of the job. Jobs. It looked like everyone out there was quietly doing his or her job, and it made Olsen content. He liked professionalism in everything, whether something as complex as space travel or something as simple as street cleaning. But parking in a handicapped spot was definitely not professional. Maybe he should do something about it. The van's rear doors opened up.

A spoonful of yogurt was en route to his mouth, just one minute before noon, when a red, mud-splattered Chevy pickup truck with oversize tires roared up from a side street and skidded to a halt behind the armored van. Two men burst out, wearing ski masks and carrying shotguns. The first one got out quickly and shot the no-longer-bored-looking guard at the rear.

BOOM! The hollow sound echoed up the narrow street, and people started screaming and running away, as if that annual Spanish bull run had suddenly dropped by. The second guy fired his shotgun and a window shattered. More screams. A guard tumbled out of the van's rear, firing off several rounds from his pistol, and a street lamp a few yards away broke to pieces. Another shotgun blast, the guard dropped, and the two robbers ducked inside the open van.

Olsen carefully put his spoon inside his yogurt container. Aloud he said, "You have *got* to be kidding me."

The two men came out of the van, screaming at each other, each holding bags in one hand, shotguns in the other. The bags were tossed into the rear of the truck. Another shotgun blast. *BOOM!* A male pedestrian across the way fell. More screams. More shouts between the robbers. Two more canvas bags tossed into the truck bed. They got back in. Smoke rose from scorched rubber as the driver punched the accelerator. The truck slewed as it roared up Main Street, clipping two parked cars.

Olsen wiped his lips with a napkin, started up his Crown Victoria, and began his pursuit.

From downtown Spencer there were at least three ways of getting onto state roads and from there, the nearest Interstate, in about ten minutes. The knuckleheads up ahead chose none of those routes.

They kept on going straight on the local Route 12, the truck easy to follow. Olsen kept his distance, ignoring the panicked chatter over his police radio. There. A quick turn up a narrow paved road, going up into the hills. Olsen slowed and made the turn as well.

It didn't take long. About a half mile up the narrow country road there was a dirt cutoff to the left. A cloud of dust was eddying in the air, and fresh tire tracks were cut into the dirt. Olsen braked, pondered his options, and decided a direct approach was best. He turned left and sped down the dirt road. It widened into a dead end. The pickup truck was next to a light-blue Ford Escort. Two men were at the rear of the truck, their faces red and sweaty, hair matted down, no doubt from having worn those ski masks.

Olsen braked again, put the Crown Vic in park, and stepped out.

The nearest guy said crossly, "The hell do you want?" as his companion reached into the open truck bed for a shotgun.

"Not much," Olsen said, as he took out a Sig Sauer 9 mm and shot the first one dead, and then from his ankle holster, quickly removed a .357 stainless steel Ruger, and did the same to the second.

A quick glance into the canvas bags revealed bundles of single dollar bills, a whole lot of bank deposits with local checks, and lots of rolled coins.

That was it.

Olsen shook his head, went back to work, and after a while, strolled back to his Crown Victoria.

"Amateurs," he said.

A month later, Olsen was back in his Crown Victoria, once again eating lunch, once again enjoying the sights of downtown Spencer. The people were out, the sun was shining, and once again, the van from IRON VAULT PROTECTION SERVICES—with two new guards—was in the handicapped spot.

He took another swallow from the yogurt. The news from last month had been shocking, but the Spencer police had quickly solved the case. Two brothers had wanted to make a quick score, but had bungled the entire thing. An argument ensued as they tried to divvy up the meager loot, ending up in a shoot-out that killed them both.

It was almost noon. Olsen put the yogurt container down, removed his new 9 mm Beretta, and started up the Crown Victoria. Earlier on, the dispatcher had once again reported the town's sole police cruiser was back in the garage. Can you believe that?

He pulled into traffic and eased up to the armored van, whose doors were now open.

Olsen stopped the car, stepped out, and went to work. In a land of amateurs, the professional was always king.

—◆—

Brendan DuBois is the award-winning author of more than 115 short stories and twelve novels, including Deadly Cove *(2011, St. Martin's Press). His stories have appeared in* Playboy, Ellery Queen Mystery Magazine, Alfred Hitchcock's Mystery Magazine, *numerous anthologies including* The Best American Mystery Stories of the Century, *and have twice won Shamus Awards and three Edgar Allan Poe Award nominations. Visit his website at BrendanDuBois.com.*

THE PROMISE

Warren C. Easley

Momma always said I slept like a nervous bird. When I heard the front door click open that night, I got up and peeked down the hall. It was Momma's new boyfriend, Duane, and he was just closing the door behind him.

He looked real surprised to see me. "Oh, hi, Sprout. Just havin' a smoke outside."

I hated it when he called me Sprout. My name's Kat. "You must have smoked a pack, 'cause I heard you go out a long time ago."

He laughed, but his eyes got kind of small and hard. "One cigarette. You were dreaming."

Early the next morning, I heard Momma's cell ring. Momma rushed into my room. "Kat, get up. Something's happened to Pop Pop." We drove over to my grandfather's house. There were lots of police cars and flashing lights. Momma told me to stay in the car. I knew something awful had happened, and my heart sort of shriveled up in my chest.

I started thinking about the day before. I was at Pop Pop's house, teaching him how to use his new cell phone:

"Punch the number in first, then press the little green light. That sends the call."

He chuckled the way he always does, 'specially when he's laughing at himself. "I'm an old dog, Kat. It's hard to teach me new tricks."

He was gray and bent with big hands rough as tree bark, but his eyes had a kindness in them that shined like a light. "You're not old," I told him, "least not to me."

Before I left he hugged me and gave me a serious look. "How are things at home?"

I dropped my eyes. "All right."

"That new fella, Duane, he's treating you okay?"

"Yeah, I guess."

"You guess?"

My face got a little hot. I didn't like Duane, but couldn't say why. "He's okay."

"Are they using?"

"I don't know, Pop Pop. I keep to my room, mostly."

He hugged me again. "Listen, now that you've taught me to use this phone, you can call me anytime, Kat. I promise I'll ans—"

I jumped when Momma opened the car door. She was all in tears. "Pop Pop got robbed last night," she said.

"Is he okay?"

"No, Kat. He's not. Pop Pop's dead. The burglar killed him."

Momma held me for a long time. When I stopped crying, she said, "Kat, the police want to talk to you. Listen, honey, they don't like Duane 'cause he's got a record. Don't say nothin' bad about him, okay?"

"Momma, he went out last night. I heard him."

She gripped my shoulders so hard it hurt. "No, he didn't, Kat. He was with me. Don't say that to the police. Please, honey. Duane's a good man."

I talked to a nice police lady and didn't say anything bad about Duane or Momma. Another policeman came in, and the nice lady excused herself and joined him across the room. I looked down at the hole in the toe of my sneaker like I wasn't listening, but I was. "The murder weapon's missing," he said in a low tone. "Something heavy, like a hammer." She told the man about Pop Pop's cell phone. The man nodded and said, "That's missing, too, along with his wallet and cash."

When everything in the apartment got quiet that night, I snuck out of my room. Duane kept his tools on a shelf next to the washer. I pulled a chair up and looked for his hammer. I'd used it just the other day and knew it had red paint on the handle. The hammer was gone.

"Whatcha lookin' for, Sprout?" I jerked around and there was Duane. A cigarette dangled from the side of his mouth, and his eyes were hard again, like little stones.

A pack of spiders crawled down my back. "Uh, a screwdriver," I answered, pulling one out of the toolbox and adding real fast, "You're not supposed to smoke in the apartment."

He blew smoke from his nose and smiled like a snake. "Things are gonna change around here, Sprout. We're gonna move out of this dump into your granddad's house."

I lay in bed with my door locked, trying to think what to do. When I finally dozed off, I dreamed about Pop Pop. He smiled down at me, held up his cell phone, and said, *"You can call me anytime, Kat. I promise I'll answer."*

I woke up and snuck Momma's cell phone from the hall table. When I tapped in Pop Pop's number, it rang several times before going to voice mail—"Hi, this is Claude. Leave a message." He did answer me! When I heard his voice, I knew what I needed to do.

I slipped out the front door and ran down Fourth Avenue till I got to the alley that cut through to Pop Pop's street. There were a few lights, but it was mostly dark and scary in there.

I started down the alley, dialing Pop Pop's number again and again. My legs were shaking, but the sound of his voice kept me going. Halfway in I heard it—the ringtone I'd put on his phone. It came from a humongous trash can. I took the lid off and pulled hard on the lip of the can, tipping it over with a crash. Dogs started barking up and down the alley. I didn't care.

I sifted through the garbage till I found a plastic bag that buzzed with Pop Pop's ringtone. The bag was tied shut, but a wooden handle with red paint on it had punched through the side. I put the lighted face of my phone up to the handle and saw a clear fingerprint in blood.

I dialed 911 and sat down to wait.

THIS STORY WAS FIRST PUBLISHED IN *EVERY DAY FICTION*.

Warren C. Easley lives on a ridge overlooking the Willamette Valley near Portland, Oregon. A chemist and former R & D executive, he is the recipient of a Willamette Writers Kay Snow Award for fiction, and his short stories have won several awards. Easley is author of the Cal Claxton Oregon mysteries (WarrenEasley.com), which will be published by Poisoned Pen Press beginning in the summer of 2013.

A STUDENT OF HISTORY

Gerald Elias

Patient? Of course I'm patient. I'm patient as a saint, so I've been told. I can watch a glacier melt, though maybe that was a better analogy back in the day. Patience is one of the great virtues. If the creationists understood that for three billion years—more or less—evolution has been the miracle that demonstrates God's patience, maybe they wouldn't be so impatient to throw it under the bus. But patience has its limits, doesn't it? After all, we let Hitler invade half of Europe trying to be patient. Get him to listen to reason. Who was it—Neville Chamberlain—that said "peace in our time"? There's a fine line between patience and appeasement. As a student of history, sometimes you have to draw a line in the sand, don't you? So you're not taken advantage of.

Then there's mercy. That's the other great virtue. I love that speech Portia gives in *The Merchant of Venice*, the quality of mercy. It's one of my favorites. Give me a sec while I put on my best Laurence-Olivier-in-drag accent: "The quality of mercy is not strain'd. It droppeth as the gentle rain from heaven, Upon the place beneath. It is twice blest; It blesseth him that gives and him that…" Am I boring you? All right then, I'll cut to the chase, since you seem to be in a hurry. Blah blah blah blah blah "it is enthroned in the hearts of kings, it is an attribute to God himself and earthly power doth then show likest God's when mercy seasons justice." Etcetera. I believe that to be some of Shakespeare's best writing. She really did screw Shylock, though. Took away everything that was important to him and forced him to be a Christian. I think there's a bit of hypocrisy going on there, but still she makes a good point, even if there's no black and white. Like when we dropped the bomb. Most of the people in Hiroshima probably didn't think we were being merciful, but then when you look at the big picture—all the others who would've died had we not done it; and don't forget Russia was on Japan's doorstep. What would the world be like now if we had been thinking of mercy in the narrow sense? I'm talking about religion and war a lot, aren't I? They seem to go hand in hand in a way. I think people have a right to believe what they want, though I'm not particularly observant. I don't approve of fanaticism of any kind. Believe me, I've seen more than enough of that for your lifetime and mine. It really is good to be home. Why did I kill her? I believe that's what you asked me. If she hadn't been a stranger, I probably wouldn't have. Let me amend that to be perfectly honest: I *might* not have. But she put her hand on me for no good reason. None that I could think of at that moment, anyway. There really was no choice. It's easy to be a Monday-morning quarterback, isn't it? At that moment I had to draw a line in the sand. Didn't I?

—◆—

Gerald Elias is an internationally renowned musician and an award-winning author. A former violinist of the Boston Symphony and associate concertmaster of the Utah Symphony, Elias has concertized, conducted, taught, and had his own compositions performed on five continents. Elias is also author of the Daniel Jacobus series, murder mysteries that take place in the murky corners of the classical music world, which have achieved popular and critical acclaim.

WOLFE ON THE ROOF

Loren D. Estleman

L yon was angry, I think.

You never can tell whether the little butterball is seriously miffed or just emulating Nero Wolfe, his role model and life's obsession.

Then again, it might have been disgruntlement over having to spend two hours playing with his tomatoes, which never need more than ten minutes' attention even in crisis; orchids are another thing, but tending to them is beyond his green thumb, which isn't green at all, but almost as fat as his torso.

Too bad. If you're going to keep a greenhouse on your roof instead of a swell patio, you reap what you sow.

But he may just have been primping for our guest, whose Prada bag and Chanel suit indicated money, and whose blonde head suggested the opportunity of my selling her the Triborough Bridge. She'd arrived unannounced, but I didn't want to risk alienation by asking her to wait, and as anyone knows who knows even one-tenth of what Claudius Lyon knows about Wolfe, nothing is more vexing to a fat genius detective than entertaining a client in his plant rooms.

"I cannot help you now, Miss—?"

"Alexandra Pring."

"I hope to cross this plum with that beefsteak and create a tomato that is both delectable and substantial. If you wish to consult me, you must wait until eleven o'clock, when I'll speak with you in my office. Mr. Woodbine knows that, but has chosen to ignore the rules of this house." He favored me with the gassy-baby's face he thought petulant.

The fake. He was tickled pink over having a client. The one thing he can't pull off about his masquerade is a convincing show of pique at the chance to flash his brain before an audience. Since he's a rotten horticulturist, and can burn a salad in the kitchen, solving mysteries is the only thing he has left.

"But it can't wait! I've lost my job, and my rent is past due. Please make an exception this one time!"

I was batting only .500. I'm sure there are plenty of blonde PhDs, but I'd sized this one up right. I flied out on the rest. In bright sunlight, the bag and suit were knockoffs; and now I was the one who was miffed.

Lyon hid his delight under a gruff litany of made-up Latin, fingering ordinary vines while drawing her out on the reason for her visit.

"I run errands for an eccentric millionaire in Queens," she said. "That is, I did. He was always complaining that he couldn't reach me because I keep forgetting to charge my cell." She opened the phony bag and showed him a cheap no-contract phone. "I admit I'm absentminded. I keep forgetting to pay my rent, and by the time I think about it, the money's spent. But I'm very efficient once I'm given an errand. Mr. Quilverton must know that."

"Ronald Quilverton, of the Boston Quilvertons?" I perked up. There might be money in the thing after all, if she was as reliable as she claimed and Quilverton was grateful to have her back.

"Yes. I said he's eccentric. That's why he lives in Queens, New York, instead of on Beacon Hill back home."

Lyon scowled in earnest, wiping black loam onto his apron.

"The solution is hardly worthy of my abilities, Miss Pring. Tie a string to your finger and remember to plug in your mobile."

"I've thought of that, of course. But how can I correct my behavior if my former employer won't take my calls asking for a second chance?"

"My dear young lady, you need an advice columnist, not a detective."

"Hear me out, please. The last time I spoke with him, I was walking down Junction. He was giving me an assignment when my phone beeped, warning me my battery had run out and the call was about to be dropped. He heard it. What I can't figure out is why he said what he said then."

"If it was 'You're fired,' I think I can educate you."

"'Steak and eggs.'"

"Once again?"

"I'm quoting. Well, I lost the signal before the second *s*, but it was definitely 'Steak and egg,' and of course no one says it that way in a restaurant, even if all he wants is one egg. What did he mean?"

"He was instructing you to bring him breakfast."

"Mr. Quilverton is a vegan. He wouldn't touch either item with a ten-foot fork.

"I tried calling him back from a landline, but he never answered. Maybe he had a stroke. I'd call 911, but if I'm wrong, he'd never forgive the intrusion. I'm as worried about him as I am about myself. He's a recluse and lives alone; he may be lying on his floor, with no one to help."

"Steak and egg; you're sure?"

"Yes."

I was thinking the eccentric was just plain nuts when Lyon surprised me by foraging in one ear with a finger. That was his answer to Wolfe's puckering his lips in and out, indicating he was near a solution. Either that or the food talk had him thinking about lunch.

"Miss Pring," he said, wiping wax onto his apron. "Did it occur to you Mr. Quilverton was imploring you not to think about a hearty morning meal, but to stay connected?"

"Stay connect—? Oh!"

"We're increasingly an aural society. 'Steak and eggs' and 'Stay connected,' the latter cut off abruptly when your cell lost power, would sound identical."

She pouted. "But I'm still out of a job." Then she brightened. "Perhaps—"

"No. Bringing a woman into this household would be like…" For once, the vocabulary he'd filched from Nero Wolfe failed him.

"Like crossing a plum with a beefsteak," I suggested.

Loren D. Estleman has published seventy books in mystery, Western, and mainstream fields. He's received four Shamus Awards from the Private Eye Writers of America; none, to his regret, for a Claudius Lyon story. His latest novel starring Detroit PI Amos Walker is Burning Midnight.

HIT ME

Christa Faust

Spanking is cheap. You want to hit me in the face, it's fifty dollars more. A hundred if you want to use a closed fist. That's not even counting the fee for marks. I charge a flat rate for parts of my body that can be covered by clothing. Double for my face, neck, and hands. When I say marks, I'm talking bruises, contusions, hematomas, burns, cuts, welts, ligature marks, or any other visible injury that takes more than six hours to heal. Try something you haven't paid for, my guard dog'll show up and treat you to a little nonconsensual role reversal. Don't like it, you can try your luck in trendy nightclubs.

Bottom line, you get what you pay for.

In retrospect I guess $800K is a fair price for a gunshot wound.

Mr. Tak was one of my best customers. He was the kind of guy who always needed something to do with his hands. When he wasn't using them to rough me up, he would fidget compulsively with a deck of cards. He and I were almost exactly the same size, but when he really let me have it, I felt it for a week and remember who's talking here. I get hit for a living.

I'm pretty sure that Mr. Tak wasn't his real name, but that's what he told me to call him. What do I care? Filthy Fucking Whore isn't my real name either.

Mr. Tak's scenario was real simple. The usual drill. He paid for fists and made me earn every penny.

That night I could tell something was wrong as soon as he walked in the door. He was antsy, eyes all over the empty waiting room. There was a maroon leather briefcase on the floor beside him. The endless flow of cards between his hands was jerky and awkward. I watched him on the monitor in the security room as he fumbled and dropped a card.

Danny, that's my guard dog, he shot me this look like he was asking if I was sure I wanted to go through with it. I gave him one back to let him know I was. I guess I should have known something was up, but it was Mr. Tak. I trusted him. Even liked him a little. As much as it was possible to like a guy who pays to beat the shit out of me.

I could see that Danny was less than thrilled. See, Danny was in love with me. I knew he went home at night and jacked off to fantasies of rescuing me and taking me away from all this. I let him. That hopeless kind of love made him a really good guard dog.

What happened next happened so fast I'm still not sure exactly how it went.

I went into the playroom, and Mr. Tak was there. He wasn't alone. There was another guy. The other guy had a gun. That's pretty much the only thing about him that I remember.

"Fuck you," Mr. Tak said to the guy with the gun.

Then several things happened at once. Danny came screaming through the door. Mr. Tak clutched his briefcase to his chest. The guy with the gun used it.

I hit the deck, covering my head with my arms. On my way down, a bullet slammed into my left calf. It hurt, but I didn't scream. I never scream unless the client requests it.

There was noise and more shots and then long, ringing silence. When nothing happened for several minutes, I looked up through my fingers. Danny was dead. So was Mr. Tak. The guy who used to have the gun didn't have it anymore. He was on the floor, trying to reach the gun with one hand, but he couldn't seem to make his fingers work right.

There wasn't as much blood as you'd think.

Mr. Tak's briefcase was open on the ground. It was full of money. Of course I took it. The way I see it, I earned it.

I still feel bad about Danny, though. Maybe I should have fucked him after all.

Christa Faust is the author of several award-winning novels, including Choke Hold, Money Shot, *and* Hoodtown. *She worked in the Times Square peep booths as a professional dominatrix, fetish model, and adult filmmaker. Faust is a film noir fanatic, an avid reader of classic hard-boiled pulp novels, and an MMA fight fan. She lives and writes in Los Angeles.*

BENEATH THE BRIDGE

Lyndsay Faye

Metal trash cans dot the dark ledge, their fires flickering with colors of piss and ash. Faint human outlines surround them. The bridge looms above, and beyond the graffiti-covered shelter the rain falls into the East River, relentless. It's always raining these days, Marion thinks, pulling her rail-thin legs closer into her body.

"Doesn't seem like he's coming," Jason says. He likewise sits on the fine layer of traffic grit covering the ledge, back resting against tags done in violent sprays of yellow and red over the concrete.

"He's coming," Marion says. She shifts dull blonde hair away from her eyes. She's eighteen, and, though she wants to be here, she thinks she might be sick.

He does come, five minutes later. Appearing as if the drizzle had parted like a curtain. The Postman is thinly menacing as ever, hunched over as if he carried a shell on his back. A cigarette glows between his weakly shivering lips.

"I heard about Sam," he says. "That sad little bastard. You can't let it get ahead of you like that, let it own you. Like I always said."

Marion nods, tugs at a lace on her filthy green canvas shoe. Both feet are covered in writing from a Sharpie she stole from a shelter last winter. Friends' signatures. Crude flowers. A quote her brother, Sam, had liked, before the powder and the needles got to be too much and they found him open-eyed and lifeless down by the shore. *Had we but world enough, and time.* Marion doesn't know where her brother heard that. She likes it, though. She'd liked everything about Sam.

"Who's the new boyfriend?" the Postman asks, jutting his chin at Jason.

Marion glares. The Postman takes too much interest in her, but, despite being brittle and glassy as a Midtown high-rise, Sam had always told him to fuck off. Now Sam is gone and all the daylight with him, and Marion doesn't feel like arguing.

"He's a customer," she says, pushing up the wall. Jason rises behind her, slouching with his cap pulled low.

The Postman cocks an eyebrow. Marion sees his sour breath when he exhales a drag from the cigarette, and she could gag on his peculiar reek of lowlife skittishness from yards away. The higher-ups smell of well-oiled power no matter the situation, she imagines. The casual dealers sweat paranoia.

"Figured you'd have moved along since Sam," the Postman remarks. Beyond, the trash fires flicker, and the hiss of a bottle opening snakes through the gloom.

"Where would I go?" Marion asks.

And fuck if she doesn't wonder as she asks it. Every piece of her is stitched up with Sam. It has been since they left home, because, well, they had to leave, didn't they, once belts and fists were replaced with boots and memorably a tire iron, but Sam rode too close to the sun, didn't he, wanted to touch the stars and feel their hard edges slice into his skin, and ever since the Postman's last delivery killed him dead, it doesn't really matter anymore where Marion goes.

"What's on offer?" Jason asks.

And the Postman launches into his vague, reedy pitch. Marion knows his entire inventory, of course. She and Sam started coming to him over a year ago. Smack and oxy are a two-minute transaction, and if they want crank, he can get it, though that's a walk to a den in Alphabet City. Jason's eyes glitter from under his cap brim. Marion reads her shoes upside down.

Shivering, Marion stares at an iron girder thrusting through the shadows like a giant's spear and wonders where Sam is buried. She'd called the police from a pay phone. But she hadn't talked to them, had watched from up by the highway. She wonders if they've found out who he was.

Now Marion also wonders if, wherever he is, Sam is angry with her.

Jason is talking and the Postman is pulling out little bags full of dreams and racing hearts and Marion has never wanted to go home but she feels as if she can't breathe until she is somewhere else other than beneath this goddamn bridge.

"Fifty dollars covers it," the Postman says to Jason. "First-time discount."

The Postman assumes Marion wants eighties, so she pays him for the pills without saying anything. Her lips feel numb. The smack he'd last sold her brother had been poison-laced, cut with God knows what. He as good as put a gun to Sam's head.

"Hope to be seeing more of you," the Postman says to Jason.

"You will be," he answers.

When Jason's gun comes out, the acid light gleams along its barrel as if it's a sword, and Marion backs away. The Postman is outraged, shrieking a metallic whine that pierces her eardrums.

Marion shoves her hands in her pockets when Jason snaps the handcuffs over the Postman's thin-boned wrists. Her empty gut churns as the cop talks to his prisoner. Jason is bigger suddenly, filling out his ratty sweatshirt, and it occurs to her that he's good at this. She'd wondered.

The Postman screams at her now, calling her a whore and a rat bitch and worse, but he's fading into the background as she fades into the shadows. Jason will be angry that she's not going to the station house as promised. That she won't be testifying. Jason will be furious that she lied to him, she thinks, as she slips from the ledge and lands in a crouch on a wet hill littered with shredded plastic and beer cans.

But the Postman will do time for possession if nothing else, and Marion doesn't live here anymore. She heads north, squeezing past chain-link guarding weed-choked lots. The rain needles to earth from the place where her brother Sam watches her now, high above the silent bridge.

—◆—

Lyndsay Faye is the author of the critically acclaimed The Gods of Gotham, *the first in a series of historical thrillers featuring New York copper Timothy Wilde, as well as the Sherlock Holmes pastiche* Dust and Shadow: An Account of the Ripper Killings. *Her short story "The Case of Colonel Warburton's Madness" was selected for inclusion in* Best American Mystery Stories 2010. *She lives in Manhattan with her husband and cats.*

THE GIRL WHO LOVED FRENCH FILMS

Christopher Fowler

Sheila grew up in Sheffield, a northern English town that had once been famous for the magnificence of its cutlery and the bravery of its air force pilots. By the time she was seventeen, its glory had faded, and the grand Victorian lady had become a disappointed drab. It still had eleven cinemas, the smallest of which showed weekly French films after the town's remaining students turned Roger Vadim's *And God Created Woman* into a surprise success.

Sheila had been taken on the ferry to Boulogne when she was seven, a day trip with her father before he was put away for running a disorderly house. Now she lived in a sooty boarding house with her mother, and her life was closer to depressing English dramas like *A Taste of Honey*. Every Friday she fled to the Roxy to watch Catherine Deneuve, Brigitte Bardot, and Simone Signoret. She learned to smoke Gitanes and Gauloises, and spent her earnings on red lipstick, high heels, and bare-shouldered blouses. She knew the Montmartre backstreets better than the alleys of her hometown. In her mind's eye, the gangs on the banks of the canal were replaced by lovers on the banks of the Seine. Looking down into fetid water filled with shopping carts, she saw only the reflected towers of Notre Dame.

She saw him sheltering from the rain, leaning against the coffee-stall counter outside the Roxy. He was wearing a gray fedora, a crumpled Givenchy suit, and a narrow tie of midnight-blue silk. He had a pencil moustache and was chewing a matchstick. He seemed to have stepped down from a Gaumont picture. Perhaps he needed his dreams just as much as she needed hers.

He studied her openly as she ordered a tea and told her his name was Jean-Guy Melville. She gave a shrug and turned her back to him while she added sugar, but only so that his eyes might linger on her bare shoulder, her exposed bra strap, the curve of her waist. He waited patiently. She had expected an over-practiced pickup line, but none came. He asked if she had seen *Àbout de souffle*. She told him it was her favorite film. They talked about *Vivre sa vie* and *Jules et Jim*. She said she was seeing *Les diaboliques* tonight, and he offered to accompany her. After, they discussed it in a café that felt French apart from the menu. There were checked tablecloths and candles in wine bottles and accordion music played on a transistor radio.

Jean-Guy explained that he had worked as a croupier in Marseilles but a problem with a colleague had forced him north. He had settled in Clignancourt and set up a business importing black-market foie gras from Perigord to Paris. Sheila could not understand what he was doing in such a town as this, and his inability to explain excited her.

He had left his wallet on the dresser in his rented room, so she paid the bill. They lingered so long in the café that she missed the last bus home, so he walked with her in the rain. When it fell too hard, they sheltered beneath the red-and-white awning of a butcher's shop, and he placed his jacket around her shoulders. He smelled of strong coffee, wine, cigarettes, and something indefinably fleshy, as if the plenitude of engorged geese lingered on his skin.

They reached the part of town where the roads split from littered ginnels to wide suburban wastes. Knowing that the rundown boardinghouse where she lived with the keening old lady would disturb the delicacy of their shared dream, she told him she would see herself the rest of the way. He elicited her promise to join him next Friday to see *Judex*.

She sold dresses in a store that owed little to the umbrella shop in *Les parapluies de Cherbourg*, but it had a place at the window from where she could watch the falling rain, and if she fixed her blonde hair in barrettes she could at least feel like Deneuve for a moment. On Friday Jean-Guy collected her and they ran through the neon puddles to the Roxy. In the café afterward he closed his hand over hers as he lit her cigarette. In the candlelight he looked a little like Jean-Paul Belmondo. She wore a dress similar to the one Anna Karina had worn in *Vivre sa vie* and tried not to cough as she smoked.

For a month she shut out the sound of her complaining mother and lived only for the cinema, the café, the walk home. As they watched *Contempt*, his hand settled in hers like a cuckoo curling into another nest. After, they drank house red and smoked, watching the rain-chased windows, and he told her he was returning to Paris. There was a deal that was too good to miss. She waited for him to ask, and waited.

Finally he said, "I thought you might consider coming with me. But I must tell you, my past is full of lies."

And she quoted Karina from *Vivre sa vie*, telling him "Shouldn't love be the only truth?"

There was no English timidity in his kiss.

As they were leaving, the café door opened and a grizzled man in a tweed flat cap bustled in from the drizzle.

"Blimey, Charlie, you gave me a fright," he said with a laugh. "I thought you was still inside for desertion. Then Chalkie told me you was up to your old tricks. This a new little chickie for your henhouse?"

A small boy fishing for eels in the canal snagged the Givenchy-clad body with his line. In 1958, Sheffield had made an aircrew release knife that had become popular in the French underworld after the end of the war. Such a knife was found buried in the man's heart.

Sheila's mother said she had no daughter, and if she did the foolish girl was probably living in Paris.

—✦✦—

Christopher Fowler is the award-winning author of more than thirty novels and twelve short-story collections, including ten Bryant & May mysteries. Red Gloves, *a collection of twenty-five new stories, marks his first quarter century in print, and his memoir,* Paperboy, *won the Green Carnation Award, with a sequel in the works.*

DAVID TO GOLIATH

Matthew C. Funk

Didee Fuller looked about half his age, slumped across from me in his pajamas with the specter of a black eye floating above one cheek. Looked about six. Small, skittish, and unafraid.

"You know who I am, Didee?" I gave him eyes as unblinking as my star tattoos under them.

Didee chuckled. Maybe more of a giggle. "Yeah. You're Jurgis."

"Why's that funny?"

He slid on a wry smile. "We got similar interests."

"You know why I'm here, then." I flipped open my notepad.

"Mhm." The smile dawned big. "You want to know how a twelve-year-old could take down Giant."

I clicked my pen. Didee got talking.

Didee spent Saturday mornings busy. When other kids were shoveling cereal in front of cartoons, Didee had already cleaned his room and sorted his comic collection.

He liked *Teen Titans* the best. Robin was his hero.

"Robin's ten times as brave as Batman," Didee told me. "Batman's a grown dude, spent all his life training how to mess somebody up. Robin's just a kid. Not much training. Not even a pair of pants. Takes a special bravery to run around, getting in fights, without pants."

Didee would be out helping charities in the Desire district by nine.

Giant came by Didee's house Saturdays at noon. Didee didn't even know why his mother was crying until he asked three months in.

He had come back from gathering strays for the animal shelter that morning, bouncy with a job well done, and asked her with a grin, "Mama, why you got to be so down on such a beautiful day?"

She told him. Not everything at first, but he kept pressing.

Didee was a curious kid. He'd stick Mentos in a Diet Coke two-liter to prove they'd blow up. Made baking soda volcanoes out at Edith Sampson Playground just to see the smaller kids goggle in wonder.

"What Mama told me," Didee said, "it was the first thing I ever learned that I didn't want to know."

"You know why Giant was shaking her down for money?" I set the pen down.

"And sex," Didee added. The word sounded like even more of a crime coming from a kid.

"Right. Why?"

"Way Giant had it, my uncle had ripped him off when he was just coming up in the game." Didee shrugged. "Stole his bike. Beat him up. Crippled his brother."

"This was payback?"

"No," Didee said "That was an excuse."

He told the rest of the story with his fists clenched pale.

It took a month of spying to get Giant's routine memorized.

"I didn't take no pictures, didn't write nothing down," Didee said. "Never write nothing down."

Then two weeks to steal enough animal tranquilizer from the kennel.

"A bit at a time, they don't notice," Didee said. "Never take nothing they'll notice."

Then another two weeks of watching Giant park his F-150 outside his last drop-off, a crack house on Law Street. Timing how long Giant visited, averaging it, doing practice runs. Checking no one was on the street. No one looking out a window.

"Had to be patient," Didee said. "Never rush nothing."

Then August 13 arrived with the 100 percent humidity of a Crock-Pot and not a soul on Law.

Giant came out to the F-150 and tried to start it. The sugar Didee put in the gas tank worked a charm. Giant cussed a few minutes and then went under the hood.

Didee came from behind the trash cans in the alley and put the syringe of ketamine in Giant's femoral.

"He went down like a pit bull," Didee said with a smile white as his knuckles. "Growling."

Giant crumpled into four hundred pounds of watery muscle. Didee hunched by his head. He took out his mama's kitchen knife.

"Never take no chances," Didee told me as I wrote another bullet point.

Didee made sure Giant's eyes saw him, slid the metal through the tight tube of his jugular vein and was back in the alley by the time Giant bled out.

"So how'd you get caught?" I asked, pen poised for the last entry.

Didee's eyes and smile went somewhere else. He hugged himself. Straightened up in those orange jail pajamas.

"Told Mama," Didee said to the parish prison window. "She got in an argument on the street and said it to scare someone. Might as well have used a bullhorn. All Desire knew by dinner time."

I flipped the notepad closed.

"You forgot the last note," Didee said, looking back at me. "Never get close to nobody."

I didn't have to write that down to live it.

"How're you holding up?" I pointed at his black eye as I stood.

"Good," he said, smiling tight again. "Just got jumped into the Grubs up in here. My reputation preceded me; ain't that how it goes?"

"That's how it goes."

"Word has it, Giant's brother's looking for payback." Didee gave up on smiling. We both had. "We'll see who gets who first."

◆

THIS STORY WAS FIRST PUBLISHED IN *SHOTGUN HONEY.*

Matthew C. Funk is a digital marketing manager, an editor for Needle: A Magazine of Noir, *and a staff writer for* Planet Fury *and* Criminal Complex. *Winner of the 2010* Spinetingler *Award for Best Short Story on the Web, Funk has work featured at dozens of sites and in printed volumes indexed on his website, MatthewFunk.net.*

THE ONE WHO GOT AWAY

Jim Fusilli

He hadn't forgotten her—what kind of moron could forget who turned him into a bum?—but now that he was laid up in the hospital, bandages wrapped around his head, she appeared in his dreams: angry, sweating, wagging a sausagey finger as she declared him useless and unwanted; in the mist he was a little boy again and she was his terrorizing fourth-grade teacher. Not that he was some kind of all-star, but he was at worst a second-rate bully, and always his classmates were asking for it, being little and laughing all the time. He taunted, he teased, he took. He didn't kill nobody.

Okay, he thought back then, I'll be through with her when the school year ends and good riddance; also I hope she dies. But then they made Sister Ellen Francis principal at St. Matthew the Apostle, and the torture continued through the eighth grade. He could hear her foghorn voice now: "Joseph Anthony!" Stomping across the schoolyard toward him, the other kids parting like swinging doors, she grabbed his ear, smacked the back of his head. Or later, taken a ruler to his palms because he was slow, no good with the books.

But not so slow that he didn't use the time in the hospital to come up with a first-rate scheme, one guaranteed to give him enough cash to get him a new start—and a shot at embarrassing the church too, seeing as they retired Sister Ellen someplace, wherever they put nuns past their prime, so he couldn't go right at her. On his back, he refined the plan. A nurse's aide brought him a map.

Finally, they discharged him, telling him the lifting hook that struck his head at the shipyards didn't do nothing but split the skin, twenty-one stitches. "Good luck, Joe," they said as he signed the release papers. He walked into a frigid cold, the second day of January 1948, on his way to a place where no one would see him as crude, dim-witted, and luckless.

Claiming he was an actor, he bought a priest's getup in Midtown, close enough to Broadway so the lie took.

A week later, Joseph Anthony Triviani boarded a bus headed north into Pennsylvania, his ticket on the cuff courtesy of the line's policy toward the clergy. Everyone on the bus nodded as he made his way along the aisle, his black fedora set to conceal his new scar, his plump chin dented by the starched white collar. "Good morning, Father," an old woman said. As the bus zoomed through the Jersey countryside, she offered him her liverwurst sandwich.

Three hours later, a priest robbed the First National Bank of Scranton. Ninety minutes after, a priest hit the First National Bank of Dunsmore. Then, back in his own clothes, Joseph Anthony Triviani bought a Ford Tudor sedan, paying cash, from a cheery Ford salesman who offered to help set him up in town. He then took down the First National Bank of Dickson City, management on the lookout for a renegade priest. With about $96,000 in the trunk, Joseph Anthony Triviani headed toward the Kittatinny Mountains of northwest New Jersey, figuring a warrant don't cross state lines. So far, so good.

The old nun teetered into the police station, a young visiting novice at her elbow, fresh snow on their black galoshes, their cheeks red from the snapping wind. A three-man squad, so they had a neighborhood woman work the desk, and she trotted around to settle the old nun. "How can I help you, Sister?"

The old nun was out of breath. Seventy-six years old, hunched and arthritic. They wanted to send her to Arizona to rest, but no, give me one last task, allow me to serve again. A distance from the Delaware Water Gap, with only a filling station and a poultry farm in sight, the old school had twenty-two students—fewer than in a single class at St. Matthew the Apostle in Narrows Gate, and she knew each one by name. She made sure their hair was combed, their shoes shined; "Good morning, Sister Ellen Francis," they sang in unison.

A sergeant came from the back of the station.

The novice handed Sister Ellen a newspaper a few days old.

The old nun sagged with disappointment. Pointing to a grainy photo, she said, "This is Joseph Arthur Triviani."

"The bank robber?" the sergeant said. The amateur snapshot was a miracle, an invaluable aid to the two-state investigation. He had a copy on his desk.

She nodded.

"Forgive me, Sister," the cop said gently, "but he's not a priest, is he?"

"Far from it," the old nun replied.

Being a moron, Triviani kept up his shenanigans, even though he had a lifetime's worth of cash in his trunk. Wearing the priest's suit, he went to diners for meals on the arm, and they didn't charge him at the movies. He walked into a bar, figuring a priest took a drink now and then, and the cops were waiting. They took him down hard, from the stool to the floor with a thud, and they cuffed him, though not before removing the black suit. The newspapers, including the *Jersey Observer* down in Narrows Gate, showed him in his boxers wading through the snow toward the police station.

The old nun waited in the lobby.

Without ceremony, they put Triviani in front of her.

"That him, Sister?"

It took a minute, but Triviani recognized the withered stick figure in black. She was a danger to nobody.

She told the cops. Yes, that's him.

To Triviani, she said, "I'm sorry, Joseph Arthur. I'm sorry I failed you."

He took those words with him to the penitentiary. They kept him awake. They echoed throughout the night.

—◆◆—

Jim Fusilli is the author of seven novels and is the rock and pop music critic of the Wall Street Journal. *His most recent novel,* Road to Nowhere, *was published in November 2012 by Thomas & Mercer.*

HALLOWEEN

Carolina Garcia-Aguilera

"You want me to find out what, exactly, you did on Halloween night?" I was slightly hungover—my longtime boyfriend, Miami homicide detective Oliver Gutierrez, and I had partied a bit too much the night before, and the two Cokes and four Advils I'd had for breakfast had not kicked in yet. "This past Halloween, on Monday, two nights ago?"

The man sitting across from me kept shifting around in the worn brown leather chair where my clients sat. I normally only took referrals, but business was slow, real slow, so I agreed to meet with him. Over the phone he had said he had found me on Google when searching for a private investigator in Miami. Although he was casually dressed in jeans, short-sleeved cotton shirt, and sneakers, his short haircut and erect bearing told me he either was or had been in the military.

"Well, you're a private investigator, right? On your website, Marisol Martinez Investigations, you list all the services you provide, and one of them is that you conduct discreet investigations. I need discretion—lots of it." He looked me straight in the eyes as he spoke, almost as if he was challenging me, sending a slight shiver down my back.

When he had called to make the appointment, he had given his name as Tom Smith, but I would have bet one of the three twenty-dollar bills that I had in my wallet that that was not it. Well, at least he hadn't chosen John Smith, as others had done before him in the fifteen years that I'd worked as a private investigator.

"It's kind of embarrassing, really." Tom looked down at his lap, then, a minute later, began speaking slowly, the words coming out as if it pained him to get them out. I was used to that, since individuals never came to see me for happy reasons. "I'm not from here—I live in Tampa—but one of my buddies, Scott, who moved down here a couple of years ago—we were in the marines together, served in Iraq—invited me down for the weekend, and Monday being Halloween, he convinced me to stay over, that Halloween on South Beach was wild and crazy, and I couldn't miss seeing it."

"Yes, Halloween on South Beach is crazy," I agreed.

"Well, my friend insisted that we had to wear costumes; it would be more fun that way. The plan was that two women, ones he had met here recently, would be joining us." Tom took a deep breath. "Scott got us costumes—he went as Dracula, and I was a pirate. The costumes were pretty good. I even had a real knife, too, very sharp, so sharp that I had to be careful holding it. The girls—Tanya and Maria were their names—went dressed as baby sheep. They looked really cute—I remember that. We met at a bar on Lincoln Road and started drinking right away. It was very crowded."

Having myself celebrated Halloween on Lincoln Road several times, I could easily picture the scene. Tom looked so miserable that I felt the need to help him a bit. "So, what happened then?"

"I don't know. I just don't know," he repeated. "That's what I came to you to find out."

"Why do you need my help with that?" I didn't understand his dilemma. He was with three other people. "Why not just ask your friends?"

"They can't help. We split up at around midnight. I never saw them again, and Scott said he had no idea where I ended up." Tom got up and started pacing around my office. "I really need your help. You have to look into what happened to me after I went off on my own. What I did."

"I'm not sure I understand why you are so worried. I mean, you don't seem to have anything wrong with you—you're not hurt. Is there something you're not telling me?" I wasn't buying the story, but then I was used to my clients lying to me—at least in the initial interview.

Tom paced some more. "You remember I told you I was wearing a pirate costume?" I nodded. "Well, when I woke up the next morning in Scott's apartment, I was wearing a Little Bo Peep costume—two ratty things that looked like sheep tails in the right pocket."

"Little Bo Peep?" I wanted to make sure I heard right. "Like the nursery rhyme?" I'd had some strange cases, but Tom was beating them all.

"Yes. A man-size costume; it fit perfectly. I looked like some kind of drag queen." Tom shuddered. "I have no idea where the pirate costume went—or the knife."

I could see why he was worried. "Okay. I'll start the investigation first thing tomorrow. Before you leave, I need you to write down everything you can recall about Halloween night. Everything. Don't leave anything out."

That night back home, I had just begun looking through the dozens of takeout menus crammed in one of the drawers in the kitchen when Oliver walked in.

"You look exhausted. Rough day?" I greeted him with a kiss.

Oliver opened the door of the refrigerator and took out a beer. As a senior detective in the homicide division in Miami, Oliver was responsible for a very heavy workload, and with the cutbacks, he was sometimes overwhelmed. Still, that night he looked especially beat up.

He took a long pull of the beer. "I swear, Marisol, you know I come across a lot of weird murders, but even for Miami, the one I worked today was memorable."

"Yeah? What was it?"

"You're not going to believe this." He finished his beer and got another. It must have been some case. "I have two dead girls in sheep costumes. Throats slit, tails missing."

The room went around for a minute. "Chinese okay tonight?"

～～

Cuban-born, Miami Beach–based Carolina Garcia-Aguilera is the author of ten books as well as a contributor to many anthologies, but she is perhaps best known for her Lupe Solano mystery series. Her books have been translated into twelve languages. Garcia-Aguilera, who has been a private investigator for more than twenty-five years, has been the recipient of many awards.

THE OLD GAL

Gregory Gibson

Her name was Darlene. The way I got to know her was that I dated Pam, her niece, in high school. We were going hot and heavy there for a while, but finally Pam dumped me. I guess I wasn't exciting enough. Then she got knocked up by a kid with a Camaro whose father owned a plumbing company, which I thought was pretty amusing. Then they moved to Georgia.

By this time I'd gotten my job at the post office so I could keep track of her by the Christmas cards she sent to Darlene, who was on my route downtown. After five or six years, Pam must've broken up with the plumber because the cards had a different return address and she'd changed her name back to the original. It was too late for me then, anyway. I had a wife and two kids. I looked Pam up on Facebook once. She must've weighted two thirty.

Darlene, on the other hand, kept her figure. And she kept her smile. She wasn't particularly good-looking—"sweet" would be the most flattering description—but she had a body, and a kind of energy. What would you call it? Not exactly sexy. More like when you were around her, you felt good. A smile from her could make your day.

She worked in the kitchen at the Head Start program, and the kids loved her. And she volunteered at Animal Aid, and they loved her there, too. Saturday nights, when my wife and I went out, I'd see her at one bar or another—lots of people around her, but she always had time for a chat with me. Everyone loved Darlene.

Her only problem was she had bad taste in men. As the years went by and she got knocked around by one loser after another, black-and-blue became a permanent part of her look. And it didn't come from Helena Rubenstein.

Finally the long train of bad men was too much even for her, and she settled down with one bad man. His name was Bill, and he always referred to her as "the Old Gal," so, for some reason, we all started calling her that, even though he was a rat and we shouldn't have listened to anything he said. He beat her up on a regular basis, but since she never complained or pressed charges, even when neighbors called the cops, there was nothing anyone could do about it.

At first we thought it was because she was too nice. She'd taken care of her niece and all those kids at Head Start, and helped so many other people around town just by her good nature and kindly spirit. We assumed she just didn't have the backbone to stand up to a creep like Bill. But after so many years of the same routine, we realized, or at least I suspected, that she dug it. She stayed with Bill because the way he treated her turned her on.

That was the theory I'd invented, anyway, as I delivered her mail to Liberty Street. Bill moved in, sponging off the money she made at Head Start. She'd keep "bumping into doors" and "falling down." Sweet lady, but a fucked-up masochist underneath.

Then after she retired from Head Start, she moved to senior housing and left Bill out on the street.

It was pretty amazing. By that time she'd been getting Social Security checks for three years at least, so depending on when she started collecting, she would've been in her late sixties, anyway.

And she'd finally broken loose. Poked up into the sunlight like weeds through the asphalt.

Then old Bill started coming around again, to senior housing, just to give her a weekly beating. It was a very discouraging development.

I've got three hundred thirty people on my route, and as the years went by, I'd had something to do with nearly every one of them. Once I saved Mrs. Alves, who'd fallen in her living room, even though her family thought I should've let her die there. I witnessed the fatal heart attack of Cummings, the ward councilor. I knew where Sammy the Rat slept it off and could follow Sammy's slime trail at eight a.m. down to the Dugout for the first of his trembling drinks with the night-shift fish packers who were just getting off work. I never delivered a baby, but I watched Dicky Lufkin get born in the backseat of a car that never even started for the hospital. After a while connections reached across the gaps and the whole route became like a spiderweb. When a gnat hit the sticky, the spider knew, and when the spider moved, the gnats knew.

I thought I'd seen everything the route had to offer. But the day I found Bill beat all.

He was in the parking lot behind senior housing, next to the Old Gal's Chevy, lying in a puddle of frozen blood with his head caved in.

I got the cops there right away, but of course there was nothing they could do except remove the stiff and clean the concrete.

The cops in our town aren't particularly nice people—maybe that's just the way cops are—but I'll say this for them. They handled the investigation of Bill's death just right.

They interviewed everyone, took notes, and gathered evidence, and, after a week or so, declared that a chunk of ice had slid off the roof of senior housing and found its way to Bill's skull.

A tragic accident. The fact that the Old Gal's car was parked in the middle of the lot never made it into their report.

The Old Gal knew that we knew, and we knew that she knew we knew, and nobody said anything. Social workers, newspaper guys, the people at Animal Aid and the bars, her neighbors in senior housing, even the cops. Nobody said a thing.

Ever.

❧

Gregory Gibson is an antiquarian book dealer living in Gloucester, Massachusetts. He is the author of three nonfiction books. His first crime novel, The Old Turk's Load, *was published in April 2013.*

NECESSITY

Ed Gorman

—Damn it, Daryl, they're just gonna send ya to back to prison for this.

—My name ain't Daryl. Now hand over all the money in that cash register or I'll be usin' this gun.

—You think just because you're wearin' a stupid gorilla mask I don't know who you are?

—You get with it, lady, I'm warnin' ya.

—An' I can hear your voice plain and clear.

—I want the money NOW!

—What if I say I won't do it?

—Then I blast ya.

—Please quit waving that stupid gun around, will ya, Daryl? Damn thing might go off accidentally and hurt somebody.

—I'm countin to five and then—

—Tell ya what I'll do. You turn around and walk out of here and I'll forget this ever happened.

—Four—three—two—

—You dumb sonofabitch. With your record, this'll get ya seven, eight years.

—ONE!

—There, ya happy now? Register's open!

—Put it all in this bag.

—Yessir, Mr. Robbery Man.

—And no smart talk.

—Nosir, Mr. Robbery Man. There ya go. Close to six hundred bucks.

—You don't move till I'm clear of the door. And stop callin' me Mr. Robbery Man.

—Sure thing, Mr. Robbery Man.

—You—!

—Billy, ya need t'hurry. Daryl actually went through with it. He's probably on his way back to our trailer park. Take three minutes to get there. He's on the end of our lane, so it'll be easy to hide.

—I kinda feel bad sendin' him back ta prison.

—I give him every chance I could tryin' to talk him out of it.

—Stupid son of a bitch.

—That's exactly what I told him. And we need the money bad as he does. Worse. He ain't married or nothing, and we got three little ones.

—I worked at that factory twenty-two years, and then they come in here and shipped all them jobs overseas.

—I tole yah, Billy. You got to let it go. You wake up in the middle of the night and sit on the edge of the bed, and I know you're stewin' about that job.

—Now even my unemployment's run out.

—Please, Billy. Just get goin'.

—You sure this'll work out right?

—Sure. He robbed me, you robbed him, and we keep the money. He sure ain't gonna tell nobody what happened. He never shoulda made that dumb-ass joke to you about maybe robbin' a convenience store. This town's so small there's only one of them, and that's where I work.

—Yeah. He sure is a dumb ass.

—Just go next door and ask Jemma to watch our kids for half an hour or so. That's all you'll need. Then go get him.

—I sure love yah, hon. Thanks for workin' them long hours when I know ya'd rather be home with the kids.

—I love you too, Billy. Now hurry.

Ed Gorman's work has appeared in magazines as various as the New York Times, Redbook, Ellery Queen Mystery Magazine, *and* Penthouse. *His work has also won numerous prizes, including the Shamus, the Spur, and the International Fiction Writers awards. He's been nominated for the Edgar Allan Poe, the Anthony, the Gold Dagger, and the Bram Stoker awards. Former* Los Angeles Times *critic Charles Champlin noted that "Ed Gorman is a powerful storyteller."*

LOST CAT

Ron Goulart

You wouldn't think burying a dead cat could cause you so damn much trouble.

The scruffy orange tomcat's name was Pumpkin, and it wasn't exactly Roger Overman's cat. It was his wife's. Although Bonnie insisted that Pumpkin was "*our* darling little pussycat."

In fact, Roger didn't like the thing, and the cat quite obviously loathed him. Had it been tiger-size, it would long since have leaped upon him, ripped him asunder, and chewed on his bones the way tigers did to their hapless victims on PBS nature documentaries. Among the things the surly Pumpkin had been able to accomplish was to bite his shanks, claw his hands, trip him by suddenly popping underfoot on numerous occasions and, more than once, by climbing up the back of the sofa to nip his right ear.

When he complained, his wife told him he simply didn't understand Pumpkin's playful nature. The cat would give him a guileless look, clearly implying that he'd once again gotten the best of Roger.

Roger had never done a bit of harm to the odious Pumpkin, who was the color of a slightly spoiled sweet potato. Well, nothing beyond an occasional kick in the backside when Bonnie was off shopping and Roger was doing the house cleaning.

He really couldn't afford to antagonize his wife. Roger was nearly fifty—well, fifty-three, actually—but he didn't always put that on his résumés. He'd been out of work for eleven months now, ever since he lost his assistant account executive job at a Westport advertising agency. They had to rely on the stocks, bonds, and annuities that Bonnie's father, who'd made his fortune from his swimming pool water-supply business, had bestowed on her.

Pumpkin went on to glory in this way. Roger, after he'd finished vacuuming, had made himself a cup of cocoa and settled on the sofa in the small, cluttered den to watch the local news channel. Bonnie wouldn't be back from her shopping trip and luncheon date for several hours. The handsome newsman was in the middle of a story.

"Three known organized crime figures in our area have suddenly vanished. Police suspect gangster conflict may be behind this. Now, Natalie, how about that recipe for homemade pizza you promised us earlier?"

Just as the chipper blonde co-anchor appeared on the small screen, Pumpkin came galloping into the den in pursuit of a catnip ball.

"Shoo," suggested Roger, standing. "Be gone."

The tom obviously had no intention of following his ball into the dusty corner next to the rickety TV stand. He instead began making that sound, a wail suggesting a banshee with a toothache that indicated you had to fetch something for him.

"Okay, all right, asshole." He crossed toward the set. Somehow his left foot got tangled in the frayed cord.

Pumpkin yowled again as the heavy old TV dived from the collapsing stand and fell smack on top of him with a thud.

"Oh, shit."

But Roger realized there was plenty of time to clean up the evidence. He'd clean the wood floor, upright the TV set. It didn't suffer as much damage as the cat, and Bonnie rarely entered the den.

Okay, what had actually happened, he decided, was that Pumpkin had pushed his cat door so hard that he broke out and ran off into the overgrown woodlands in back of their house. He'd search the woods, calling out, "Pumpkin, dear Pumpkin." They'd take out an ad in the local paper, put up a sign in the post office: "Lost cat, friendly and amiable, answers to the name of Pumpkin."

But he couldn't bury him in the woods because Bonnie would obviously scour them.

"Ah," he said aloud, pointing a forefinger ceiling-ward. "The New Beckford Nature Preserve." It was forty acres of rundown, overgrown forest. The town hadn't had the budget to take care of it for years, and nobody went there except for teenagers late at night. "Perfect."

Roger didn't anticipate that *perfect* was not the apt word.

Roger put the remains of Pumpkin in an old gunnysack. Parking his six-year-old Toyota on a narrow street with two foreclosed houses on it, he walked a quarter mile to the thick, overgrown forest. He'd first wrapped the cat's remains in a plastic bag, so there was no blood showing on the sack he carried in his right hand, swinging it to and fro. The garden trowel he used to do his weeding was also in the sack.

He shifted his grip on Pumpkin and pushed his way into the welter of trees, brush, and weeds. Thorns scratched his sleeves while fallen twigs crackled beneath his feet.

After struggling through the forest for more than ten minutes, Roger decided he'd gone far enough.

Just then he heard voices from up ahead and saw two men in dark suits about twenty yards away. They were digging a large hole in a patch of earth in a narrow clearing. And lying on a small stretch of mixed wildflowers, face down, was the body of a man with two large splotches of dried blood on the right side of his candy-striped dress shirt.

"Oops," murmured Roger, grabbing up his sack, clutching it to his chest, and commencing, very quietly, to back away.

Crackling, thrashing sounds started off to his left. A third man in a blue suit emerged from the trees. He had a revolver in his left hand. "Too much noise, friend," he said in a soft voice. "We heard you sneaking up on us five minutes ago." He pointed the gun directly at him.

"No. Nope. I wasn't sneaking up on anybody. Just taking a hike in the woods. "

"Thing is, we can't really let—"

"Enough already," called one of the men with a shovel. "Shoot the guy."

Just before the gunman pulled the trigger, Roger said, "That goddamn cat got the best of me again."

— ✦ —

Ron Goulart is a cultural historian who has written extensively about pulp fiction, including the seminal Cheap Thrills: An Informal History of Pulp Magazines, *and has written dozens of novels and countless short stories, spanning genres and using a variety of pen names, including Kenneth Robeson, Joseph Silva, and Con Steffanson. Goulart's* After Things Fell Apart *is the only science-fiction novel ever to win an Edgar Allan Poe Award.*

SUNDAY IN THE PARK WITH SARGE

Chris Grabenstein

"Sarge?" cried the dame they called Trixie. "Hey, Sarge. That you? Yeah! Over here."

Sarge ambled over. Reluctantly.

"What is it this time, Trixie?"

"It's Moose and that bunch."

Sarge let out a long sigh. "Moose Murphy?"

"Yeah, yeah. Murphy. Him and his trouble boys have been bothering that old guy, you know, the mug with the missing leg—Lucky they call him. Lucky Rabinowitz. You know Lucky, right?"

"Yeah, I know him. What's Lucky doin' out here? I told him last weekend, certain stretches of this park are too shady for an old-timer like him to be nosin' around in."

"Hey, leg or no leg, the guy has his pride. We used to run together, Lucky and me."

Sarge wasn't surprised. Trixie was the kind of dame who would run with just about anybody, even if they didn't have enough limbs to *really* run anymore.

"Come on, Sarge. You know Lucky Rabinowitz still has his pride. He ain't gonna tuck his tail and sulk home just on your say-so."

"Then tell him, for his own good, to keep far away from Moose Murphy. Like somewhere in the next zip code."

"I did, Sarge. But that ain't how it works with Moose and that bunch. They sniff out you're old or weak, they move into your territory, and boom, they grab everything that ain't nailed down."

"Well, I'm sorry to hear it, Trixie. But I gotta go. Nice bumping into you. Enjoy your day."

"Hey, hey, hey. You're leavin'?"

"Yes, Trixie, I'm trying to."

"What about Lucky?"

Sarge let out another, longer, sigh.

"There's nothing I can do."

"Sure there is."

"Look—tell your pal Lucky to call the cops."

"Ah, come on, Sarge. You know the cops don't care about you, me, Lucky, or none of us. Not like they used to, anyways. Not like they did when you was on the force."

"That's ancient history, Trix. I'm not a cop anymore."

"Sure you are, Sarge. Once a cop, always a cop, am I right? That's why you're still out here every weekend patrolling your old beat."

"I'm not patrolling anything, Trixie. It's Sunday. I'm just trying to grab a little fresh air."

"Cut the chin music, Sarge. Save that noise for someone who don't know you no better."

"I'm telling you straight up: I'm done. I'm out of all that."

Trixie looked at Sarge hard.

"This is on account of what happened to your partner, ain't it?"

"Trixie?"

"Yeah?"

"We're friends."

"I know."

"You want to maybe stay that way?"

"Sure I do."

"Then drop it."

Trixie flicked her hair to the side. She always did that when she was annoyed.

"When are you gonna get it through that thick skull of yours that what happened to Joe weren't none of your fault?"

"Oh, really? Try telling that to Mrs. Amodio. Or their three kids."

In a flash, it all came back.

The night down in the subway. Sarge and his partner tailing two suspects. The thugs getting the drop on Joe, a good cop with the bad habit of walking where he maybe should've looked first. Shots were fired. Both officers went down.

Sarge still carried a lead souvenir in his left hip. He hadn't lost a leg like Lucky. But he did lose the best partner any cop ever had.

"We were together a long time, me and Joe," said Sarge, biting back the hurt the memories always stirred up.

"Then do this thing for him. Help a sad sack like Lucky Rabinowitz get back his stuff from Moose Murphy. Joe Amodio sure would."

Sarge heaved one last sigh. "Where'd this incident go down?"

"Over this way. By the bench near the garbage can."

Trixie scampered over to the spot. Sarge loped after her.

"Hiya, Sarge!" The big lug Lucky limped out of the shadows under a tree. "Thanks for taking my case."

"What'd they steal?"

"The only thing my kid ever gave me!" whined Lucky. Then he started whimpering.

"Ease up on the waterworks," barked Trixie. "Sarge don't need no more emotional baggage. He's already over his limit. Am I right, Sarge?"

Sarge ignored her. Studied the mud.

"Moose and that bunch sure left a lot of prints. A one-year-old could follow this trail."

"That's because they knew nobody had the guts to chase after them," said Trixie.

Sarge looked to where the path made its curve around the oval-shaped lawn.

A pack of six rough mugs were tossing a ball back and forth under the shade of a towering oak tree.

"That's my ball," said Lucky. "The one my boy gave me. It's got great sentimental value, you know?"

Sarge nodded. "Yeah."

One of Joe Amodio's kids had given Sarge a ball once, too.

He took off. Dashed up the pathway. Weaved his way through the Sunday strollers.

Moose Murphy saw him coming. Grinned.

"Well, hello, Sarge. Funny runnin' into you out this way. I heard you quit the copper life."

"You heard wrong."

Sarge snarled. Just once.

Moose Murphy acted tough. Made like he wouldn't mind having Sarge chase him around in circles.

Sarge was in no mood for circles.

So he bared his fangs and lunged forward.

Tasted fur.

Moose yelped and dropped Lucky's ball. The thing was slimed with drool and a little chewed up but otherwise okay.

"Hey!" shouted one of the people holding a leash. "Keep away from my Moose!"

It was the Murphy dame wearing a fanny pack and a fancy Ivy League sweatshirt.

"Whose dog is this?" she shouted like she owned the park. "*Whose dog is this?*" She went to protect Moose.

Sarge smiled.

He knew whose dog he was: Officer Joe Amodio's. Late of the NYPD K-9 Unit. Sarge Amodio was a dog who'd always track down the bad boys like Moose Murphy to protect the weaker mutts like Lucky Rabinowitz.

He picked up Lucky's ball with his snout.

Trixie had been right.

Once a cop, always a cop.

Chris Grabenstein is the Anthony and Agatha Award–winning author of the John Ceepak/Jersey Shore mysteries for adults, the Haunted Mystery series for kids, and the Riley Mack comic capers, also for kids. He has also co-authored a pair of middle-grades books with James Patterson.

NAILS

James Grady

Eleanor was like any long-retired schoolteacher who believes in punctuality, punctuation, propriety, and that the universal bar code on everything everywhere is the Mark of the Beast. Lord knows it must be so, or why else would she be marching over the sidewalk on a Tuesday morning past second-rate stores on her way to shoot two people? She wore sensible shoes, a blue pantsuit under her formal tan overcoat, and not a fleck of makeup or a dollop of dye in her gray hair.

Just because the day requires crime doesn't mean everything gets thrown out the window.

Eleanor, of course, had been on time for the robbery.

7B was late—*running late*, she told Eleanor when they met by the elevator in the pine-ammonia-smelling hall outside their apartments.

"Could you help me?" lied Eleanor, who'd been standing at the elevator with feigned innocence for twenty-four ticking-clock tardy minutes. "My hands. Arthritis. I can't push the call button."

7B looked at the old lady she talked to half a dozen times a week—more, actually, but 7B seldom noticed this gray-haired woman who was so slight the wind off the cold river could blow her away. 7B had her yoga mat plus gym bag slung over her left shoulder, and that hand clutched a metal coffee cup logoed by a save-starving-children charity of which Eleanor approved. The frayed shoulder strap on the attaché case cut into the right shoulder of the business suit 7B wore down to her properly pantyhosed knees. A cell phone filled her right fist.

7B put the cell phone in her suit's side pocket, stretched across the old lady to push the elevator summons button—and didn't feel Eleanor's deft fingers slip the cell phone out of 7B's pocket and into her own black purse.

"Thank you," said Eleanor. "For helping with the elevator, I mean."

"No problem," said 7B.

Eleanor said: "We all take care of each other."

The elevator arrived.

As 7B let the old lady enter first, she heard a motherly voice say: "Your coffee is getting cold."

Lord please don't let the cell phone ring!

The power of prayer got the cage to the lobby in blessed silence.

Eleanor watched her neighbor stride off to her doom in the coming End of Days and, before then, to the sorrows of this life someone should do something about, then went on her own dreaded way.

The alley alongside the grocery store where young men awaited temptation held only the thug called Knucks. Eleanor's eyes leveled at the chrome cross dangling from his rhinestone-speckled neck chain.

Knucks stared at the twenty-dollar bill the old lady gave him and what she held.

"You want me to show you how to use that? Don't you watch TV?"

"There is no substitute for direct instruction."

"What's keeping me from *direct* taking you off an' taking that?"

"You are smarter than you think. You know a risk should equal its gain."

Knucks blinked.

"Your cross is on upside down. Lord knows it is not for me to judge anyone's faith, but the cross bar belongs at the top. Do you know why?"

Knucks shook his head.

The little old lady stuck her arms straight out from her sides. Waited.

Fifth grade is forever. Knucks stuck his arms out like hers.

"Your arms are wide because the nails make you hold your own weight."

Knucks showed her what she wanted to know: "Just point and shoot."

Eleanor sat on that Brooklyn park bench until noon. Then, like most days, to the park fountain came the handsome lawyer who'd been squiring 7B for nineteen months and was the "he" in overheard elevator cell phone calls about "when was he *finally* going to ask." Next came the black-haired receptionist for the nearby museum, who Eleanor first saw having an apparent business meeting in a hipster coffee shop with 7B's intended—innocent until the receptionist slid the lawyer's hand up her skirted thigh to the strap of her black garter belt, which Eleanor spied through tea's steam and realized that she herself should have said yes more often to long-gone Hank, an epiphany she now luckily could do nothing about.

What she could do something about was God's challenge. If she walked past the sin of betrayal, was she not condoning, even committing that sin? And as Hank's direct instruction in divorce had taught her, what crime is worse than betrayal? Was committing one sin to battle another worse than doing nothing at all?

The nails make us hold our own weight.

Eleanor reached into her black purse as the lawyer and receptionist kissed.

Used 7B's cell phone camera to point and shoot, shoot, shoot.

Strolled back to the front desk of their apartment building where she watched the doorman call 7B's emergency numbers until a human answered and took the information about the anonymously found cell phone that Eleanor was certain 7B would check if not tonight then soon, so before the end of this world, she might find someone worth loving.

➤◄

James Grady's first novel, Six Days of the Condor, *became the Robert Redford movie with only the loss of three days. Grady has published more than a dozen other novels and as many short stories, been an international investigative reporter, a screenwriter, an Edgar Allan Poe Award nominee, and a recipient of the Grand Prix du Roman Noir (France) and the Raymond Chandler Award (Italy) for his fiction career.*

LYE

Derek Haas

You should know, first off, I'm a coward. I get squeamish, and if there's a choice between fight or flight, well, it's really no choice for me.

The con goes like this: Coombs and I explain we're with the property board, and we need to survey the measurements of the house to make sure the homeowner isn't paying too much in taxes. I tell the mark to hold a piece of string standing at the front door while I take the other end to various rooms inside the home and call out measurements to Coombs, who writes them down on his clipboard. What I'm really doing is cleaning out any drawers of silver, jewelry, or knickknacks, or whatever I can find that I can slip into my tool sack. I have free rein of the house because I know the homeowner is on the other end of that string. When I return, we tell the mark, "The city will talk to you soon," and we're in Coombs's car and down the road before anyone knows what's what.

I have no idea if there's a "property board." Neither does 99 percent of the housewives and hillbillies living in single-level homes around major cities in Texas. We're not scamming rich people…too many alarms, too many safes, too much house, too many problems. Nope, we hit people who are scratching by but still own homes. You'd be surprised how many of them have jewelry worth pawning stuck in the back of their sock drawers.

On this particular day, the woman who opened the door was dressed as skimpily as a prostitute and said her name was Devin. I went through my spiel, and she lapped it up and took her end of the string, but I saw her making eyes at Coombs, and I was already thinking, "This is no good."

Coombs has one of those dimples in his chin that gets women steamed. I'm not ugly by any stretch, but I have a forgettable face, so I have no problem blending into the wallpaper. Why I partnered with someone with a dimpled chin is beyond me.

We were locked up in county together, shot the shit for a couple of hours, and when we both were released, we ate some barbeque at Vitek's, sort of laid out this grift, and here we were five months later.

The string was tight, and I called out, "Four ninety-five," which didn't mean anything, and rummaged through the kitchen but didn't find squat. I walked on to the first bedroom, which had been converted into a pathetic office—sagging desk and five-year-old Mac sandwiched between filing cabinets—not expecting to find much of value. I opened the first drawer of the desk, nothing. My hand must've grazed the computer mouse because the monitor clicked on, and at first I didn't look at it and, to tell you the truth, I wish I hadn't. I saw the browser open, and the website displayed an order for a one-pound bag of lye, which struck me as odd. The only thing I know lye is used for is making soap or soft pretzels or bodies disappear.

I still felt the string tight in my hand and realized I hadn't said anything for a while, so I called out, "Six twenty-one." Usually Coombs calls back the number so I know we're good, but if he parroted it back to me, I didn't hear it. I should probably have moved on to the next room, but instead I moved the cursor up to the History tab and clicked it. Here were the search terms: "acid," "dead body," "disposing of a dead body," "body decay," and "lye."

I blanched and gave a lookie-loo out the window to the backyard, and I'll be damned if I didn't see a mound of freshly plowed dirt. Scratch that. Two mounds, side by side, three feet apart, six feet long. Right then, the string went slack.

"Wilson!" I called out, which was the code name I used for Coombs, but he didn't answer, the string limp in my hand. I felt my cheeks go hot the way they do when I'm nervous, and I called out again, "Wilson!" but I only heard a grunt and the sound of a body collapsing on the furniture coming from the front.

I swallowed hard and poked my head out in the hallway, which gave me a clear sight line to the front door, but all I saw was the other end of my string lying slack on the floor.

I tiptoed as quiet as a cat down the wooden slats of the hallway, hoping to hell one of those boards wasn't loose, and maybe I could make it out the front door before Devin got me like she got Coombs.

My pulse was racing like a locomotive, and I could hear it in my ears as I moved toward the front door. I heard more grunting, and I told myself to keep moving, but I looked over into the living room, and on top of the couch Devin was on top of Coombs, pounding, pounding, and I realized she wasn't stabbing him, she was riding him like a thoroughbred. He was having the time of his life. He spotted me over her shoulder and gave me the thumbs-up. I couldn't process what I was seeing, and I think I gave him a slight nod, but it's not too clear in my mind.

I left him to it and headed outside toward the car. As I stepped into the street, I saw a giant man pull up in a plumber's truck and get out from behind the wheel, fisting a massive wrench. He nodded at me, neighborly-like, and headed toward Devin's door.

I'd love to say I helped Coombs, but I'm a coward, Detective. You gotta believe me. I'm telling the truth.

❦

Derek Haas is the author of The Silver Bear, Columbus, Dark Men, *and* The Right Hand. *He also cowrote the screenplays with his partner Michael Brandt for* 3:10 to Yuma, Wanted, The Double, *and the NBC show* Chicago Fire, *which premiered fall 2012. He is the creator of the website PopcornFiction.com, which promotes genre short fiction. He lives in Los Angeles. Follow Derek on Twitter @popcornhaas, or "friend" him on Facebook.*

THE PLEDGE

Parnell Hall

He didn't want to do it. It went against every fiber of his being, taking another person's life. He wouldn't have even considered it.

And yet…

He wanted to get into Delta Pi, the most elite fraternity on campus. They took only a few students a year, and then only when the alumni got tired of banging the co-eds and moved on, leaving a vacant room. For Kevin, who had spent his whole life on the outside looking in, it was everything he ever wanted, status, recognition, the impossible dream. One few achieved.

And now he knew why.

Kevin couldn't believe it was true, thought it must be some sick hazing stunt. Even if a pledge were depraved enough to go through with it, surely at the last moment the frat brothers would step in and stop it, the young man's willingness to commit the act all that had been required all the while. Even so, Kevin couldn't plan a person's death, whether he intended to go through with it or not.

Then he heard Jeremy talking during lunch.

Some things, Kevin thought, were omens, signs from the gods. Jeremy was carrying on about the bums who panhandled from the students on their way to class. The security guards tried to chase them off the campus, but they were like cockroaches, kept coming back. The students ignored them for the most part, just went about their business as if they weren't there.

It was not surprising Jeremy was unable to ignore them. A brilliant student but socially awkward, he was a ripe mark for a panhandler, and there was one loathsome creature who wouldn't leave him alone. The man was easy to spot in a filthy red shirt, so usually Jeremy got away. But not today, and so he sat in the dining hall, bruised, beaten, and babbling about the dangerous psychopath who terrorized him, saying how he felt like following the bum until he drank himself into a stupor and passed out, then sneaking up on him and hitting him on the head.

For Kevin, it was a weight being lifted, the answer to a prayer. He could never kill another human being. But an inhuman monster, a sadistic, psychotic menace?

Which is how Kevin found himself all alone at midnight, scouring the doorways down by the waterfront with a steak knife in his pocket. Kevin had gone on the Internet, googled "fatal stab wounds." The consensus was that the best bet was in the left chest, piercing the heart. The front was far superior to the back, the neck, or the head, though it occurred to him now, as he fingered the knife in his pocket, that slitting the throat might be *more* effective.

Kevin kept walking, trying to stifle second thoughts and trying not to look over his shoulder, where he knew the frat boys were. They would be tagging along to confirm the kill. They would see him when he did it. Or they would see him when he chickened out. They would be there to witness his humiliation and his shame.

It would be hell if he didn't do it.

If he could just *find* the guy. And it didn't look like he was going to. He'd found bums in doorways, bums in cardboard boxes, one bum behind a Dumpster, even one bum passed out in the street. But none in a red shirt. Could he have changed it? That would be the ultimate bad luck, the typical kick in the head. The thought crossed his mind: would it count if he went back and killed the bum passed out in the street?

And there it was. On the corner, just ahead, curled up against the metal loading door of a factory building, a flash of red. Could it be?

It was. A shirt so dirty it could have passed for brown. The hair stringy, greasy, spread out like a huge furry spider around the head.

Could he do it?

Yes, he could.

He slipped the knife out of his pocket.

In the front. Not the back. But he's facing away. He'd have to turn him. Maybe the throat was better. Maybe he should slit the throat. Would a steak knife do that? Why didn't he spend more time on the Internet?

Goddamnit, they were watching him. They were standing there watching him hesitate. No time for thought. He had to do it now.

Kevin crept forward, stealthy, crouching, the knife in his right hand. He reached the man, knelt down. Throat? Chest? The body was lying by his left knee. He would have to reach across himself to slit the throat. If the man were lying in the other direction, Kevin's left hand could hold the head, but from this angle his left hand was near the man's belt. Slitting the throat was out. It had to be the chest.

Kevin raised the knife, rolled him over.

Kevin didn't know what it was—the pain in his chest. Divine intervention? His conscience kicking in? Or cardiac arrest, his heart literally bursting?

He felt excruciating pain.

Then nothing.

Jeremy rolled off the body in disgust. He clambered to his feet, pulled off the greasy wig. He bent down, pried the steak knife from Kevin's lifeless fingers, and then wrapped Kevin's hand around the knife in his chest, as if he'd made one futile gesture to pull it from his heart.

Jeremy stood up, slipped Kevin's knife into his pocket, and then stripped off his thin rubber gloves. Out of the corner of his eye, he could see the frat brothers moving in to confirm the kill.

Jeremy couldn't wait to pledge Delta Pi.

Parnell Hall is the author of the Stanley Hastings private eye novels, the Puzzle Lady crossword puzzle mysteries, and the Steve Winslow courtroom dramas. His books have been nominated for the Edgar Allan Poe, Shamus, and Lefty awards. Parnell is an actor, screenwriter, singer/songwriter, and past president of the Private Eye Writers of America. He lives in New York City.

GAMES PEOPLE PLAY

Bruce Harris

She wore short shorts, sneakers, white socks, and a tank top. No bra. Her blonde ponytail rested on Mr. Perfect's broad shoulder. They listened as I stood next to my Saturn, explaining my actions to a cop whose shined shirt-pocket name tag read "Ortiz." He nodded. "Go on."

"Like I was saying. I was out of milk, and Stephanie, that's my wife, asked me to head to the grocery store for a gallon. I was steering my car with one hand, trying to find the Cubs game on the radio with the other, and then I saw her." I pointed to No Bra Girl. "Jogging, blonde ponytail bouncing up and down, but no one in hell was looking at that, especially me. Excuse my bluntness, but even Stevie Wonder can see she isn't wearing a bra, and her boobs were practically hanging out of that top. Damn.

"I slowed down, maximizing the time I had to admire her, my prurient thoughts raging. I shifted my gaze to the side-view mirror as I passed her. I'm still watching her ass as she jogs out of my life, when I see a black pickup truck pull up alongside her. She stops and peers into the truck's window and, in an instant, she's gone! Shit. I just watched some guy drag her into his truck. I do an immediate U-turn and head for the pickup truck. At first I can only see the driver, but seconds later I see her blonde head, but it quickly disappears again. From about five hundred feet away, it appears that they're struggling. I floor it. I think the bastard is hitting her as he speeds up, but I'm not letting him out of my sight. He swerves right to avoid a UPS truck, and I can see him looking back at me through his rearview mirror. I give him the finger. I smack into the truck's rear bumper, and again the guy looks back at me. He's cursing. I slam into him again. Now, she's in sight, staring at me. She looks petrified. She's screaming something, but I can't make it out. He's shouting, too. I'm playing bumper cars with this fucker's, excuse my language, truck, but I'm not really playing. The radio is between stations, so I shut the damn thing and reach for my cell phone and dial 911. Before it connects, I hear your siren and see flashing red lights approaching. Someone else must have called you. Within minutes, you cut him off, and here we are, all three vehicles are stopped on the side of the road. Good, I figured, now the bastard's going to get what he deserves."

"Boy, am I glad you came in time, Officer. This fucking guy is crazy. Look what he's done to the back of my truck! He nearly drove us off the fucking road." Ortiz looked away from Perfect Man toward the damaged vehicle and shook his head.

"Watch your language, sir. Keep it civil." He turned to me. "Do you have anything else to say?"

"Officer, I watched this guy pull this young lady off the street against her will. I was just trying to stop him and help her, you know, trying to be a Good Samaritan and all that. That's the truth." The policeman looked at the couple with raised eyebrows.

Now it was Braless's turn. Pointing to me, she said, "This guy is out of his mind." The perfect couple hugged again. "This is my boyfriend, Officer. We were just having a little fun playing a game, keeping things exciting between us. It was nothing more than a little harmless sex skit we were acting out. The next thing we know, this nut is ramming the back of our truck. I called 911, and thank goodness you showed up."

A moment later, a second squad car pulled up. A black cop named Brown sauntered over, said, "Whatcha got, Ortiz?"

Ortiz motioned to the couple. "This guy was harassing this young woman. Get him the hell out of my sight, Terry."

I watched two jaws simultaneously drop. Before either could say a word, Officer Brown escorted a handcuffed Perfect Body into the backseat of his police cruiser and drove off. "What the hell are you doing?" shouted Ponytail. "That's my boyfriend!"

Ortiz slapped her face, cuffed her wrists, and pushed her into the backseat of his car. "Get in there and shut up. You, Good Samaritan," he pointed to me, "in the front seat."

"Are you crazy? What the hell do you think you're doing? I want a lawyer!" Ms. Boobs in the backseat was crying.

Shit, a lawyer was going to help her about as much as the boogey man was going to scare Ortiz. Ortiz was as crooked as an arthritic finger. I'd seen his type plenty of times. We left the sobbing blonde in the locked police car as we belted down close to a dozen cold ones at a local tavern. Ortiz told me shit I didn't want to hear about his childhood and stepfather. After nearly two hours, he grabbed a fistful of peanuts and said, "Let's go!" We were both drunk. He had trouble opening the patrol car's rear door, stuffed his face with nuts, loosened his belt and grabbed the girl. Spitting peanut shells, he said, "If you say a word about this to anyone, you'll think this was Christmas morning compared to what I'll do to your boyfriend." Ortiz undid her handcuffs and positioned himself inches away from her face. His uniform pants dropped. "You know what to do!" She did. When Ortiz screamed "Yes!" the poor bastard was too drunk to notice Blondie had removed his gun with her newly freed hands. She fired. Twice.

THIS STORY WAS FIRST PUBLISHED IN *DEADLY CHAPS*.

Bruce Harris is the author of Sherlock Holmes and Doctor Watson: About Type *and a chapbook,* The Man and the Mark. *Visit the author's website at BatteredBox.com.*

BUILT WITH LOVE

Jamie Harrison

Paul's grandmother Ruth had been a gardener, and his grandfather Matthew had begun a greenhouse for her, but she had
left anyway. Paul had never known her, but he knew, from his
father, that Ruth had been the only person Matthew had ever
loved.

Everyone had baggage. Now Paul stood in the humid sun
measuring the frame for glass for the third time, as if the metal
might have bent and warped overnight after forty years. The
greenhouse had been no more than a skeleton and a flagstone pad
for most of his life except for a brief period when Matthew had
topped it with willow branches as a sort of ramada. He'd built it
on the edge of Maiden Lake, and on high-water years it was possible to jump directly into the water from the pad. Paul and his
brother had played foursquare and table tennis during summer
visits, though the table warped quickly in the constant rain, and
the location was hard on every kind of ball.

Paul finished and went inside. Julia, the live-in aide, was in
the kitchen; she was the reason he didn't mind this long visit. "Are
you ready to guess?" she asked.

"Yes."

"Turn around and shut your eyes."

He already had, even though he wanted to see her. Honey-colored hair, big gray eyes, the nose a little hooked. She liked to read books. She liked what they did and seemed to like who he was. He had to figure out how to stay, or how to move them to Montana. Her to Montana—Matthew couldn't last much longer.

"It's not hot," she said. "Open up."

"Chickpeas," he said.

"Of course," said Julia. "But what's in there? What's the edge?"

"Cayenne and salt."

"More."

"Garlic?"

"No. Preserved lemon, drizzled with a little sesame oil. I used the garlic press, so maybe there is a touch there."

"Sit on my lap," said Paul, opening his eyes.

She slid on, facing him. Through the glass patio doors, they could see Matthew watching the water, the frame of the never-glassed greenhouse cutting through the view.

Many people with Matthew's condition lost their sense of taste, but food had been his greatest love, after the late, great Ruth. Since Paul had arrived two weeks earlier, everything Julia had cooked had boggled and seduced. When Matthew, an obsessive, seemed to want rice, she'd made Persian rice and paella and sticky rice balls, stuffed cabbage, rice pudding, and avgolemono. A sudden desire for halibut brought on grilled grape-leaf packets and red-cooked halibut cheeks and tacos and chowders. The pork run, which preceded this relative diet, nearly killed Paul—and sealed his adoration.

Matthew couldn't speak but wrote notes: *nectar of the gods, the heart is an interminable artichoke, who ate the first oyster?*

The next day the glaziers arrived, and by afternoon the greenhouse was finished. The idea had been to recreate some idea of happiness, finish the project Matthew had started to remind him of the notion of love or joy. He'd written notes: *She preys on my mind. She wanted the greenhouse.* Ruth hadn't left for some fresh life: she'd been clinically depressed, frayed from shock therapy and problematic drugs; she had found an unfindable place to kill herself.

That didn't diminish the fact that her husband had loved her enough to build most of it before she left. Matthew had been upset until Paul reassured him that they wouldn't cut down the trees around it, wouldn't change the path or the view from the house. The first plant in the greenhouse would be the last one to survive Ruth, a stunted Turkish fig that Matthew had managed to keep alive in the den. It produced one fig a year, and every year he chopped the fruit into pieces and fed it to the flickers.

That afternoon they maneuvered the fig tree onto a dolly and rolled it down the path, then fetched Matthew and some glasses and champagne. It was trickier getting the tree through the door than it was the man in the wheelchair. "Where do you want it?" asked Paul.

He was asking Julia, but Matthew pointed. The flagstones were bumpier than Paul had realized, and the cork was tougher to pull than Julia had expected. Paul paused to open the bottle, then pushed a little too hard on the fig tree, rather than on the dolly. The massive pot tilted and crashed against the stone.

"The tree's okay," Julia said. "It's okay. We can wiggle it into place now."

"Watch your feet," said Paul. "Don't you see what happened?"

What had happened: the stone had cracked, and the cement around it, and the whole area, had sagged. He lifted the rock away and saw that the metal screen underneath had rusted to a red powder shadow and lay over a cavity where the base gravel or dirt

BUILT WITH LOVE — 197

had subsided. "Fuck," he said. "This is going to be a complete pain in the ass to fix."

Matthew made a sound; Julia smoothed his hair without looking.

"It reeks," she said.

"Just old," Paul said. "Let it air out."

"What'll you do?"

"Clear it away, refill, repour, try to relay the stone."

Matthew was crying; they'd botched the christening. Julia poured anyway. Paul plucked away the rotten wire and slivered wood under the broken concrete, wondering if the structure could handle the weight of the glass. He saw more wood and pulled out a piece, and dropped it next to his champagne.

It was a leg bone, a tibia.

"That's human," said Julia.

"Jesus, Papa, who built this thing?"

Matthew waved a hand, and Julia handed him the pad. Matthew wrote slowly, big jagged letters. He mantled over the paper, and Paul could only make out one word, *fucking*, and braced for another rant. It had been a few days, but this mess would set him off.

I did it myself. She wanted a fucking greenhouse.

—◆—

Jamie Harrison is the author of The Edge of the Crazies, An Unfortunate Prairie Occurrence, *and two other mysteries. She lives in Livingston, Montana, with her family.*

THE GUN WITH TWO TRIGGERS

Rob W. Hart

The digital readout on the dash of the rental says the outside temperature is ninety-seven degrees. The sun went down three hours ago. I tap the plastic—like that'll make the numbers drop.

Fucking Texas.

I kill the engine. The air conditioner stops chugging, and heat creeps in like the cold air wasn't even on. When I open the door, the swelter rushes up and clocks me across the jaw.

I hate this kind of weather, but in this economy it's hard to say no to a job.

Especially when Ginny Tonic gives it to you.

The aluminum briefcase next to me is still cold. I hold it at arm's length, try to guess at what's inside. I can't, so I drag myself into the parking lot as sweat breaks on my brow.

I hit the lock button on the key fob. The car beeps, and the sound bounces off the empty stretch of road and the laundry across the street. There's nothing else around besides that, a streetlight, and the building in front of me: a vegetarian restaurant, in Texas.

The door is unlocked. Inside the lights are off and Muddy Waters is growling from the overhead speakers. Robust air-conditioning makes me chilly and thankful.

THE GUN WITH TWO TRIGGERS — 199

There's a bar and a grid of heavy wooden tables. A man is seated at a table in the center of the grid. He doesn't move when I shut the door. He doesn't stand as I walk toward him. He just nods at the seat across from him, pulled out and waiting.

He's got a half-eaten garden salad in front of him that he doesn't acknowledge. He's small but hammered out of iron. Tight military-style haircut and rigid shoulders. Even in the dim light, it looks like he's vibrating. I set my feet in case he takes a dive at me.

He doesn't, so I toss the briefcase onto the table and sit. He cocks his head.

"From Ginny," I tell him.

"I know." His voice echoes like it's coming from another room.

"I got the first number for you."

"She didn't give you all three?"

"Wasn't my job to look inside."

Ginny was specific. When she slid the briefcase across her desk in Hell's Kitchen, back where the weather behaves at night, she said: Deliver it and don't open it. Acknowledge the contact was in receipt of the contents. Then come home.

She gave me the first number to the lock and said the other two were in Texas.

I did ask Ginny what was inside. She said, "A second chance."

She didn't need to explain what that meant. The last job I did, the job I fucked up, I thought that was the end, and my next living situation was on the bottom of the Hudson.

Ginny doesn't dole out second chances. This was a generous offer and the whole ride down I wondered if it was too generous.

The guy cocks his head again, like it's the only way he can express himself. He asks, "The number?"

"Three."

He nods, rolls the other two numbers in place, and then clicks the top open.

He smiles. It's the smile of a kid on Christmas morning, and for people like us that can only mean one thing.

I don't even wait. I pull the Walther PPK from my waistband and put a bullet in his forehead.

The ringing in the air drowns out the music. The salad is on the floor, but I don't know how it got there. He doesn't fall off the chair, just sprawls back, his arms outstretched, palms to the ceiling.

I wait for something else to happen, and nothing does. Then I turn the briefcase around. Inside is a Smith & Wesson Model 500. A gun this big would have blown a hole through me, and then the back wall of the restaurant.

The silver gun is heavy in my hand. Maybe I'll take it when I go visit Ginny. Because after this, she's due for a visit.

I turn it over and find something stuck to the grip.

A magnet, the size of three stacked dimes.

I roll it over in my fingers. Ginny doesn't do anything unless it's on purpose.

Then my body erupts in sweat, sucking the warmth out of my skin under the strength of the air-conditioning.

I think I know what this is.

Under the red felt lining of the briefcase I find another, different kind of digital readout. These numbers are dropping, but not in a good way.

I look at the dead guy across from me.

"I guess we both fucked up."

❧

Rob W. Hart is a blogger and columnist at LitReactor.com. His writing has appeared at Shotgun Honey *and in* Needle: A Magazine of Noir. *This story was originally published as "Second Chance" and was published in* Shotgun Honey *on August 17, 2011. You can learn more about him at his website, RobWHart.com.*

BLINDFOLDED

John Harvin

She fastened her seatbelt, reached for the ignition, looked up, and stopped. Puzzled, she stared at the three small wires hanging where the rearview mirror should have been. At almost the same time, she felt the gun at the side of her neck and heard the man behind her say, "Don't move, Judge Evans. Both hands on the wheel. Don't turn around."

"Okay," she said. Her voice sounded higher than normal. She'd been to a class once on how to react in a hostage situation. She tried to calm herself. "What do you want?"

"Put that on your head," the voice said. A small black silk bag floated over the seat.

"Now what?" she asked, voice muffled by the bag.

"Now you drive," the voice said.

"I can't see."

"But you've driven your driveway a thousand times. It's only, what, a quarter mile out to the road? Drive!" He jammed the barrel of the gun deeper into her neck.

Slowly she felt for the gears. She released the brake and pushed the accelerator. The engine revved, but the SUV did not move. She bumped the shifter down one and eased backward. A moment later she felt a thump, and slammed the brake.

"Hope that pot wasn't expensive." The voice laughed. "Tell you what. I'll help you out. I'll say 'stop' if you're about to blow it. I don't want you driving off one of those nice stone bridges and killing me. But here's the deal. Only three times. The first three are free, the fourth time you die. Now drive!"

She shifted, slowly released the brake, and felt the car roll forward. Concentrate, Elizabeth, concentrate. She pictured the fountain and the slight curve to the right as she left the courtyard, then felt the transition from stone to blacktop under the tires and held her breath, waiting.

She heard a laugh. "Very good, Judge."

Slowly she rolled along, trying to visualize the hard right curve at the end of short straight. She pictured herself driving at night in a heavy rain. Or in the snow.

"Stop!" said the voice. "You need to turn right now or we go into the woods."

She took her shaking hands down from the wheel and wiped them dry on the tweed skirt, turned the wheel sharply to the right, eased forward, and released the wheel on the count of a thousand-ten.

"What is this about?" she asked.

"Shouldn't you be concentrating on the road, Judge?" The voice laughed. She could smell him now in the closeness of the car.

The driveway curved back to the left at some point, she knew. Without replying, she slowly eased the wheel to the left and counted to five, then released it.

"Good."

She ran the movie of the road in her head, felt the rise and fall of the first bridge right where she expected it.

"Is this about the Riley case?" she asked.

"Bravo, Judge."

She licked her lips. She should feel the second bridge any moment now.

"Stop!" the voice said. "You're about to drive us right into it. Move left."

She slammed on her brakes and felt his weight against the back of her seat. Slowly she backed up, cocked the wheel a fraction, and drove over the second bridge. Mentally she ran down the remaining road. Four curves. At the last curve, a forty-foot ravine. And at the highway, if they made it that far, traffic and a stone wall directly across from the mouth of the drive.

"What did you say at the sentencing?" the voice asked.

She stammered, trying to concentrate both on the road and to remember her words. "I don't know."

The gun jammed into her neck, forcing her head to the left. "Remember!"

"I said…"

"Stop! There's a ditch. You need to turn left."

Slowly she corrected and moved on. The temperature rose inside the hood, and she felt the silk sticking to her sweaty forehead. The air tasted moist and stale.

"That's three, Judge. No more chances. Now what did you say today?"

Suddenly she remembered the shock on the face of the heavyset young man sitting in the third row as she handed down the maximum sentence. "I said, 'Three strikes and you're out.'"

They should be approaching the third turn now. She eased the wheel to the right and counted, holding her breath. At twenty she let go and straightened up.

"You're getting pretty good at this," the voice said. "How does it feel to be out of strikes?"

"I didn't do what Riley did," she said.

The voice in her ear almost screamed, "You have no idea what Riley did or why he did it."

"I trust the system."

"The system," snarled the voice. "I know all about the system."

"What do you want?" she asked simply.

"I want Riley freed." Still too loud.

"I can't do that," she said. "You know I can't do that."

Then, "I need to concentrate for this next turn."

She slowed and felt his weight against the seat. In her mind's eye, she pictured the curve and the ravine. Slowly she eased the wheel to the right, and counted. At thirty she straightened.

"I never thought you'd make it," the voice said. "Not that it matters."

When she heard the click of the hammer, she floored the accelerator. The huge Mercedes leaped forward. She heard a gasp and felt the gun fall away. A horn blared, and then she felt the shuddering impact of the stone wall, the chest strap cutting into her, and her face sinking into the air bag. A weight flew by her right shoulder. She heard him slam against the dash.

Her airbag deflated, and she reached up and shakily pulled off the black bag. The man lay in a crumpled heap on the passenger floorboard. A hand pounded on the driver's side window.

"Are you okay?" someone yelled.

She patted the air bag console. "You have to trust the system."

❖

In addition to blogging on politics and society (under the pseudonym Otherwise at ScholarsandRogues.com) and writing, John Harvin works with the CEOs of major corporations on strategic problems. He splits his time between his apartment in Chicago and various countries and cities around the world. This year he will attempt his fourth Ironman triathlon.

PRESENT COMPANY

Michael Haynes

Detective Collins straightened his jacket before entering the residence. He'd pulled Maple Hill's first homicide in years and wasn't about to walk in looking like a slob. He took one more swipe at his hair and stepped inside.

"What have you got for me?" he asked those already at work.

"Deceased is Margot Harris," an officer named Hoffman said. "She lived here with her husband and two children."

That children lived here was apparent. Toys were scattered on the floor—here a plastic dinosaur, there several random building bricks.

Collins looked at the corpse. Dressed for a day at the office, but blood stained her clothing. A purse was on the floor, and yet another toy, a stuffed animal, sat by her left hand. It, too, was bloodstained.

"A maid comes in once a week," Hoffman continued. "She found Mrs. Harris like that and called 911. We had to have her taken down to St. Paul's; she was awful shook up."

Hoffman gestured at the body. "The techs say she was stabbed multiple times. She either moved herself or was moved before she died, but not far."

Collins crouched, thought. "Where was Mr. Harris when this happened?" he asked.

"We're still trying to get in touch with him. A neighbor says he takes the kids in to school before going to work."

A tech stepped between Collins and Hoffman, bagged up the purse and bloodied toy, took them away as evidence.

"So, hubby and kids leave," Collins said. "And sometime between then and when the maid shows up, Mrs. Harris is killed."

"That's what we've got so far."

"Not much, is it?" Collins stood up. "Call me when you have something new. And get me the address of where Mr. Harris works. I'm going to pay him a visit."

Collins entered the offices of Harris & Parker Accounting shortly after ten. In the reception area, a well-dressed man talked with the woman behind the desk.

"Pardon me," Collins said, showing his identification. "Could I speak with Mr. Harris?"

"He's out for coffee," the man said. "Can I help you?"

"Actually, he just came back, Mr. Parker," said the receptionist. She spoke quietly into her phone, then directed Collins to Harris's office.

Half an hour later, Collins left, certain that Arnold Harris wasn't their guy. He seemed stunned when told his wife was dead. Naturally. Anyone who'd watched a TV knew to act that way. But he also had people who could vouch for his movements all morning.

Collins also met with the maid when she came into the station to give her statement. A tiny middle-aged woman with thin hair and a premature stoop to her shoulders. No chance she overpowered Mrs. Harris.

He went home feeling like he'd gotten nowhere. That evening he spread the case file contents on the dining table. His wife, Claire, walked by. She muttered something he didn't catch.

"Hmm?" he asked.

She gave a nervous laugh. "Oh, it was just…A joke in poor taste."

"What about?"

"That photograph."

Normally Claire avoided talking about his work. She said she preferred not knowing.

"What about it?"

Her face flushed. "I said you could rule out Yak Yak Bird kidnapping as the motive."

"I don't understand."

"The doll there. It's a Yak Yak Bird. They were hot last Christmas."

"Never heard of them."

She smiled crookedly. "Maybe if you'd helped me shop for your nieces and nephews you would have."

"Huh. So, what was the big deal?"

"Oh. They talk."

Collins shrugged. "Haven't there been talking toys since we were kids?"

"No. I mean they talk back to you, repeat what you say."

Claire kept talking, but Collins didn't hear. He looked at the photo again. The bird sat by Harris's hand. And the techs said they thought she'd tried to move herself…

He called the station. Frank Butcher took the call.

"Frank," he said, "Could you sign out one of the pieces of evidence for the Harris case? I want you to check something. It's the toy, a stuffed animal."

Collins waited while Frank was away.

"I've got it. Ugly thing, ain't it?" Frank said.

"Yeah, listen…What I need you to do is…" He realized he had no idea and put his hand over the mouthpiece.

"Claire, how do you get the thing to talk back to you?"

She thought about it for a moment. "Squeeze the wing."

"You're sure that won't erase the recording?"

Claire nodded brightly. "Oh yeah, you have to push in its tummy to do that."

Collins shook his head. This was nuts. Still, he uncovered the mouthpiece. "You got gloves, Frank?"

"Yeah."

"Get 'em on. Then squeeze the bird's wing."

There was a long silence. Butcher finally answered, "It's got two wings, Detective Collins. Which one do you want me to, um, squeeze?"

"I don't know. Try one, then the other. Let me know what happens."

There were some rustling sounds as Butcher followed his directions. Moments later, Collins heard everything he needed to hear.

"Whoa. Is that…" Frank said.

"Yes."

The recorded voice of a woman making her dying declaration echoed through Collins's head.

"Get it back to the locker right away," he told Butcher. "And whatever you do, don't press on its tummy…its stomach. I need to get some warrants."

Collins went down to the holding cell.

"Want to tell me about it, Parker?"

"There's nothing to tell because I didn't do anything." Parker picked at his shirt cuffs. "I'll be out before lunchtime, Detective," Parker said. "What makes you think you can arrest me for this?"

"Because I know you killed her. Because she wouldn't help you cheat your partner, her husband, out of the partnership's profits. And because she wouldn't leave him for you."

Parker's eyes gave his fear away, but he still snorted a laugh. "Right. And where'd you get that idea?"

Collins smiled as he turned to leave. "A little birdie told me, Parker. A little birdie."

THIS STORY WAS FIRST PUBLISHED IN *EVERY DAY FICTION*.

Michael Haynes lives in central Ohio, where he helps keep IT systems running for a large corporation during the day and puts his characters through the wringer by night. An ardent short-story reader and writer, Michael has had more than twenty stories accepted for publication during 2012 by venues such as Orson Scott Card's Intergalactic Medicine Show, Daily Science Fiction, Nature, *and many others. Visit his website at MichaelHaynes.info.*

THE EINSTEIN DIVORCE

Gar Anthony Haywood

Through the bedroom door—*his* fucking bedroom door!—
Lester could hear them inside. Laughing. Cooing. Moaning.

He gripped the gun in his hand tighter, all reservations gone now.

The sonofabitch had been right. This was the only way.

"She's fucking around on you, isn't she?"

Lester had spun around. "What?"

"I know, I know. It's none of my business," the guy had said, nine days ago, "but I kinda recognize the look. I've been there myself, man. I used to see that face in the mirror all the time."

He'd taken the next seat at the bar without Lester noticing. It hadn't been much of a trick: Lester was here for the liquor, not the company, and nothing else had warranted his attention.

The stranger, a shaggy-haired beach-boy type who had to be Lester's junior by ten years, held out his hand. "Scotty Henson."

Lester shook the hand but didn't offer his own name, too inebriated to tell yet what this was.

"It does something to a man, the pain," Henson said, sounding as if he'd already had a few drinks himself.

"The pain?"

212 — GAR ANTHONY HAYWOOD

"Finding out your woman is doing some other guy. This the wife or your girlfriend?"

Lester thought about lying, decided there was little point. "The wife," he said.

Andrea. Eleven years of marriage. A home, two cars, money in the bank. All the clothes and shoes to wear she could want, and no kids to pin them down. The bitch should have been happy. Sure, Lester played around on her, but so what? Sex was nothing to a man; it was as strictly physical an act as taking a leak. But for women? For Andrea? There had to be feelings involved. Andrea couldn't watch sex on television unless the people having it were madly in love.

"The wife, that's rough," Henson said, emptying his glass. "That's, like, the ultimate betrayal. And it's not like you can just walk away, right? Without rewarding her ass with half of everything you own?"

Lester was finally getting irked. What did this punk know about it? "Hey, look…" he started to say.

But Henson wouldn't quit, oblivious to every attempt Lester made to shut him up. Before Lester knew it, the guy was buying them round after round of fresh drinks as he rambled on about the inequities of divorce and a man's need for some greater form of justice when his woman had slipped another man's joint between her legs.

Not talking about Lester's situation at all, Lester realized, but his own. Some woman somewhere had fucked him over, too, and Henson was still feeling the sting.

"So what do you suggest?" Lester asked him, his voice dripping with sarcasm. "Murder?"

Truth be told, Lester had been thinking a lot about murder that day, ever since he'd found the bottle of scented sex jelly buried at the bottom of Andrea's workout bag that morning. But murder was just a pipe dream, because a man couldn't kill his wife and get away with it. His obvious motive would always make him the cops' prime suspect, and they wouldn't stop digging until they'd found a way to nail him for the crime.

What Lester hadn't considered was Henson's ingenious, if somewhat costly, solution to the problem: not worrying about "getting away" with murder at all.

Premeditation was the key, Henson had said. Planning the murder over time was what always brought the law down hardest on a man's head when he killed his wife, but when he killed her in the heat of passion, at the very moment he discovered her infidelity? *That* was a man the court could pity. He'd do some time, sure, but probably not much; it was the difference between a lifetime behind bars and two or three years, maybe even less.

Was that too high a price to see Andrea dead, Lester wondered?

A criminal record wouldn't destroy him. He could start over. And when he did, he could have all the women in the world without feeling the slightest bit guilty about it. There'd be no more Andrea to complicate matters.

He'd be free.

"She'll bring the asshole home eventually," Henson had said. "They always do. I'd catch the two of 'em in the act." He was speaking only hypothetically, fantasizing out loud, but Lester wasn't thinking in those terms. "I'd go through the door and empty a gun into the fucking bed. I wouldn't talk, I wouldn't hesitate, I'd just empty the gun, because every minute I waited they'd say was time I had to reconsider."

It all made sense to Lester. Too much to ignore. So here he was now, outside his bedroom door with a loaded gun in his hand. Just as Henson had predicted, Andrea had brought her lover to Lester's bed; she'd gotten sloppy and dropped just enough clues for Lester to suspect today was the big day, and sure enough, it had been.

After this was over, Scotty Henson would have to die too, of course—loose ends always had to be tied—but first things first.

Lester threw open the door, saw Andrea sprawled across the sheets, naked as a newborn, and started firing.

When Lester was done shooting, a half-naked Scotty Henson slipped up behind him and cracked his skull with a golf trophy he'd taken from the fireplace mantel, killing Lester on the spot. Self-defense, he'd tell the cops, and they'd buy it. He then stepped over Lester's body into the bedroom to turn off the porno movie playing on the TV, silencing all the loud laughter and exaggerated moaning. Andrea, dead as she was, didn't seem to mind.

She was going to end their affair. She loved Lester, not Scotty, she'd decided. It had been more than poor Scotty could bear. He would rather see her dead than with another man.

Luckily, it turned out her husband felt the same way.

—◆—

Gar Anthony Haywood, whom Booklist *has called a writer who belongs "in the upper echelon of American crime fiction," is the Shamus and Anthony Award–winning author of twelve crime novels and numerous short stories. He has written for both the* New York Times *and* Los Angeles Times*, and he blogs about writing regularly at www.murderati.com.*

FRINGE BENEFIT

Jeremiah Healy

O n a warm weekday afternoon, Martha was standing just off the curb of her assigned corner. She wore a chartreuse safety vest and held the splintery handle of a white-on-red cardboard "Stop" octagonal stapled to the underlying wood at both top and bottom. In short, she was the perfect image of minor—and, even then, only ephemeral—authority.

But the full-length mirror at home couldn't hide other, equally evident, truths.

Begin with middle age.

Add mousy hair.

Ditto dumpy frame and sagging breasts.

Then subtract any way to reverse the effects of growing older, much less to defeat the law of gravity.

Martha always strove for the earth mother look, and by sheer force of personality and sympathetic understanding, she occasionally reaped that role's delightful rewards. However, Martha more often thought, apply grotesque makeup, pull on floppy shoes, and you'd pass for a circus clown.

Nevertheless, she watched carefully for the middle-school students who, during brief periods twice a day, were her charges. Martha never believed being a crossing guard amounted to a calling, but the job did carry one fringe benefit that she genuinely treasured.

The clique that Martha had labeled "Princess Diana's" began to move from the driveway of their campus and down a hedge-bordered sidewalk toward her intersection. Martha's heart prepared itself to skip a beat. Princess Di—her real name didn't matter yet, and might never—was a seventh grader who, sexually, could have been going on twenty-eight. Blonde hair, blue eyes, and a Lolita smile over budding breasts and a coltish undercarriage, she was the clear alpha female of her crew. Laughing a little too loudly, vamping a lot too much. And inappropriately touching boys to the point of "Why don't you give me a try?"

The Princess's likely future wasn't hard to picture: deflowered within a year, knocked up before two more. The perfect target for a ninth-grade Romeo–rebel without a clue, his extra male chromosome eager—even driven—to perform stud-duty on the cutest mare in the herd.

Which ordinarily would make the girl a perfect candidate for Martha's protection. But the crossing guard's heart would have to wait if it still wanted to skip that beat.

Princess Di was not leading her amoeba-like entourage. In fact, the delectable muffin wasn't to be seen, period.

Martha stepped into the crosswalk, brandishing her stop sign against oncoming motorists as though it were a crucifix warding off four-wheeled vampires. The Princess's clique flowed around Martha like she was just a traffic pole planted in the macadam. A couple of geeky boys trailing within the cool kids' wake actually thanked the crossing guard for being there, but Martha was searching the foreshortened horizon, hoping for a glimpse of Princess Di to confirm that she was indeed—

Abruptly, a royal "spotting." White tank top, blue denim minishorts, and cork platformed sandals, the last elevating and accentuating calf muscles that eventually would project original sin vibrating in four-inch stilettos. A horny humper's dream come true, but, oddly, the Princess was by herself. She also seemed to choose her walking route to avoid being noticed by her worshippers, though they were now far ahead of Martha and apparently oblivious to anything occurring behind them.

Then, from a partition in the sidewalk's bordering hedge, a lanky, mop-haired boy dressed in grunge jumped out and clamped the Princess in a bear hug, spoon-style. Probably the quickest way of impressing upon her the burgeoning heft of his manhood.

Martha wanted to spit, but refrained.

The boy spun Princess Di 180 degrees, so that she now faced him. They kissed in that sudden, sloppy way adolescents do, thinking that tongue-lashing the other's mouth showed they were already sophisticated in the ways of love. She broke off the kiss, and he gestured toward the gap in the hedge. Princess Di quickly scanned the surrounding blocks. Then, apparently not gauging Martha as a concern, the girl took the boy's hand and let him nearly drag her to the hedge, where he used his free palm to shove those barely clad buttcheeks through the partition and out of sight.

Martha felt that particular mourning that nested somewhere between disgust and resignation. It had certainly happened with prior "princesses," beguiled and defiled by some clumsy, pubescent caveboy before a tender and surprisingly adept crossing guard could introduce her virgin of the moment to the exquisite—and utterly safe, never messy—lore of an alternative love.

Necessarily, however, Martha also recalled the...others. Princesses who actually had spurned their male predators in favor of the crossing guard's gentle touch, leading them up far more civilized paths to sexual heaven.

And Martha fervently hoped that they *were* in heaven, since she obviously couldn't let them live after being with her. It'd take just one, revealing to school officials or confessing to parents. And, certainly, the newly initiated would share the magical details of that experience with their girlfriends. No, better that a still-shuddering princess become an early angel instead, allowing Martha to stay out of jail, keep her job, and enjoy its wonderful…

Wait a minute.

Through that gap in the hedge, one foot in a cork platformed sandal, followed by a hip in blue minishorts. And, finally, the white tank top, raggedly torn from left shoulder to right waist like her wardrobe choice had been diagonally—and brutally—slashed by the clothes police.

Princess Di, face in her hands, began stumbling and then loping awkwardly toward Martha, the offending boy neither appearing nor pursuing. The older woman took a deep, soothing breath. As she exhaled, her heart skipped that delicious, welcome beat.

It looked to be a long, late afternoon, sweetened and spiced by the crossing guard's favorite fringe benefit.

Jeremiah Healy is the creator of the John Francis Cuddy private investigator series and (under the pseudonym Terry Devane) the Mairead O'Clare legal-thriller series, both set primarily in Boston. Of his eighteen novels and more than sixty short stories, sixteen have won or been nominated for the Shamus Award. Visit his website at JeremiahHealy.com.

WYOLENE

Sam Hill

He finished the mug of buttermilk and used his sleeve to wipe the white moustache from his lip. "I'm going to take the wagon into Waycross tomorrow," he drawled.

She looked up. "Do you think I could go, RW? We need a whole bunch of stuff. Everything, really. Kerosene. I could help you with the tobacco."

He shook his head, "No reason for you to be going to town. Too much work to be done here. I'll get what we need after I leave the auction barn." RW stood, pulled the overall straps up over his shoulders, and snapped them into place. Reaching down, he used the last fragment of biscuit to wipe the egg yolk from the plate, crammed it into his mouth, and walked out, still chewing.

After washing the dishes, she pulled a pair of tattered overalls on over her cotton dress and left the small unpainted house, walking past the unmarked place where she'd buried the dog in a shallow hole, to the small grave bounded by whitewashed logs. She knelt and pulled the tiny sprigs of grass starting to peek through the sandy soil. She straightened the cross. As she worked, she kept an eye on the track, just in case RW came back for something. He did not like her tending the grave.

At noon, they ate mostly in silence. Finally, RW looked up and said, "You could probably come if I knew you wouldn't tell them crazy stuff. But I can't count on that. You haven't been right since your baby died. I can't count on what you will say half the time."

She shook her head emphatically. "No, RW, I am all right now. You can count on me to be all right. You can," she pleaded.

He stared back at her, chewing with his mouth open. "I can, can I?"

He stood up and stomped outside, the screen door slamming behind him. A minute later he appeared with the Mason jar in his hand. He placed it on the table. A piece of cheesecloth tied with twine covered the mouth. The thin coral snake lay quietly. Beautiful alternating bands of color. Red and yellow, kill a fellow. "What do you call this, Wyolene? Is this what somebody who ain't crazy keeps hidden under the corner of the house?"

Her face went pale. "It's a pet, RW. The cat ran off, and you had to shoot the dog." She paused.

"And our baby died. That's what you were going to say."

"Please, I just need something," she begged. "It's a peaceful snake. It isn't like a rattler."

He shook his head. "Animals are for working. They are to serve man. Like it says in the Bible. You don't need no pets. Especially no snake."

He picked up the jar and turned. She grabbed his arm. "Wait, RW."

He swung his arm back, catching her just above the corner of the eye with the jar, sending her backward across the raw flooring. "What do you think you're doing grabbing hold of me?" He pulled the cheesecloth from the top of the jar, and turning it upside down, dumped the snake on the floor between them. Before it could move, he used his heel to grind its head into the floor. "There's your pet, Wyolene. Go bury it like you did the damned dog." He left her sitting with her back against the wall, the blood from the cut running down and mingling with the tears.

After supper, she read the Bible to him before going to bed. He stayed on the porch, smoking and drinking clear liquid from a jar, occasionally waving at the persistent mosquitoes. Later he lurched in and stood over her. "I didn't kill that baby. I found her like that. I told you a hundred times."

He studied her a moment, then raised his voice. "Stop pretending. You ain't asleep." Her eyelids fluttered.

"You don't need no baby. You don't need no pet or nothing. You got me," he bellowed, spittle flecking the wall behind her. Her eyes popped open. With one huge hand, he covered her mouth and nose. She kicked and thrashed, her small fingers digging at his arm. When at last her body sagged, he leaned close to make sure she was still breathing.

"I had Ophir Strickland write a letter to your people saying you died of the typhoid. You don't need them either," he whispered, hiking her flour-sack shift up to her waist.

In the morning he washed in a basin on the back porch and shaved with a straight razor using the small round mirror. He cut himself like he always did and, without a word, took the clean rag she offered and dabbed the cuts. After breakfast he pulled on the worn, clean, and starched white shirt, and tried to button the sleeves.

"There's a button missing," RW said.

"Let me fix it," she answered.

Sweat poured down his face, and he worked a finger into his collar. "There's something wrong, Wyolene. I don't feel right. My face is tingly."

She worked on his sleeve. "Ouch, you stuck me with that needle," he said thickly.

"The poison is making you tingly, RW," Wyolene said quietly, "It was on the rag, and it's on the needle, too."

His breathing was ragged now, and his eyelids drooped. He tried to speak, but it came out in a slurry.

She spoke again. "They say a half a drop of coral snake poison will kill a man. But you're a big man." She pricked another hole in his wrist a quarter inch from the first one, and used the eyedropper to squeeze a white drop onto each wound. "It took me weeks to get six drops. To be sure."

He panted, watching her through slitted eyes.

"I'm sorry, RW." She patted his hand, stood, walked to the basin, and washed her hands twice. Then without looking back, went to change her dress for town.

◆◆

Sam Hill lives with his wife, dog, and two cats on a farm just outside Bloomington, Indiana. In addition to the critically acclaimed novel Buzz Monkey, *he has written and published an additional four books and more than thirty short pieces, both fiction and nonfiction. He is working on his third novel,* Stonefish.

AKA

Steve Hockensmith

BRRRRRING! Hey! America! Wake-up call! The "War on Terror" is a sham! Join us, the Aryan Knights of America, and strike a real blow for freedom! The AKA has the will and the means! So rise up, patriots, and smell the bitter coffee of deception! Nourish yourself with a tall glass of righteousness! Breakfast is the most important meal of the day! Let's break some eggs! 812-555-2783!

—*The River City Herald-Times*
Page E-13
May 26, 2007

The ad worked. Once Hightower waded through the cranks ("Is *Mrs.* Hitler home?"), he had three candidates. He just needed one to fill out the ranks of the AKA. One true believer to stand by his side.

One martyr.

They came out to his farm. An old man, a young man, and a girl. Joan wasn't around to cook anymore, so Hightower put out microwave popcorn, and they stood in the kitchen talking politics.

The recruits said the right things—mostly "Yes! Exactly!"—as Hightower philosophized about the UN and the Zionist Occupation Government and how bin Laden had ruined everything by making America look for enemies *out there* instead of right here.

The recruits passed the first test—they stayed and listened—but Hightower liked the young man best. His *exactly!*s were the most fervent, and you've got to respect a man in a These Colors Don't Run T-shirt. Plus, Hightower didn't like the way the girl said "Umm…is this everybody?" or the fact that the old man was old. Old men might complain, but all they really want is comfort. A young man has the passion to sacrifice himself for Right.

So when it was time for the second test—the *real* one—Hightower took the young man aside.

"Play along. We're gonna weed out the weaklings."

"Yes, sir," the young man said, looking like he was about to salute.

Wonderful. Hightower was 99 percent sure he had his man. The one who'd help him ride a 1981 Ford Econoline to glory. (*You* try loading a van with a thousand pounds of ammonium nitrate and nitromethane when you have a bad back.)

"Come on," Hightower told the others a minute later. "I want to show you something."

The ammonium nitrate was under tarps at the back of the barn. The guys from Hoosier Feed & Fertilizer had given Hightower funny looks when they'd unloaded them. They could see his farm wasn't growing anything but mold anymore. That's why he had to move fast.

He looked at the young man, the old man, and the girl. Back in the Clinton era glory days, he'd had dozens of comrades in arms. Now he had three, all strangers.

At least he wasn't alone. At least he could choose who to die with.

"Friends," Hightower said, "there's a traitor in our midst."

He pulled a gun from under his windbreaker and pointed it at the young man.

"Whoa!" said the young man.

"Wait!" said the old man.

"Aaa!" said the girl.

"I heard him calling his handlers," Hightower said. "He's an ATF spy."

"That's crazy!" the young man protested. "I'm a patriot!"

He didn't sound very convincing.

Good. He was keeping his head, acting the part.

The young man was still the front-runner. But the test wasn't over.

"Come here," Hightower said to the girl.

"Me?"

"You. *Come here.*"

The girl moved to his side with hesitant steps.

Hightower kept the gun pointed at the young man with his left hand while his right grabbed the girl by the wrist.

He forced her to take the gun.

"Shoot him."

"What?"

"We're in here with enough explosives to blow the Indianapolis Motor Speedway to China, and he's about to call in the storm troopers. Shoot."

The gun was shaking in the girl's hands.

She turned it on Hightower.

"Look," she said, "my name's Hannah Fox and I write for the *Herald-Times* and my editor knows I'm here working on a story about your ad so you'd better let me leave without any trouble or—"

Hightower pulled out his other gun and pointed it at her.

"Your safety's on," he said.

"Huh?"

"Get the gun. Quick," Hightower told the young man.

He did as he was told. Of course. The girl's betrayal hurt, but at least Hightower was about to have his winner.

"Now," he said, "*you* shoot *her.*"

The young man swung his gun toward Hightower instead.

"Drop it." He offered Hightower a grim grin. "ATF. Really."

Hightower's heart was breaking even as he said, "You stupid Zionist goon. Don't you know a BB gun when you're holding one?"

The young man's grin disappeared, leaving only the grim.

Hightower turned toward the old man, about to sigh. "Guess it's down to you."

The old man's fist smashed into his face. By the time Hightower hit the ground, the gun had been ripped from his grip.

The old man gave him a moment to clear his head, then said, "My name's Erie. I'm a private investigator. Your ex-wife was worried you were up to something foolish with that money you owe her. Looks like she was right."

Damn, Hightower thought. *You can't trust anybody anymore.*

The ATF thug was going to drive Hightower to a police station.

"You're by yourself?" the PI asked him. "No backup?"

"It's not people like this we're worried about anymore."

Salt in the wound.

The goon turned on the radio as they drove off. To discourage Hightower from talking, he figured. Fine. He just listened.

On the radio, they were yakking about some senator running for president. His name wasn't Osama bin Laden, but close.

It actually cheered Hightower up.

A Muslim in the White House? Let 'em try! Then America would drop the United We Stand mask and show the world what it was truly made of.

Hightower watched the houses and farms zipping by.

He wasn't *really* alone. He still believed that.

Maybe he just had to wait.

Steve Hockensmith is the author of the Holmes on the Range mystery novels, as well as the New York Times *bestseller* Pride and Prejudice and Zombies: Dawn of the Dreadfuls. *His short fiction has been nominated for the Derringer, Shamus, Anthony, and Barry awards, and three collections of his stories are available:* Naughty, Blarney, *and* Dear Mr. Holmes. *He lives in Alameda, California. Visit him at SteveHockensmith.com.*

HIJACKERS

Chuck Hogan

He had pushed it as far as he could go—farther, actually. He'd hoped to begin the next morning on the other side of Denver but needed to get off his bike. Cities had limits; so did he.

The Days Inn looked like a good place to disappear for a night. He parked his bike and checked in, then carried his helmet and saddlebag straight into the lounge.

A sign above the backlit bar advertised a discount "for members of our armed forces," but to him it was worth the extra 10 percent not to have to deal with that yet. He experienced a singular moment of joy when he saw the overhead television showing the opening minutes of a Lakers-Nuggets game and dropped his bag and helmet onto a bar chair.

"Pretty bike."

She wore a scoop-necked black T-shirt and faded jeans, cleavage being a standard feature of the hotel bartender's uniform. He sensed somehow that she was a person in transition, but whether her life was moving from worse to better or the opposite, he could not know. His Screamin' Eagle Fat Boy was visible through the window blinds, two-tone red and black.

"I can still feel the vibration from the road," he said, flexing his numb hands.

She reached across the bar to grip the fingers of one hand and quickly pulled back, feeling it. "You need a drink," she said.

"Stoli, rocks."

The bottle was near. "How far you going?"

"LA."

She poured. "What's in LA?"

"Palm trees. Earthquakes. More street gangs and museums than any other city in the world."

She set his drink on a Days Inn napkin in front of him. "What's in LA for you?"

He picked up the glass, holding it there without spilling, commanding his hand to be still as though proving something to himself. "Home," he said, and brought it trembling to his lips.

Muffled applause came from behind the closed double doors of a nearby function room.

"Food, too?" she asked.

"Give me a few minutes," he said, and the bartender went to key in his drink order, and he settled back to focus on the game— for the moment, blissfully content.

The double doors opened, and the attendees exited in a wave of energetic chatter. White males in their thirties, handwritten nametags affixed to their shirts. A training seminar, or maybe a hobbyists' convention. He was determined to tune out their shop talk as they crowded tight around him.

But instead of unwinding, they remained on a group high, loudly carrying on. Like bits of gravel kicked up underneath his helmet visor, certain key phrases breached his consciousness:

"*Controlled demolition…*"

"*Building Seven…*"

"*…jet fuel…*"

He drained half his glass, ice and all, in one pull.

There was more. Box cutters and Saudi double agents. Missiles disguised as passenger airplanes. Cell phone signal range. The Mossad. Holograms.

The bartender was busy pouring drinks and taking food orders. He flexed his sore hands at his side. He wouldn't go back to his room. He could be alone right here if he worked at it hard enough.

"This guy. Let's get his opinion."

Iverson put a spin move on Fisher, but the ball rimmed out.

"Hey?" one of them said. "Excuse me?"

He couldn't hear the play-by-play anymore, but a graphic told him that Odom and Camby were in early foul trouble.

A hand rested on his shoulder. He turned as though a wasp had landed there.

The man to whom the hand belonged had soft cheeks and a tight smile.

"We were just wondering, I mean, you're not here for TruthCon, right?"

The motorcyclist said nothing. The attendee, intoxicated by a day of groupthink, was further emboldened now by the growing attention of his fellow hobbyists. "You look like a real guy, an average American…and I'm just wondering…I mean, regular people, people on the street…planes don't just disappear when they crash into buildings, right? I mean, at the very least you know…there's more to it. Am I right?"

The others hung on his response. The motorcyclist felt pressure from the crowd. A simple yes would grant them the satisfaction they craved and return to the motorcyclist his privacy, though not his solitude.

"People are afraid of the truth," he said.

The attendee nodded heartily, as did others around him. "You can say that again."

"They reject facts that threaten their worldview. They want simple answers to complex questions. They are immature and wish to remain that way."

More enthusiastic nodding. "True, that."

The lounge had fallen nearly silent, all focus on the motorcyclist. "Here, I think, is the real question," he said, addressing the faces turned his way. "If some secret entity could seed charges throughout twin one-hundred-and-ten-story skyscrapers without anyone knowing…if they could frame nineteen Arabs as terrorist hijackers…if they could fake a plane crash at the Pentagon and shoot down a passenger jet over Pennsylvania…if they could pull off all this and more in front of billions of people watching on live television…then how can they allow any dissenters to live? I ask those who have exposed the real truth—why haven't they come for you yet?"

The attendee's resolve flickered, his brow furrowing as he formed his response.

"What if…" the motorcyclist said, stopping the attendee before he could answer. As he did so, he pulled out his brand-new mobile phone and rested it atop the bar, like a detonator. "What if they have been waiting years to get you all together, in one location? What if, this time, they sent in just one guy, to finish the job…?"

The bartender emerged from the kitchen two minutes later with a large tray of chips and appetizers in her hand—and stopped, looking aghast at the empty lounge.

Only the motorcyclist remained, his eyes on the overhead television.

"What happened?" she asked.

"Kobe got fouled on a three." He finished his drink with a steady hand. "I think I'll order something now."

Chuck Hogan is the New York Times *best-selling author of several acclaimed novels, including* Devils in Exile *and* Prince of Thieves, *which was awarded the Hammett Prize and adapted into the 2010 hit film* The Town. *He is also the co-author, with Oscar-winning filmmaker Guillermo del Toro, of the international best-selling* Strain Trilogy. *His short fiction has twice been anthologized in* The Best American Mystery Stories *annual.*

FULL BLOOM

Wendy Hornsby

The old apple tree in the back corner of Stella Mary's garden began to bloom early in the spring. By late June its branches were heavy with ripening fruit.

"Funniest thing." Arlo Holbrook, Stella Mary's next-door neighbor, leaned his elbows atop the fence that separated their yards and eyed the tree. Eyed her, too; nosy, horny bastard, she thought. "All these years, that scraggly tree never produced anything but dead leaves for Fred to rake in the fall. Now look at it."

"I'll have a pie or two from it, that's for sure." Stella Mary continued troweling fresh mulch into the soil around the base of the tree. She knew from the way that men—Arlo among them—had begun to take particular notice of her again that the tree wasn't the only thing in her garden that had blossomed that spring.

"Yep, that puny tree used to piss off Fred," Arlo said.

"A lot of things pissed off Fred," she said.

"What do you hear from him?"

"Not one word since October, Arlo." She raised her chin enough to see his face. "Remember, I have a restraining order."

Arlo had the grace to blush. "I told you before, I'm sorry I asked him to come over that day. It's just that Fred's a real strong guy and I needed some muscle to help dig out that big ficus tree—roots you know, fouling the sewer line. Jesus, seems like we dug down halfway to China before we got them all."

"I remember."

"Anyway, frame of mind Fred was in at the time—getting served with the divorce and all—it wasn't a good idea for me to put an ax in one hand and a can of beer in the other. I guess it just didn't occur to me…" He seemed properly chagrined.

"Don't know that I ever thanked you for returning the ax, Stella Mary. Your back door looks good as new."

"Uh-huh," was all she said, and went back to work.

"Your garden puts mine to shame this year." He surveyed her yard, took in the fat red tomatoes spilling over their frames, the lovely cukes and peas, the masses of ripe blackberries hanging heavily in the corner bramble. "It's almost like that ficus poisoned the soil; nothing wants to grow back there. Don't know what I'm doing wrong. What's your magic?"

"No magic, Arlo, just dig, fertilize, water, pray."

He studied the fresh soil around the base of the apple tree. "That what you did here? Dig?"

"Root-bound," she said. "Like all living things, the tree needed room to grow and breathe."

Arlo was silent long enough that Stella Mary began to hope that he had come to the end of his conversational string and would go tend to his own business. She had been so perfectly happy that morning, working in solitude under the shade of the tree, the air perfumed by sun-warmed apples and fresh-turned earth. Until Arlo showed up.

She raised her chin and found him still there, staring at her.

"The guys at the club were talking about Fred the other day," he said. "No one has heard from him since that set-to last fall. When he didn't show up to be Santa Claus at the Kiwanis Christmas banquet, well, folks understood; still embarrassed about the restraining order and all that. But when he hadn't bounced back in time for the club's Memorial Day golf tournament..."

There was something accusatory in Arlo's voice, in the intensity of his expression as he studied her. Stella Mary sat back on her heels and wiped her cheeks with the cuffs of her garden gloves—pretty new ones—as she met his gaze. Surely Arlo understood that Fred's constant "bouncing back" after she filed for divorce was the reason she had to get a restraining order.

He said, "I have this gut feeling that something bad has happened to Fred."

"Knowing Fred as I do, I wouldn't be at all surprised." She rose and dropped her trowel into the pocket of her gardening apron. "Tell Cora I'll save her enough apples for a pie."

She turned and strode purposefully toward the house. The blessedly tidy, quiet house.

The table was laid for her supper when the doorbell rang. On the front porch she found a trio of uniformed policemen with shovels, a cadaver dog, and a search warrant.

"I would never have suspected my neighbor to be possessed of such a lively imagination," she said as she led the officers around back to search under the apple tree. They promised not to harm either the tree or its burgeoning crop, and so, leaving them to their task, she went inside to enjoy her meal.

"Sorry you were inconvenienced, ma'am," the sergeant in charge offered as he finished the fresh blackberry cobbler Stella Mary served the men when they had finished their search. "But since your neighbor is on the city council, well, certain pressure was brought to bear."

"I understand," she said as she wrapped a basket of blackberries for the officer to take home to his wife.

"I hope there isn't bad blood after this," he said.

"There's no bad blood," she said, handing him the berries. "Not on this side of the fence."

><

Wendy Hornsby is the Edgar Allan Poe Award–winning creator of the Maggie MacGowen series and is the author of many short stories. Her ninth mystery, The Hanging, *was released by Perseverance Press in September 2012. Her first seven books are now available from MysteriousPress.com in electronic-reading formats. When she isn't writing, she teaches history at Long Beach City College. Visit her website at WendyHornsby.com.*

THE BLACKMAILERS WANTED MORE

David Housewright

He heard the fear in her voice the moment she recognized his.

"No phone calls," she said. "We agreed to communicate only through chat rooms."

He assured her that it was an emergency and directed her to a park they both knew.

"Are we in trouble, Kevin?" she asked.

"Yes, Emma. I'm sorry."

He was sorry, too. Sorry for her, but mostly sorry for himself. A year ago, Kevin was named the youngest vice president in the firm. Old Man Torrance himself had taken notice and often invited Kevin and his beautiful bride, Lisa, to gatherings at his fabulous estate—that's where he was introduced to Emma, Torrance's long-legged trophy wife. Unfortunately, he and Lisa had drifted apart, mostly because of the grueling hours Kevin worked and the long trips Torrance sent him on. They hadn't enjoyed sex in weeks. Kevin decided if she was going to be that way… He met Emma in the elevator. She was willing, so he slept with her that evening. Kevin meant for it to be a one-night stand, something to remind him that he was still desirable to women. Yet he saw her again the following week and then a third time three days later—never at the same place twice. They had been very careful.

Emma was waiting for him on the park bench. He could see the anxiety on her face. He answered her nervous questions by presenting a letter that he'd discovered in his mailbox. *I know about your affair*, it said, and: *I will tell Torrance unless I'm paid $10,000.* The letter was accompanied by three laser-printed photographs. The first was taken through a bedroom window and showed Kevin and Emma embracing. They were embracing in the second photo as well, although Emma's yellow sundress was now lying at their feet. In the third photo, Emma's bra and panties had joined the sundress.

"What are we going to do?" she asked.

"Pay him. He's threatening to take away my wife, my job, probably my career. What would you lose?"

"Everything. The way our prenup is written, and Roger—his temper—you can't imagine his temper. And his kids…What was I thinking, sleeping with you?"

"Good question." Kevin was attempting to sound blasé yet was surprised at the ache he felt. He liked Emma and thought she liked him. "I can come up with five thousand dollars."

"I can find the rest, but what if he wants more?" Emma asked.

Turned out the blackmailer did want more. Kevin had followed his instructions impeccably—the cash was sealed inside a white envelope with *Room 1242* written on it and brought to the front desk of a downtown hotel. Kevin gave the envelope to a clerk. He tried to learn who was staying in 1242, but the hotel had a policy against revealing information about its guests. Two weeks later, Kevin received a second letter. The instructions were identical to the first except for a change in room number and hotel.

"What are we going to do?" This time it was Kevin who asked the question. "I can't keep withdrawing five thousand dollars in cash from our accounts without Lisa finding out."

"Sooner or later he'll betray us, anyway," Emma said. "I know he will."

"Maybe we should just go to our spouses and explain…"

"No, no, no, no, no. When I married Roger everyone accused me of being a gold digger, a blonde bimbo from the wrong side of the tracks who was using her looks and sex to snare a rich husband. It wasn't true. I married Roger because I genuinely loved him. There's no way he's leaving me. No way I'm leaving him. They were right about one thing, though. I am from the wrong side of the tracks. I know people."

"What's that mean?"

Emma glanced cautiously around her. When she was sure no one was watching, she dipped into her bag and produced a white envelope. She told Kevin to take it and follow the blackmailer's instructions. Roger knew what it was, yet asked anyway.

"It's a letter bomb," Emma said. "We're lucky because the blackmailer expects the envelope to be thick with cash. It allows us to pack it with more explosives. Otherwise it would just pop and flash like a firework."

Kevin held the bomb as if taking a deep breath would be enough to set it off. Emma told him to relax, but he couldn't. He gave her a long list of reasons why they shouldn't do this.

"We have no choice," Emma said. "Besides, it's the blackmailer's fault. He started it." Kevin still wasn't convinced. She kissed him, kissed him passionately. "Do this and I'll sleep with you one last time," she said.

An hour later, Kevin delivered the envelope to the downtown hotel designated by the blackmailer. The next day, he was arrested for murder.

The case was smartly presented. First, the prosecutor described how Kevin had withdrawn $5,000 in cash to buy the bomb. Next, he presented security footage of him handing the envelope to a hotel desk clerk who passed it to a bellhop. The bellhop testified that he carried it to room 4786 and gave it to Roger Torrance. Finally, the medical examiner explained how Torrance opened the letter, detonating the bomb that killed him as well as the woman he had been meeting at the hotel once a week for six months—Kevin's wife, Lisa.

Kevin blamed Emma. Emma denied everything, and since the letters and photographs had somehow gone missing, Kevin couldn't even prove they'd had an affair much less that it was she who plotted the crime.

"I loved my husband," a teary-eyed Emma testified at a pretrial hearing. "It broke my heart when I learned he was cheating on me."

Kevin believed her. In the end, he exchanged a guilty plea for a chance at parole in 210 months. That same week Emma inherited half of her husband's estate.

❯❯

A reformed newspaper reporter and ad man, David Housewright has published fourteen crime novels. Penance *won the Edgar Allan Poe Award from the Mystery Writers of America and* Practice to Deceive *and* Jelly's Gold *won Minnesota Book Awards. The Dark Side of Midnight will be published in June 2013. Find a complete list of his books and stories at DavidHousewright.com. Follow him on Twitter and Facebook.*

NOTHING LEFT TO LOSE

Dana C. Kabel

Farmer was sweating like a bastard. Goddamned Thailand. The native sitting across from him must have been born without sweat glands; he was dry as a bone.

The guy didn't speak a word of English. And Farmer didn't speak Thai. That was okay, the game they were playing didn't require the opponents to speak to each other.

The Thai pushed the deck of cards across the table. Farmer reached out with a trembling hand and drew a card. He flipped it over and shouted. "Fuck me!"

The Thai smiled, showing a row of crooked and rotting teeth. On the card there was a picture of a hand. Farmer sighed and took a couple of deep breaths. He spread his hand out on the table, palm down.

The Thai was so fast that Farmer saw a blur of motion and didn't know what hit him. The Thai's knife stabbed through Farmer's hand and stuck in the wooden tabletop.

Farmer pounded his other fist on the table. He didn't want to scream, didn't want to give the bastards that.

"Out...out...take the fucking thing out already."

The referee, satisfied that all of the bettors around the table had seen Farmer's bleeding hand, pulled the blade out. Coming out was definitely more painful than going in.

Farmer's hand bled profusely, and he pulled a handkerchief out of his pocket to stanch the blood. Some of the bettors cheered; their fast-spoken chatter language sounded like an orchestra of giant birds. How the hell did they understand each other?

It was the Thai's turn to draw. He flipped the card over and breathed a sigh of relief; the card was blank.

Farmer drew the next card. He flipped it and saw a picture of an arm. "Fuck my luck," he said.

The Thai grinned and said something to the men around him. There was laughter and more chattering until the General ordered silence.

The effect was immediate. The General spoke rough English to Farmer. "You want quit now before bleed to death? I put you back in rat cage if you like."

Farmer growled, not in response to the General's offer, but in an effort to push the pain away. He still had enough blood left to keep going.

He took deep breaths, tried to relax. He held out his left arm and nodded.

The Thai yelped and sunk the blade into Farmer's flesh. This time there was no controlling it; Farmer screamed. The blade went right between his bicep and tricep.

"Out, you little yellow motherfucker."

The ref nodded; although he spoke no English, he knew he was being disrespected, and when he pulled the blade out of Farmer's arm he used a little torque to increase the pain and damage.

Farmer jumped out of his chair and smashed his elbow into the referee's nose. It crunched and blood gushed out of his nostrils.

The ref shouted and drew his gun. He jammed the barrel against Farmer's forehead. He chattered at the General. The General chattered back. The ref put the gun away.

The Thai drew. His card had a picture of an eyeball. The Thai cursed, and Farmer laughed at him.

"Ain't so funny now, is it?"

The Thai spit on the dirt floor.

"Close your eyes, sweetheart. This's going to hurt."

Farmer thrust his blade into the Thai's right eyeball and made him scream. Farmer laughed and held on to the knife until the referee slapped him in the face.

The ref pulled the knife out, and the ruined eyeball came out with it. Farmer started singing the Popeye song.

The one-eyed Thai shouted something in his face. Farmer figured the guy was telling him to shut up.

"I'm gonna call you Si. Si, the one-eyed Thai." Farmer almost fell off his seat laughing.

Tears streamed down his face. He was losing his sanity over their lack of humanity.

He drew the next card. It was a picture of a pinky. How the hell was his opponent going to stab his finger? The light clicked. "Oh…no, no, no, no, no," he said.

The General nodded, and one of the men standing next to Farmer grabbed his arm and clamped it to the table.

It was the one-eyed Thai's turn to laugh. He stood up and grabbed Farmer's pinky. He used his knife like a saw to cut through the tissue and bone.

Farmer screamed and banged his head against the table.

"Whiskey," he shouted. "Now! I want some fucking whiskey."

The General nodded and said something to one of his men. The guy left and returned with a bottle. It was some kind of liquor he had never seen before. There was a small viper in the bottom of the bottle, the same as a worm in the bottom of a tequila bottle.

Farmer opened it and took a long pull. When the guy who brought the bottle tried to take it back, Farmer hugged it against his chest to let him know he intended to drink more. The General nodded, and the man backed off.

The one-eyed Thai drew and howled. It was a picture of a family. Worst card in the deck.

"This mean, you go his home. Kill wife and children. Brothers, sister, whoever in house."

Farmer knew what the card meant. His brother-in-law drew the family card playing in this same game a week earlier. His opponent killed the brother-in-law's wife and children. Unfortunately, Farmer's wife and children were in the house and the guy took them out, too.

That was what brought Farmer into the game. He had nothing left to lose.

—◆—

THIS STORY WAS FIRST PUBLISHED IN *OUT OF THE GUTTER*.

Dana Kabel has written several short stories for such online publications as The Flash Fiction Offensive, Yellow Mama, Shotgun Honey, A Twist of Noir, *and* Out of the Gutter, *to name a few. He recently relocated to New Jersey with his wife and youngest daughter, where he plans to continue work on his novel.*

IN THE HOURS BEFORE HER DEATH

Michael Kardos

By evening he'd erected the volleyball net, scraped the grill, and stuffed the fridge with potato salad, slaw, hot dogs, thirty pounds of ground beef. He'd bought Kool-Aid and cola. A keg of Heineken. Burlap sacks for races.

He'd even rented a PA system, twelve hundred watts of ass-kicking power, and a stage for the lawn. Bill Valero's band had never gigged before. The point was always to jam in the garage and drink beer. But it was now or never. Eons ago, the big bang had ushered everybody into the world. Tomorrow night, as the planet spun toward its fierce conclusion, the Rusted Wheels would usher everybody out.

Now, eleven thirty p.m., Bill sat on the bed. Allie lay beside him, running her hand up the thigh of his jeans, stopping at his limp cock.

"I should've bought horseshoes," he said.

"You've done plenty." Allie believed he was throwing himself a birthday bash a week early. He didn't have the heart to tell her the truth.

"You know horseshoes is the best outdoor game." He slapped his leg. "And I need to get the porch umbrella out of the shed!"

He was almost at the door when she said, "Bill." She'd lit candles. Worn the black, crotchless number from Frederick's of Hollywood. "You'll be right back—deal?"

He felt revved up, like on speed, only this wasn't chemical. It was cosmic, and bigger than sex. Bigger than everything.

"Wish I could," he said, "but you can't imagine how much ground beef is downstairs."

After opening the umbrella and sweeping the porch, he started pounding beef into patties in the kitchen. Easy to imagine each patty as the face of David Magruder, a TV weatherman living around the corner, who was screwing Allie while Bill was on the road. Easy to imagine enacting every revenge.

But no need. Tomorrow, all nine planets would line up—a "superconjunction," it was called—and suck away the Earth's gravity until there was no life left.

He'd learned about the superconjunction that same October day when he learned about Magruder. After hearing a new Aerosmith song on the radio, he'd pulled his big rig over at a gas station, called his drummer from the pay phone, and informed him that they must learn this song right away, and if he *hadn't* heard it yet—

"Shut up a minute," his drummer said. "Listen, buddy…I saw something."

Driving past Bill's house, he'd seen Allie in the walkway with Magruder, his arm around her waist. Before going inside, they'd kissed.

"A real kiss?" Bill asked.

"What do *you* think?"

Driving west across Pennsylvania, Bill imagined Allie in bed with Magruder and wondered: Were there *other* other men? He stopped seeing the highway and saw Allie with every leering accountant and dentist in the neighborhood. He saw the tools in his shed—blunt tools, sharp tools—and imagined using them on her when he returned home.

How lucky for everyone, then, that before the day was out he'd meet this fellow trucker outside Pittsburgh who'd lend Bill his paperback full of science—solar flares, plate tectonics—long enough to read the underlined parts. Armed with the knowledge of scientific prophesy, Bill knew that he wouldn't have to do one damn thing. On the night of April 23, 1983, in just six months, God would take his own tools out of the shed and set everything right.

After refrigerating the burgers, he wiped down the counters, scrubbed the downstairs bathroom, and went into the den with his Gibson guitar and a pair of headphones. He shut his eyes and strummed—the Stones, Skynyrd, the Doors, the Dead—nothing less than the soundtrack to his whole life, everything electric and tinged with blue.

Come on, baby, light my fire.

Wild horses couldn't drag me away.

Lately he'd sensed all the human struggles—wives and husbands, rich and poor, Communists and capitalists—fading away like the diminishing squawk of his CB radio. He'd begun to feel a current in the atmosphere, always—the tug of galactic forces nudging everything into place, including him.

As he strummed he thought about his childhood: the bruises, the bags of weed, the stolen Corvette, the night of his sixteenth birthday spent in the drunk tank. Plenty to regret, yet this rough start had led him to Allie, candy-striping where he was recuperating from a bar fight. Their love led him to a job, a peaceful home, and, of course, to Maddie. He imagined their daughter, now asleep upstairs, all grown up. A school principal, maybe, doling out punishments to delinquents like Bill.

Sad, how this future would never come to be. But not overly sad. The superconjunction made him realize that we were but small critters on a small planet in a huge universe with laws that existed regardless of our understanding of them. A planet forms and then it dies, end of story. The closer the end came, the more Bill felt resigned, like when a movie's credits roll and you accept the ending, even if it's not the ending you'd choose.

At 6:20 a.m. he returned to the bedroom. The candles were out, lights off. Twenty-eight, and Allie still slept on her belly, same as the kid.

He looked through the curtains. He couldn't see those eight other planets dragging themselves mindlessly into position, but he could feel it, the inevitability.

He considered frying up some eggs, serving Allie in bed. She was going to die tonight—this he knew with scientific certainty—but in the hours before her death he wanted to treat her right. Yet she looked comfortable, and there was still so much to do: propane to buy, and those horseshoes. A firepit to dig in the backyard, in case the evening became chilly. A big, deep pit. He'd chop down the half-dead cedar for firewood.

The ax needed sharpening—so there was another task.

He would dig a deep pit. He would sharpen the ax.

And tonight, his whole world would change.

❧

Michael Kardos is the author of the novel The Three-Day Affair *and the story collection* One Last Good Time. *He is originally from the Jersey Shore and currently lives in Starkville, Mississippi, where he codirects the creative-writing program at Mississippi State University.*

ARSON AND OLD LUCE

Marvin Kaye

Hilary Quayle is not an armchair detective. Technically, of course, she's not any kind of investigator; she runs a PR firm, for which I'm secretary. She never had the patience to serve the apprenticeship needed to become a sleuth, but I've still got a PI's license, so from time to time we've done some symbiotic detecting together.

But the day we lunched at the Fifth Avenue Club with Scott Miranda, president of Trim-Tram Toys, Hilary reluctantly agreed to play secondhand sleuth for a friend of Scott's—perfectly understandable, considering that Trim-Tram is our biggest PR client.

A bushy-haired gent in brown tweed joined us. "Hilary, Gene," said Scott, "this is my pal, Mike Prendergast. He's an insurance investigator, and he needs your help."

"Luce Novelties," said Prendergast, "took out a hefty insurance policy last summer. The size of it surprised us because Benny Luce is the biggest tightwad since Scrooge. Cut to New Year's Eve: the Luce warehouse burns down."

"And you're understandably suspicious," Hilary said. "Fill me in."

Prendergast bit a breadstick and consulted a yellow legal pad. "Here are the facts: This year, Benny added a line of Christmas decorations—Italian Nativity sets, strings of Japanese tree lights, garland, tinsel, the works—but the line tanked. The cost must have killed him, but he sent out mailing pieces, ran an incentive contest, even set up a giant Christmas tree outside and lit it up every night—still, the company ended up with a crappy season."

Hilary brushed a strand of blonde hair away from her sky-blue orbs (she'd finally listened to me and stopped tying it into a back-knot). "Tell me about the fire."

He nodded. Luce had been moving inventory down to the basement all day on December 31 to make room for spring merchandise. He was tired and knocked off early, locking up at five thirty. His wife had nagged him for weeks to take her to dinner on New Year's Eve, so he did, but, halfway through the meal, his son phoned and told him the warehouse was burning down. Benny jumped up and ran out.

"I arrived on the scene a few days later," Prendergast continued. "The night watchman said he'd discovered the fire shortly after seven p.m., while Benny was out dining. It was just getting dark out, and the watchman turned on the Christmas tree lights, then stepped over to the coffee machine in the building entry. He got a cup, sat down, and was drinking it when he smelled smoke. By the time the engines arrived, the place was nearly gutted."

Prendergast paused while the waiter served him coffee and a snifter of Glenlivet. He didn't notice Hilary's lip twist, but I did; she's a bit of a single-malt snob.

After a sip of the scotch, he proceeded. "Of course I talked to the fire chief. The blaze started in the cellar. Benny recently received a shipment of defective angels' hair from overseas. Evidently it was not flameproof, and he'd stowed it in the basement prior to shipping it back. The fire reached it, and the stuff went up so fast that if the watchman had been downstairs, he would have been incinerated PDQ."

Hilary fidgeted. "This is all suggestive, but weren't there any clues as to how the fire started?"

"Yes, one, maybe. I don't know how it fits. The fire chief found this badly charred block of black wood in the middle of the floor. It was nearly reduced to ashes, but part of it survived. In it there's a circular depression and a smear that might have been copper wire." Turning his legal pad around, he made a sketch.

Hilary asked me if I recognized it.

"Looks like what's left of a magician's flash pot, which could certainly touch off a fire. A flash pot has a treadle, which has to be pressed. It shoots a charge of electricity from a battery through a short length of wire into this round hole where explosive powder is placed."

"Yes," said Prendergast, "but Benny's son is an amateur Houdini and keeps—kept—his equipment in the basement. And if anybody was near enough to step on that treadle, he would have burned to death. So I'm stymied."

"It's definitely arson," said Hilary Quayle, "and I think you might be able to prove it."

"How do you know?"

"It hinges on Benny Luce's stinginess. Assuming he did commit arson, he would do it before the end of the year for tax purposes. He'd surely pick a night when he had to take his wife to dinner. When his son called him and he jumped up and ran out, I'll bet he left her to pick up the check.

"Motive? A bad year because of an unprofitable line.

"Means? His son's flash pot and lots of flammable angels' hair, which arrived suspiciously late in the season. And since it was defective and had to be shipped back, why would he move it to the basement?

"Most important, he had string upon string of unsold Christmas tree lights, which means an ample amount of copper wire. All he needed was to splice wire together and run it outside to the Christmas tree, which he knew the watchman would turn on after Benny quitted the premises. I suggest you look for traces of that wire. With any luck, you'll find some."

Prendergast turned to his friend. "Thanks for having me talk to her, Scotty. She's as good as you said!"

"*De rien*," Scott demurred. "But I don't see how you put it all together, Hilary."

She laughed. "It was that outdoor tree. Why would a tightwad like Benny Luce run up his electric bill and turn on that tree every night through December 31—*six days after the Christmas selling season was over*?"

➵➵

Marvin Kaye has written sixteen novels, including The Last Christmas of Ebenezer Scrooge, *optioned as a feature film, and* The Passion of Frankenstein. *He has edited many mystery and fantasy anthologies, including* The Fair Folk, *which won the World Fantasy Award for Best Anthology of 1996. He edits* Sherlock Holmes Mystery Magazine *and* Weird Tales.

DADDY'S GIRL

Nicola Kennington

"Daddy?" I call out from a safe distance, just in case.
The man in the denim jacket and the faded cords sitting at the blackjack table and looking like he's gotten used to handing over his chips, turns around. It's him. Christ. After nearly twenty-five years and so many false leads, I've finally found my daddy.

I feel a vibration in my pocket, and I slip around the corner of a line of slot machines. I peer back as I retrieve my cell—the man has a puzzled look on his face, but he soon returns to his game. One of the doll-faced hostesses offers him a beer on the house. He takes two. He won't be going anywhere soon.

"Yes?"

"Hey, Chicken, how's it hangin', baby?" Shit, it's Paolo. Why didn't I check caller ID?

"Hey, Paolo, just takin' a break," I say.

"Well, here's the thing, Chicken. I hear you ain't been workin' for a coupla hours." I hear him take a deep drag and exhale slowly. "Could even be more than that."

That may be true—I've been combing Cleopatra's Casino since dinner, and Vegas since forever. Everyone ends up in Vegas. Some never leave. Like me.

"I'll get back to it, baby," I say. "It's just that—"

"It's just nothin', Chicken," Paolo says pleasantly. "Now, get back to work an' stop moping. Time is money. *My* money." He takes another drag. "If you don't wanna, remember what happened to Lola."

Everyone remembers what happened to Lola. She slacked off, tried to get herself a real job 'cause of her little girl. She got visited by two friends of Paolo and now wears a permanent smile, ear to ear.

"Okay, baby, I wanna," I say.

"Good girl," Paolo says. "Go suck me some dick, lie back and pretend it's me humpin' ya, and remember who keeps you safe around here."

I return the phone to my pocket. Shit, stop shaking, calm down. I look around again, just in time to see him getting up and heading toward one of the exits. Seems like Lady Luck isn't on his side tonight. I tail him—it's not difficult; he's walking the careful walk of the slightly hammered.

Once outside, he finally pauses by a Dumpster and slumps against it. He burps, loudly. I go up to him and gently touch his arm.

"Hey, Daddy, it's me," I say. "It's Rosie. Your little girl." He stares at me with out-of-focus eyes.

"Wha' the fuh?" His breath stinks of beer and nachos. His belly strains at his T-shirt, faded AC/DC decal and stained with something bad.

"You must remember me," I say. "You used to read me stories at bedtime? Bathe me and Cassie when Mom was out working?"

"Sorry, lady, I think you want someone who gives a shit." He's sobering up quickly, confronted by a madwoman. He shakes his head, snorts, and tries to shuffle away.

The redness descends on me—my scalp starts to burn and crackle, and my heart is pounding like a drummer on acid. I grab the photo out of my back pocket and thrust it in his face.

"That's me and Cassie!" I cry. "The last time we were happy! When you used to love us and tell us that we were your only girls and that no one made you feel like we did! We didn't tell, Daddy! We didn't tell!"

Now he's scared, eyes wide, and he's trying to run, but I kick him—hard—in the leg and he goes down. "I didn't know Mom would come home early, I didn't know she'd throw you out! You shouldn't have left us, you motherfucking bastard!"

I stand over him, raise my foot, and then bring it down, over and over and over, just to stop the screaming. *Whumpf!* That's for Mom, who cried herself to sleep for weeks, steadily drank herself into a stupor and out of a job, and then calmly stepped out in front of a train at Mayhew Crossing one bleak Thanksgiving.

Whumpf! That's for Cassie, who felt so mixed-up and confused that she got herself pregnant by the first hick who snuck his hand down her pants, and who now has five snotty brats, a trailer home in the asshole of Crapsville, and a husband who beats her up on a regular basis to remind her how lucky she is.

The final heel in the face is for me, one of the hardest-working whores in Vegas, who has to keep turning tricks before her face and body give up on her, because she knows no other fucking trade, because somewhere and somehow a guy has to love her the way her daddy loved her. I turn over the sniveling wreck with my toe. Better make this look like a robbery. I feel inside his jacket pocket and pull out a wallet.

I take the bills and shove them down my shirt. I pull out his driver's license. Hmm, so he calls himself Mike LaSalle now. Then I check his date of birth.

Oh no.

Fuck.

He's only twelve years older than me. He can't be my daddy. But he looks like him.

Doesn't he?

I turn to Daddy—Mike—and I can't be sure but I think he's stopped breathing.

Shit, not again.

THIS STORY WAS FIRST PUBLISHED IN *OUT OF THE GUTTER*.

Nicola Kennington is a pseudonym. She is based in the United Kingdom, but has a soft spot for San Francisco. She gets inspiration from news and songs, and conversations that she overhears on trains and buses. She wrote her first crime story just to see if she could do it, and is now scared that others are clamoring to get out of her head. Still, as her mother says, better out than in.

COUNTDOWN

John Kenyon

10…

We were so close that her heart and my heart were touching, as if fused together. She looked up at me, her eyes clouded with confusion.

"What do you mean?" she asked.

"I have a confession," I said. "I'm afraid it's going to tear us apart, but I can't keep on like this."

"Oh God. I should have known," she said. "Too good to be true. What, you're married?"

"No. Remember when you said it was the worst thing and the best thing to ever happen to you? Well, please keep both possibilities in mind."

9…

It was the first time we had made love with the lights on. It wasn't teenage apprehension or the shame of flabby thirtysomethings gone to seed. There were simply things she didn't want me to see. I knew they were there. They didn't affect me. At least not the way she thought. She was worried about the surface, how she looked. But I was in love, and appearances didn't matter. She was beautiful, and the flaws did nothing to take away from that. She was baring herself to me. I felt like it was time to reciprocate.

8...

"I really don't mind the scars."

She stood looking at herself in a full-length mirror affixed to the back of the bedroom door. She turned this way and that, twisting to find the right angle to take in another part of her body. In bra and panties, the scars were clearly visible. They snaked up her forearms, made red splotches on her lower legs and angry welts along her neckline.

"You don't mind them, do you?" she asked.

"No," I said. "Now come to bed, and this time let's leave the light on."

7...

"I don't know how I would have gotten through this without you," she said.

She sat next to me on the couch in my apartment, her legs up under her, her head on my chest. I didn't respond, simply ran my fingers through her hair. It had grown out into a bob that made her seem younger.

"I kind of feel like I'm falling for you," she said.

"That's not a surprise," I said, taking her by the shoulders and pulling her upright. "I've been taking care of you."

"No," she said. "It's something more."

6...

Mr. Jennings paced back and forth across the back room. I caught a glimpse of collegiate flesh through the door to the front of the tanning salon.

"Is this going to be a problem for us?" he said.

"No, sir. It's under control. It's strictly professional."

"It had better be," he said, stopping directly in front of me. "There's no room for guilt in this business, David."

I nodded. "It was my mistake. I'm just trying to make it right."

"Just don't make it any worse."

5…

"You're doing what?"

Chris had just gotten back from picking up payments. We were sitting in the back of the salon.

"It's only until she gets on her feet. I'm responsible, so I thought I'd help her out."

"Well, she is hot. Saw her picture in the paper," he said. "What did the fire do to her?"

"She has scars, but the doctor said they'll fade with time."

"Guess she won't be coming in here anytime soon," Chris said with a laugh. "These piece-of-shit beds would finish the job."

4…

"Did you get that from me?" We were on my couch, watching TV. She had pulled aside the collar of my button-down to reveal a small, red scar in the shape of a heart.

"I guess. It's just like yours," I said, pointing to her neck. "Your necklace must have heated up in the fire and branded both of us when I carried you out."

"I still don't know how to thank you."

"There's no need," I said. "Right place, right time. I was lucky."

"No," she said. "I'm the lucky one."

3…

I wheeled her to the hospital door and then helped her up and led her to my car. "You're sure you want to do this? I'll be getting in your way."

"Nonsense. I have plenty of room."

"Okay," she said. "I guess I should expect no less. You didn't miss a day the whole time."

"Figured you could use the company. Now I figure you can use the help."

"My guardian angel," she said, rising onto her tiptoes to give me a kiss on the cheek.

"Something like that."

2...

I rushed in, pulling my jacket over my head to repel the flames already licking along the walls. The screams were coming from a bedroom in the back. I kicked in the door and found her trying to open a window that had been painted shut. I grabbed a blanket and picked her up in my arms. Holding her tight against me, I rushed back through the blaze and toward the sanctuary of the front yard.

1...

I packed the explosives next to the natural gas line that fed the furnace. It needed to burn so hot that no one could determine a cause. Mr. Jennings had made that clear. I wasn't sure if it was an insurance thing or something more. He assured me the house would be vacant.

I stepped out to my car parked halfway down the block, and whispered a countdown under my breath. I fingered the trigger, heard a muted blast, and then everything was aflame. Then I heard the scream.

THIS STORY WAS FIRST PUBLISHED IN *ThrillsKillsnChills.*

John Kenyon is executive director of the Iowa City UNESCO City of Literature organization, edits Grift Magazine *(GriftMagazine. com), and has contributed crime-fiction short stories to a number of publications. His story collection,* The First Cut, *is available from Snubnose Press.*

ATM: GET CASH INSIDE

Jonathon King

This morning was the first and only time I ever lied about it, and wouldn't you know it, the falsehood could have gotten me killed.

I'd always told friends, acquaintances, my mom, the cops, anyone who asked if I carried a gun on the job: "No. It's not worth it. It would only cause more trouble. Screw the NRA. You pull one, they're gonna pull one." So why lie today?

Mine is a unique occupation. I work for an independent ATM company. I fill and fix cash machines in Miami-Dade County. I do this alone; no partner, no armored car, no uniform, no box or bag. I walk into Kwik Stops, 7-Elevens, Brotherhood Grocery, U-Gas, the Pink Pussycat, and dozens of other joints with thousands of dollars in unmarked twenty-dollar bills in my pockets. I open the machines with keys on a ring, the safe doors with combinations stored in my head. I try to be unassuming when I take the bricks of cash from my cargo pants pockets and transfer it into the interior dispensers. But who am I kidding? Everybody who takes two seconds to notice me opening and crouching down at an ATM knows what's up. The guys hanging out at 60 Liquors in Liberty City call me "money man," as in:

"Sup, money man? First of the month, *papi*. Load it up good."

Incognito? Bull. Not in this world. So I do what I do two dozen times a day. And even though some people say I'm a fool, I say it's an honest job. Or it was until this morning, when I lied.

I pull up at ten a.m. I've stopped at this store a hundred times. It's the corner business of an old strip mall on a street used more as a pass-through than a destination. The locals come here. Off-brand cigarettes, malt liquor by the can in plastic buckets filled with ice, extra-long T-shirts in black or white, toilet paper by the roll, canned food, junk food, processed cheese food, and a permeating odor of industrial-strength cleaner poured on something gone bad that probably wasn't so good to begin with. It's called, simply, "the Market."

On this morning I walk in, nod at the Indian counterman as usual, and do a quick scan. Nobody else in the place. Just the way I like it. The ATM is in a direct line to the glass front doors, so I can see anyone arriving while I'm down on one knee, the open safe door shielding my hand full of money while I load. It won't take two minutes. But what do they tell you about how long two minutes is when the shit hits the fan?

The stickup guy walks through the door, and when I look up I notice two things—one perplexes me and one scares me.

First, he's wearing his baseball cap the way they were meant to be worn—the bill of the cap is forward, shading the eyes. In this neighborhood, hell, in every neighborhood these days, guys from six to sixty wear their caps turned backward like what, avoiding a sunburn on their neck? Secondly, he has his right hand tucked up under his shirt at his waistband. We don't make eye contact because I can't see his eyes; the cap brim and the sun coming in through the doors behind him leave his face dark. He's a shadow figure, no details but for that damn hand concealing something he doesn't want to show, not yet anyway.

He takes two more steps in, glances once at the counterman, dismisses him, and takes another toward me.

"Stand up! Gimme what you got!"

The line comes with a jerk of whatever's bundled in the shirtfront.

My employers have gone over this. Give up the money. It's insured. It isn't worth it. Back off and let 'em have it. And that was my philosophy before they ever said it.

So why am I a fool this morning? Why don't I stand up with my hands in the air, step away from the machine—even turn my back so I don't see the face—and tell this asshole to go for it, take the money and go?

But I don't. I stay right where I am, crouched behind a three-foot-tall iron door, nothing but the upper half of my face showing. Instead I lie.

"Hey man. I got nothing behind this steel door but a racked nine millimeter. And I ain't standin' up."

I'm as surprised by the words coming out of my mouth as the robber, who seems silently befuddled, or the clerk who takes advantage of the stunned air to instantly duck into some hidey-hole behind the counter.

"You fuckin' hear me?" the shadowed guy manages to say, but now the anger in his voice wouldn't convince a schoolgirl. He's five yards away, but doesn't move.

"Just turn around and leave, man," I hear myself say again, with a remarkably steady voice that I do not recognize. "If you're going to shoot me with whatever's in that shaky hand, you better be able to hit my forehead 'cause I ain't standing up from behind this steel.

"And if you take another step at me, you got a lot bigger target right on your chest, and believe me, I can use this nine, man."

Silence rules. Maybe two seconds, maybe five, maybe that eternity they like to talk about. He doesn't show the gun he might have, and I don't have anything *to* show.

"Fuck you, *papi*," the guy finally spits out, but he delivers the curse while his left foot moves back toward the door. His hand never comes out from the folds of the shirtfront. He repeats the epithet, maybe all he has left of his bravado, and in the parlance of the cop who shows up twenty minutes later to take a report, flees the scene.

—◆—

Edgar Allan Poe Award–winning author Jonathon King is the creator of the Max Freeman crime series set in the Everglades and urban South Florida. He has also self-published a historical mystery, The Styx, *which won a Florida Book Award and his latest series book,* Midnight Guardians, *was published as an e-original by Open Road Media.*

TESTIMONY

Andrew Klavan

My friends, I tell you, only a miracle could have saved this sinner's soul—and a miracle is what it was. I had come to Brother Jeremiah's healing service as a mere mocker—a scoffer—a seeker of curiosities. I thought that, after the many attacks against this man of God—the exposés on television and the Internet—no one of any sense could take his promises seriously. And so imagine my surprise when none other than Amanda Gallagher rolled her wheelchair down the aisle of the auditorium toward the stage.

I confess to you in all shame that I had harbored lust in my heart for my neighbor Amanda for many years—yes, lust in my heart despite the fact that she was tied in bonds of holy matrimony to Orrin Gallagher, the sheriff of our county. I had wrestled vainly with the devil of my desire, hunkering in my darkened house night after night, looking in secret through Amanda's windows across the way. I had railed in my soul against her rightful husband, cursing his cruelty to her, horrified by the brutal beatings and obscene enforcements he visited upon her with crushing regularity.

All these I had witnessed from my house. And yes, of course, I had called the police. But they would do nothing to curtail their colleague's violence. I had even confronted Sheriff Gallagher in person, only to find myself looking down the barrel of his service revolver, threatened with death. In the end, I was forced to look on helplessly as he tortured and tormented that sweet and beautiful creature—to look on helplessly even on that awful night he hurled her down the stairs. She never again rose from her wheelchair after that. As I myself testified at the inquest, she became a virtual prisoner in her second-story bedroom. I could see her up there, I told them, sitting helplessly by her window during the incident in question.

I would like to call that incident a tragedy, but I simply can't. I know that any man who harbors anger against his brother shall be subject to judgment, but I harbored anger against Brother Orrin, I admit it. And when, in a fit of drunkenness, he sat himself down at the kitchen table and lifted his revolver to his head and blew his brains out, I was not sorry for it. I was glad—yes, glad—though I witnessed the whole gory spectacle. I could see the sheriff's crippled wife in her bedroom prison upstairs; I could see the man himself in the kitchen right below her, struggling in the coils of his guilt and shame. When I saw him begin to toy with his gun, I called the police from my phone at home. I was in my house, on that phone with them, even as the final shot was fired.

It was in the aftermath of Orrin's suicide, my friends, that I recognized the emptiness of my life. It was then that I began a search for…I didn't know what—didn't know at all until I walked into Brother Jeremiah's service at the old Belmont Theater on State Street. It was there I saw Amanda roll her wheelchair down the aisle; there I saw Brother Jeremiah lay his hands upon her and command her in the name of the Almighty to rise and walk. And I tell you now, my friends, Amanda struggled from the confines of her chair to stand on her own two feet. Yes. Full of the spirit, she walked with faltering steps back up the aisle, past the awestruck faces of the gasping and applauding believers. With tremulous tears of joy and faith and gratitude, she stumbled to where I stood at the back of the auditorium—where I stood marveling in very wonder at this mighty miracle. And as she fell exhausted into my arms, she cried in a loud voice to the multitude, "I can walk! Hallelujah! I can walk again!"

And I tell you in that moment—in that very moment—I believed and I was saved.

Can I get an amen?

Andrew Klavan is the author of such internationally best-selling crime novels as True Crime, *the basis for the film of the same name directed by Clint Eastwood,* Don't Say A Word, *made into a film, starring Michael Douglas, and* Empire of Lies. *He has been nominated for the Mystery Writers of America's Edgar Allan Poe Award five times and has won twice. He has published best-selling thriller novels for young adults and wrote the screenplay for* A Shock to the System, *starring Michael Caine.*

LOSING MY RELIGION

K.A. Laity

"I could do it," Tony said as I started the engine. "Believe me. Easy."

I backed the Subaru up, then eased away from the curb. An old lady in a Ford pulled into the spot almost before I got out. Life in the congestion zone. "Might better open up a car park. You'd get rich a lot quicker. Especially around here."

Tony shook his head. "A car park is a finite investment. There's no end of growth potential for religion."

"Growth potential? You've been watching those YouTube videos again."

"Sidney, the knowledge of the ages is free for the taking if you know where to look."

I checked the map and made a right at the corner. "What, Wikipedia?"

Tony sighed. He thought I lacked ambition. "You really need to develop your online presence."

"I'm not getting on Friendface." I shot him a look as we idled at the light.

"Facebook! Criminy, you don't even know what it is. You might as well live among the Neanderthals."

I shrugged. "I got plenty of friends. They drink at my local. Why would I need friends I can't drink with?" A muffled shout from the boot made us both turn around. Some impatient stockbroker behind me tooted the horn of his Mercedes, and I stepped on the accelerator.

"Think we need to pull over?"

"Nah, it'll be all right."

Tony turned around to face front again. "You might be content with your lot in life—"

"I am."

"I've got ambition, Sidney. I want something better."

"Your own religion?"

"Small investment, low overhead at the start, then huge results."

I laughed. "What about those vows of poverty?" The evening sky had that pink glow that never lasted for long but made the old city look new again.

Tony laughed. "That's for the low-level minions. You ever been to the Vatican? Untold wealth. Same thing for all major religions. Mecca. Taj Mahal. Crystal Cathedral. Scientologists."

"They got a church?"

Tony shot me a look of withering scorn. "They've got the whole of Hollywood! Hands in everything. All those rich actors and directors—they're all dues-paying Scientologists."

"Not Jason Statham."

"Well, no," Tony admitted, "but then he's not really Hollywood, is he?"

Another muffled scream from the boot, more of a sob really. "So what's your religion going to be about?"

When he thinks he's got a world-beater, Tony gets this smug look that begs for a punch to the kisser. "Happiness. What everyone wants and nobody's got."

"I got it."

"You don't count, Sidney. Most people are miserable. Hold out the possibility of happiness and riches, and you'll have people eating out of your hand."

"You don't say." I looked at the map again as I found myself facing the wrong end of a one-way street. "You're going to offer them riches? Won't that deplete your own quickly?"

Tony sighed. He could sigh for England. "You don't give people riches. You hold out the possibility of riches. Like car commercials that hold out the possibility of sex with supermodels. You ain't getting it, but you think you might."

"So you'll be advertising?" I slowed the car, squinting into the thickening dusk.

"All modern religions advertise. I'll have my own website, Facebook page, and YouTube channel. I'll be an Internet sensation." Tony looked properly smug.

"We're here," I said, turning into the building site. I pulled around behind a large skip filled with rubble. Old Bill said they would be pouring concrete in the morning. All seemed quiet.

"Looks wet." Tony sighed.

"Well, let's dig first, then see about the baggage after," I suggested, opening the rear door to grab the shovels. I handed one to Tony, who frowned at it. "They don't come with golden handles, mate."

He scowled and pointed. "Here?"

"Looks good to me." The dirt was wet, but the shovels cut through it with ease. Nonetheless, we soon sweated profusely. "Not so young anymore, are we?"

"Speak for yourself," Tony retorted. "Prime of my life."

"Think it's deep enough." I scanned the horizon. All remained quiet. People having their tea about now, surely. "Let's get the baggage."

"So what was he?" Tony stared at the face without recognition.

"Someone who made a serious error in judgment. You want feet or hands?" We dragged him over and dropped the baggage in the hole.

"Face down so he can see where he's going," Tony snickered.

"Will there be a hell in your religion?"

Tony considered the thought, which meant he leaned on his shovel and let me do the work. "Carrot and stick really, eh? You need to have both."

"Dig."

"If there were no fear of punishment, more people would end up like this baggage. But you can't have it too grim or people won't be attracted. Gruesome punishments but easily avoided."

"Like fairy tales." I heard a sound and whipped round. The biggest dog I ever saw stood by the skip, hackles up, a low growl rippling from its throat. I lifted the shovel, figuring I could bash it with the blade. Tony stared.

The dog crept closer. I wondered if he were diseased or something. Tony joined me, keeping the corpse between us and the mutt. The dog lunged forward and grabbed the baggage's hand in its mouth and started pulling at it, growling even louder.

"S'pose it's his? Trying to rescue him?"

"Bit late." At least the dog didn't seem to want to attack us. Inspired, I leaned forward, brought down the shovel, and sliced through the wrist. The dog, who'd shied away at first, made a lunge and sank his teeth into the hand. Then he turned and ran off with his prize.

I laughed until I cried. Tony scowled. "What are we going to tell Old Bill?"

"Nothing. He won't mind him being a hand short. Or is that against your religion?"

"Maybe my faith needs a dog."

"Well, dog spelled backward—"

"Stop that."

"Hand of glory—"

"Shut up and shovel."

❖

THIS STORY WAS FIRST PUBLISHED IN *SPINETINGLER*.

K.A. Laity is author of Chastity Flame, The Claddagh Icon, Unquiet Dreams, *and more, as well as editor of the Fox Spirit Books' anthology* Weird Noir. *Her stories have appeared in* Drunk on the Moon, ACTION! Pulse Pounding Tales, Off the Record 2: At the Movies, Spinetingler Magazine, Pulp Metal Magazine, Shotgun Honey, *and more. She divides her time between New York and Dundee, Scotland. Visit her website at KALaity.com.*

THE TENTH NOTCH

Jon Land

Kerr had nine notches on his M4A1 Special Operations–model assault rifle, one for each of the kills he'd recorded behind enemy lines in Afghanistan. There were other kills for sure, plenty of them, but he deemed only nine of them to be worthy of notches—those being the targets he'd hunted himself. Through the blistering heat of summer in the 'Stan and bone-chilling cold of the winter. Tracking Al Qaeda and Taliban insurgents who'd made the mistake of targeting his fellow troops. But Kerr wasn't into counterinsurgency or mending hearts and minds.

His job was to rupture them.

Kerr was known as an HK—hunter/killer. Plain and simple, no further elaboration necessary. So far those lurking behind the curtain like some murderous Wizards of Oz had sent him out nine times, and he'd come back with a notch on his rifle for each of them.

He'd been plucked from the SEALs and dropped into the HKs because, well, killing came so easy to him. He took to it with the ease of a game hunter. It was sport, a human video game played out in mud, ice, snow, sand, and stone.

And he was nine for nine. Batting a thousand. A one-man death squad, which was just the way he liked it.

But this latest assignment was different, something special. A whole bunch of kills had been committed on base or encampment premises; someone finding his way in to kill the first soldier he saw, and then off he went before anyone was the wiser. Security was doubled, then tripled, but the kills continued.

Very bad for morale.

So the Wizard poked out from behind his curtain and called for an HK, and in came Kerr to pick up the trail that reeked of the remnants of Al Qaeda.

Kerr had been on the trail for three days, tracking the animal to his lair in the rugged mountain terrain. Gadgets were fine— he had a whole assortment stuffed into his pack. But this was a retro war, and HKs like Kerr had learned to adapt fast. Fuck range finders and motion detectors—what Kerr needed now were the lessons he'd learned in SEAL camp from a Native American who taught him how to track, *really* track. And the prints of his latest quarry were easy to follow.

The AQ limped, likely on something akin to a clubfoot; Kerr could tell that from the distance between steps. He also realized that his quarry was wearing *khuf*, tough socks with a sole thick enough for walking.

Walking very quietly.

It figured, didn't it? Kerr thought, beginning to form a mental picture of how this particular AQ had managed to sneak past security and leave bodies behind before disappearing—

POOF!

…into thin air.

But he'd left a trail. And HK Kerr was on it, his tenth notch soon to be added. He made them small to leave room, lots of room, for the kills to come.

The khuf prints broke sharply to the left, and Kerr followed the trail, banking upward toward a nest of caves that made the mountain face he was approaching look like rocky swiss cheese.

Until stones rustled ahead.

He twisted toward the sound with the M4A1 leveled, ready to shoot. Senses keyed, mouth gone dry. The volume of the world cranked up into the red, the sight of it sharpened to crystal clarity. Feeling the assault rifle start to grow hot in his grasp, expended 7.62 mm shells about to do their airborne dance before clamoring to the gravel and stones below.

A mountain goat pranced onto the path, regarded him briefly, and then moved on. But the goat had done him a favor. Really. Its hooves had disturbed the ground enough to reveal fresh khuf prints stopping at a steeply angled rock face that led to a trio of cave mouths peeking out from a narrow ledge.

HK Kerr moved on. Got safe from view of the cave mouths and ducked between twin boulders to wait for nightfall. When it came he retraced his steps to the steep path rising up the rock face. Climbed it slowly, pushing with his legs and pulling with his hands.

Three cave mouths.

I'm the AQ. Which one would I hide in?

The first in the row—no. The last—also no. The middle made for the most defensible position. The middle provided the extra second that could make the difference between dying and killing.

HK Kerr headed for the middle. Looping in from the side to leave no hint of shadow or shape ahead of him. He lurched into the cave mouth, built-in major candlepower light piercing the darkness with flashbulb brightness. A cascade of bullets ready to follow down the iridescent tunnel, when his finger froze just short of squeezing.

Because the light had found a boy, twelve or thirteen, huddled against the cave's rear with a crutch lying by his side. Grime coated his face. Fear filled eyes that looked too big for his face. He tried to speak, but all that emerged from his trembling lips was air. All the toes on his left foot were missing.

I almost shot Tiny Tim.

It would've been funny if it wasn't so damn sad. Kerr's tenth notch would have to wait.

"Sorry, kid," he said, lowering his M4A1 and starting to turn.

Never saw the kid grab his crutch and fire it. Felt something intensely hot and then frigidly cold hit his spine even as he hit the cave floor facedown, eyes open and sightless.

The kid rose, limped toward him, supported by the crutch that held a rifle in disguise.

Never saw that coming, did you?

The kid kicked at Kerr's body, making sure he was dead. And only then did he raise his gun-crutch enough to dig a nail into the sawed wooden butt that fit neatly under his arm.

Adding a tenth notch to the nine already in place.

Jon Land is the critically acclaimed author of thirty-two books, including the best-selling series featuring Texas Ranger Caitlin Strong that includes Strong Vengeance *and the forthcoming* Strong Rain Falling *(August 2013). He has more recently brought his long-time series hero Blaine McCracken back to the page in* Pandora's Temple. *He lives in Providence, Rhode Island.*

THE EAR

Joe R. Lansdale

It was a third date. The first date had been dinner and a movie and a kiss good night, dropped off at her door, that sort of thing. The second they ended up in a hotel room. Tonight, she was at his place, had driven over. They were going to have dinner at his house, then go to a movie. All very casual. Nothing highly romantic. She liked that. It made her comfortable; two lovers who were starting to know each other well enough not to do anything fancy.

When she got there he let her in before she could knock, like he had been watching. The place was lit up, and she could hear the TV going and could smell cooking. He was wearing one of those novelty aprons that said "Kiss the Cook."

"This is it," Jim said, waving his arm at the interior of the house. It was nice. Nothing fantastic, but nice. He was neat for a guy, especially a traveling salesman who went all over the states and didn't stay home much.

"You wore the earrings?" he asked.

"You asked me to. You like them that much?"

"Liked them when I bought them for you," he said.

"Date three, thought they might get a little old," she said.

"Not yet. You want a drink?"

"Sure," she said, and followed him into the kitchen. The TV prattled on in the other room. He poured her a drink.

"You know," she said, "we could stay here tonight."

Jim was at the stove, stirring spaghetti in a pot of boiling water. He turned and looked at her. "You want to?"

"You got some movies?" she asked.

"Yeah, or we can order one off the TV."

"Let's do that, and then let's go to bed. You can fix me dinner tonight and breakfast in the morning."

"That sounds fine," he said, smiling that killer smile he had. "That sounds really nice."

"I hoped you'd think so," she said. "Bathroom?"

"Down the hall, around the corner to the left."

She walked down the hall and turned the corner, opened the door to the left. She had missed the bathroom. It was the bedroom. She started out, saw a dresser drawer slightly open. He was neat, but not that neat. She, on the other hand, had a thing about open doors and drawers. She slipped over quickly, started to push it shut, saw what was blocking it. An ear.

Taking a deep breath, she thought, surely not.

Sliding the drawer open, she got a better look. There was a string running through the ear. She pulled it out of the drawer. There were a number of dried ears on it. They had a faint smell, a combination of decay and the smell of pickles; they had been in some kind of preservative, but the flesh was still losing the battle. Something sparkled on one of them.

"It's from the war," he said.

She turned, gasping. He was standing in the doorway, his head hung, looking silly in that apron.

"I'm sorry," she said, because she didn't know what else to say.

"My brother, he was in Afghanistan. Brought it home with him. This will sound odd, but when he died, I didn't know what to do with it. I kept it. Thought I had it put away better. I should throw it away."

"It's pretty awful," she said, lowering the ears back into the drawer, pushing it shut.

"Forgive me for having it, for keeping it."

"He died in the war?"

"Cancer. Came home from the war with his collection, those ears. Come on, forget it. I'll throw them out."

She went back to the kitchen, and later they ate dinner. When he went into the den to pick a movie, she slipped out the front door and drove home, trying to remember if she had told him where she lived, then thinking, even if she hadn't, these days it wasn't so hard to find out. Easy, really.

In her house, sitting in the dark with a fresh drink, she felt stupid to have fallen for Jim so quickly, to not know him as well as she should have. A guy like that wasn't a guy she wanted to know any more about.

She finished her drink and went to bed.

In the middle of the night she was startled awake, sat up in bed, her face covered in a cold sweat.

She remembered Jim said on their first date he was an only child, but tonight he said he had a brother, said the ears were from Afghan warriors. Several thoughts hit her like a barrage of arrows. She hadn't just awakened. She had heard something moving in the house; that's what brought her awake with her mind full of thoughts and questions. That sound was what woke her up. And in the moment she realized that all those ears had been small and one of them had something shiny on it. She knew now what it was. She had only glimpsed it, but now she knew. A woman's earring. Not too unlike those she had worn tonight.

Something banged lightly in the other room, and then her bedroom door opened.

━◆━

Joe R. Lansdale has written thirty novels and numerous short stories. He is a member of the Texas Institute of Letters, writer in residence at Stephen F. Austin State University, and has had several stories filmed. His novel The Bottoms *won the Edgar Allan Poe Award for Best Novel in 2000. His most recent novel is* Edge of Dark Water *from Mulholland Books.*

THE IMPERFECT DETECTIVE

Janice Law

Mike Brinley closed his notebook and turned to me. "I think that will do it, Chief. I'll run the piece next Thursday for your last day, and I'll drop off some extra copies for the grandkids."

"Thanks, Mike. I'm sure you'll make me sound like the Valley's answer to Sherlock Holmes."

He laughed at that. "Your record's pretty damn good. No perfect crimes in Fisher Valley, eh?"

That was a question I didn't need to answer, but I heard myself say, "There are no perfect crimes, only imperfect detectives."

He had the notebook out again, quick as a lizard's tongue. "Perfect," he said as he scribbled. "Just the right note to end on."

We shook hands, and I watched him drive away: a good friend and a good reporter, off with a quote more apt than he could imagine. But true, and standing there on the porch in the summer sunshine, I was once again back at the start of my career, bouncing over the frozen ruts of a farmyard to find the corpse of Charlie Dunmore, a bastard and a bully who had gone to his final reward via a chunk of ice.

That's what his wife, Edith, had screamed over the phone. "Come, come right away. The ice hit him. I can't move him. Please."

THE IMPERFECT DETECTIVE — 283

So there I was, standing in the Dunmores' farmyard. Icicles hanging three and four feet long off the house. Ice backed up in all the gutters and hanging off the cowshed. Ice underfoot and wet snow in the air.

I walked around the side of the house to where Charlie was lying under an old tartan rug. Footprints everywhere—man, woman, and dog—plus a trail where she'd tried to move him. I uncovered him and saw a scrape across his temple and found blood on the back of his head. Two icicles. Odds of that? I noticed chunks of ice now half buried in the snow. The light was fading, and I thought it was going to be mighty hard to tell which ones had hit him.

"He was trying to clear the gutters." I turned to see Edith Dunmore. She was a slight woman who had once been pretty. Now she was thin and pale with a darkening bruise under one eye and a couple of missing teeth.

Inside I called for the ambulance. Frozen as he was, Charlie wouldn't fit in the backseat of my cruiser. Then I sat at the kitchen table and took her statement. She'd been busy with the day's baking because the hotel wanted extra for the holidays. Charlie said he'd try to clear the gutter, and she hadn't noticed how long he'd been gone. Then she went out and found him.

As we talked, she iced trays of streusel and coffee cakes. I noticed the big earthenware bowls and the heavy pots on the stove. Edith Dunmore was slight, but she had strong arms and capable hands.

I looked at her black-and-white spaniel, too. It lay on a blanket in the corner, whimpering and licking its right front leg. Broken, I guessed, from the way it was limping. I was being the perfect detective, and I had a little scenario all worked out: Charlie had hit her once too often—or maybe he was hurting the dog—and she'd followed him out, picked up one of the fallen icicles, and let him have it. That was the perfect detective's scenario, though I didn't yet see how to prove it.

Edith finished the icing and cut me a thick slice of one of the pecan cakes. I should mention that she was the best baker west of Paris, France. The perfect detective hesitated.

"Go to waste anyway," she said. "Charlie never let me drive the truck. No way I'll get this stuff to the hotel."

I took a few bites, and I could feel perfection slipping away. "I could drop them off."

"I'd sure appreciate it," she said, and she went over to comfort the dog.

"What's wrong with him?"

"He broke his leg. Ice got him."

I made up my mind right there. If she'd been coldhearted, she'd have made something up or kept him out of sight. But now there was doubt, and the imperfect detective decided to run with scenario two, where Charlie Dunmore went out and started pulling off ice and got hit in the temple and cracked the back of his head when he fell.

I tried that scenario on Doc Wilson later after I had delivered the various pastries to the hotel and the dog to the vet. We were in the morgue, looking down at the earthly remains of Charlie Dunmore, a man hard on his wife, his dog, his stock, his neighbors.

Wilson adjusted his thin, wrinkled face a couple different ways until he found an expression that suited him. Basically he was thinking over the case. We could have an investigation without a weapon and no evidence except two bumps on the head, an investigation that would probably go nowhere and leave a bad taste and very likely deprive us of one of the few reliable pleasures of the town, namely Edith Dunmore's pastries.

Or we could abandon all hopes of investigative perfection and come in with death by misadventure. After a few moments, Wilson said, "Unlikelier things have happened," and signed the certificate.

Behind me the door opened, and my Edie looked out. "Mike gone already? I have his favorite muffins."

"Deadline to meet."

"Any interesting questions?"

"He asked if I'd ever known a perfect crime."

A pause, something in her eyes. I'd never asked her, and she'd never raised the subject. But now I knew.

"And what did you say?"

"I said that there are no perfect crimes, only imperfect detectives."

She gave the slightest smile. Edie has a partial plate now and a better smile than she had at twenty-five. "I think that's about right," she said.

◆

Janice Law's first novel, The Big Payoff, *was nominated for an Edgar Allan Poe Award. Her short stories have appeared in* The Best American Mystery Stories, The World's Finest Mystery and Crime Stories, Alfred Hitchcock's Mystery Magazine Presents Fifty Years of Crime and Suspense, Riptide, *and* Still Waters. *Her most recent story collection is* Blood in the Water and Other Secrets. *Her most recent novels are* The Lost Diaries of Iris Weed, Voices, *and* The Fires of London. *She lives with her husband, a sportswriter, in Hampton, Connecticut. Visit her website at JaniceLaw.com.*

MICHAEL COALHOUSE

Adrian McKinty

Michael Coalhouse's war against the council began when the refuse collectors refused to empty his yellow recyclable bin because it contained nonrecyclables. When he got home from work at the foundry, he found a notice pinned to the bin explaining that it "contained a nonrecyclable plastic bag" into which Coalhouse had thrown all his old beer bottles.

He called the council's help line, but it was busy. He left messages on the council's Facebook page, but got no response. On the fourth day, he went down to the council offices on High Street and was told that he needed to make an appointment by e-mail. He tried to make an appointment by e-mail, but the municipal website was experiencing technical difficulties. He went to Councillor Smith's constituency surgery and told her all about his problem, but she sided with the refuse collectors and gave him a leaflet on eco-consciousness.

On the seventh day, the binmen came back and again did not empty his bin. On the eighth day, Coalhouse attended the meeting of the council's Sustainability and Waste Management Subcommittee. He demanded to be heard, but he was tossed out by security. At work the next day, he was formally cautioned by a police officer. When the cop had gone, the foreman said that he didn't want any troublemakers and Coalhouse was "let go."

Coalhouse brooded. On the fourteenth day, his bin was again not emptied. He drove to the council offices and protested. He was accused of "making a threatening gesture" and was asked to leave. He did so. When he got home the police were waiting for him, so he circled the block and drove out to his storage locker near the reservoir. He filled fourteen vodka bottles with petrol and put a rag in each of them. That night he firebombed the council offices and left a message with the local paper letting them know who had done it and why.

He lived in the bush for the next eleven months, coming into the city only to mount lightning guerrilla strikes and get supplies. He attacked the recycling plant on Gaia Street and destroyed the council vehicle depot on Evergreen Terrace, an incendiary attack that wiped out the city's entire fleet of bin lorries. He sank a garbage barge anchored in the bay by means of a homemade limpet mine. He released baby alligators into the storm drains and used on-site methane to blow up the city's main sewage plant. Two days after that outrage, Mayor Cunningham returned home from the Single Mother Initiative Open Day to find his house on fire and his garden gnomes beheaded.

You didn't need to be Foucault to read the death-spiral subtext.

Peace feelers were sent out over Community Action Radio. Helicopters dropped leaflets on the forest where Coalhouse was suspected of being holed up. Coalhouse agreed to surrender himself if his yellow bin was emptied and Jimmy Carter, Stephen Hawking, and Fiona Apple were brought in as official witnesses. Only Carter was available, and Coalhouse said that that would do.

Coalhouse surrendered the same night and was remanded in custody without possibility of bail. He faced multiple counts of arson and criminal damage and a possibility of thirty years in prison.

The recyclable bin was emptied on the fifteenth. Jimmy Carter officially certified the fact a day later.

—◆—

THIS STORY WAS FIRST PUBLISHED ON *ADRIANMCKINTY. BLOGSPOT.COM.*

Adrian McKinty was born and grew up in Carrickfergus, Northern Ireland. He emigrated to the United States in the early nineties, finding work as a barman, gypsy cab driver, and construction worker. His first novel, Dead I Well May Be, *was shortlisted for the 2004 Ian Fleming Steel Dagger and his novel* Fifty Grand *won the 2010 Spinetingler Award. His most recent book is* The Cold Cold Ground, *the first book in a prospective trilogy about DS Sean Duffy.*

DOG

Charles McLeod

When I was twelve my dad stole a payload from auger mines, a county north of where we lived. Mom had fallen off a truss bridge drunk the summer prior, and nothing, small or large, would bring her back. So my dad took to driving to battle the sadness, but gas costs good money, and to support his habit he began filching coal. His main problem was there aren't many places to sell coal back to, except for other coal plants. Early mornings he'd wait near the tall link gates of the companies he knew of, the back of his pickup weighed down so heavy it looked like it might snap. He was brain-soft from the loss of his wife and best friend, and the foremen and plant managers and rig drivers would laugh at him while he stood there, soot covered and true, his tarnished flask in his flat, big hand.

No one ever bought the coal, but his story got around. We bred hounds to make ends meet, and our house was covered in red dirt that their paws tracked in. We spoke of the normal things a father and son can without a mother to run translation. On weekends Dad would drink heavy and we would line dance in our living room, a station from Lexington reaching our transistor. Behind the house the coal pile widened. Dad kept it under a green tarp next to the kennel, the plastic weighed down with rail pins. The parents of a boy from school won small at state lotto and soon after bought a cable dish for their television. This family would invite me over, and we'd watch, in full color, all the things that got beamed in.

The dogs grew and got sold or had new dogs. The first weekend of springtime the two men broke in. They'd fed the hounds pills past midnight and returned before dawn and killed them. They explained this to me and my father while they tied us with wire to chairs. I was scared and thought about my mother and some of the shows that I'd seen on television. One of the men took my dad's socks off and pulled his big toes back and broke them. I knew this was happening on account of the coal, though the men never said so. Outside the winds snapped the tarp.

When light broke the two men untied me. I don't remember what either of them looked like, aside that they looked like men. Both of them had guns and chrome on their belt buckles. The taller man ejected the clip on his gun and handed the weapon to me. My father was passed out where he sat.

You're gonna hit him until he gets awake, and then you're going to hit him back to sleep again, said the man who handed the gun to me. If you don't, I'll put the clip back in.

I was barefoot and could feel the red dirt between my toes. I took the gun by its barrel and hit my dad across the face with it. He woke up and tried to move his arms against the wire and almost tipped the chair over. I was crying. I kept hitting at him. My eyes were closed, and I could hear the metal on his face and head. He made sounds but never told me to stop what I was doing. I went at it like that until one of the men grabbed my shoulders and took back the gun. Their pickup had a Virginia plate with a *T* and a *2* in it. I told this to police on the phone when they'd gone.

I live in North Dakota now, some miles west of Bismarck. I never married and do not want to. A wife will lead to children, and I've seen what they're capable of.

—➤

THIS STORY WAS FIRST PUBLISHED IN *FRIED CHICKEN AND COFFEE*.

Charles McLeod is the author of a novel, American Weather, *and a collection of stories,* National Treasures. *A Hoyns Fellow at the University of Virginia, he is also a Pushcart Prize winner and series editor for the new, annual anthology,* California Prose Directory: New Writing from the Golden State.

SLOW ROASTED

M.B. Manteufel

Not that it mattered, but he wondered if the private investigator called him a loser behind his back, knowing now that his client couldn't hold on to his wife. He chided himself for thinking about it. So what if some wannabe cop with a laminated license and a telephoto lens talked about him? He reached into the cupboard for a mug.

As he poured his coffee, he wondered what his in-laws would think once this was over. His own parents were long dead, but hers were as healthy as the day he first met them, going strong, he theorized, on the life they sucked out of everyone else around them. He imagined they would curse him. He stirred some cream into his cup and shrugged.

He thought about how his coworkers might react when they heard the news. Some would express shock. Others would smugly declare they saw it coming. He placed his spoon next to the gun on the kitchen table and took a sip of the hot liquid.

He wasn't bothered this time when she burst into the house with all the grace of a water buffalo, slamming the front door and dropping her bags and shoes in the hall with her usual disregard. She would assume, of course, that he would put them away, as he always did. As he placed his cup down on the table and rose from his chair, he wished she knew just how wrong she was.

He was curious as to why she seemed shocked when he grabbed her around the neck and put the gun to her head. She was intelligent. Her vision was good. Hadn't she discerned in his voice, seen in his eyes, the smoldering, bottomless, rabid hatred that had been brewing in him for so long?

He wondered how long it would take the neighbors to call the police after hearing the gunshot. Given that the nosy hag next door reveled in knowing their every move, he figured it was just a matter of minutes. He set the gun down to take one last sip of his lukewarm coffee, ignoring the blood and bits of gray matter that covered his hand.

He listened numbly to the shriek of the approaching sirens. He hoped when they came in, they wouldn't trip on the clutter in the hall; there just wasn't time to clean up. He set his cup down, picked up the gun, put the barrel to his temple, and pulled the trigger. He sighed when it jammed and blamed that on her, too. Even in death, the bitch. Holding the gun in plain view, he headed for the door.

He wondered if the young cop shakily pointing his gun at him liked his coffee black or with cream. Maybe he didn't even drink coffee, as young as he was. Probably fresh out of the academy. He raised his bloodied pistol and hoped the rookie had scored well during his firearms training.

He needn't have worried. The double-tapped bullets found their target. As incoming waves of unconsciousness slowly but steadily smothered the fire in his chest and the light in his eyes, he had one last thought. He wondered, did he remember to turn off the coffeepot?

Not that it mattered.

⋯

THIS STORY WAS FIRST PUBLISHED IN *YELLOW MAMA*.

M.B. Manteufel is a freelance writer with published credits in a variety of print and online magazines. A former federal law enforcement agent, she has always been drawn to things danger- ous, deviant, and disturbing. In her current incarnation as a writer, she now enjoys indulging those interests worry free of being shot, stabbed, maimed, or sued. She makes her home on the dry side of Washington State.

SATURDAY NIGHT LIVE

Paul Newman

"Waddaya mean he's not dead? We all saw him hanging up there! He was up there all damned day!" Peter said.

Thomas shook his head. "Don't take it out on me. I'm just telling you what Luke said. It looks like he's gonna pull through!"

There were cheers in the small room. Peter shook his head and buried his face in his hands.

Matthew was the only other one that seemed to understand. "Shut up, you idiots, shut up all of you! Don't you get it?" He turned to Peter. "Is it too late to call it off? At least a delay?"

Peter did some figuring on his fingers before he slumped his meaty shoulders and shook his head. "Nope, it's too late. The girls are supposed to meet us there in just a couple hours. You know what we have to do, don't you?"

Matthew cleared his throat and looked away.

Peter thought a moment. "John? Hey, John? Come up here for a minute." A young man in the back looked up from his drink. His eyes were red and his face streaked from crying. He sniffled before he answered.

"Is it true? Is he really alive?" The wine and tears slurred his words into mush.

Peter reached in his belt and pulled out a couple of silvers. He handed them to the boy. "I'm sure we'll get it all figured out. Never mind that for now; we're almost out of wine, and it's your turn to run and get it. Why don't you pick up some chips while you're out?"

John trudged up to the front table and pocketed the money, then slunk out the door. Peter waited to make sure he was gone, then continued.

"All right, everybody; listen up! We don't have a lot of time. I guess you guys heard what Thomas had to say."

A few heads bobbed up and down.

"You all know the plan. You all know what was supposed to happen next."

More nods.

"Then you know that this mucks everything up. We all took the oath—you know what we're gonna have to do." He picked up a clump of straw from the floor and sorted out a handful of pieces, each a few inches long. He took one out and snapped it in half, then bundled them all in his closed fist so no one could tell the difference. "Everybody's gonna draw a straw. It's the only way to be fair. The short straw has to do it. Come on up, all of you. One line. Single file."

Matthew went first. Peter made sure it was a long one. Thomas drew a long straw and let out a deep sigh. Judas went next and pulled out half a straw.

"Aw, dammit! Me again? Why do I always get stuck with the shit duty?"

Peter smiled over at Matthew. "Must just be bad luck, Judas. Do you know what you need to do?"

The other man nodded, then reached in his belt for a long, curved dagger. He grinned so wide it showed his back teeth.

"Put that thing away! Now hurry, before John gets back!" Judas nodded and hurried out the door into the night.

Matthew cleared his throat and got Peter's attention. He asked a question with his eyes, Peter nodded. Matthew stood and spoke.

"I know it's been a long night, brothers. It's been hard on all of us, but sometimes the hard choices have to be made. Remember why we're doing this! Remember the greater good! Remember your oaths to Yahweh and the Glorious People's Revolution!" Peter saw a few of them start to nod as Matthew continued. "Now, there's just one more piece of bad business, and then we can get back on track. We're going to have to deal with Brother Judas." He paused and looked around the room. "Any volunteers?"

Every hand in the room went up, even the ones in the back. Matthew and Peter smiled at each other over their heads. Maybe they had a chance after all.

◆◆

THIS STORY WAS FIRST PUBLISHED IN *GRIFT MAGAZINE*.

Paul Newman lives in Northern California with his wife, daughter, and a neurotic beagle. He sleeps with the closet light on and keeps a cricket bat next to the bed...just in case.

DEALER SETS PRICE

"I'm telling you, when he's out, he's out cold. All we gotta do is get someone to buzz us inside the building."

"It'll never work."

"It'll work, I'm telling you. He keeps his shit in that little plastic box with his scale." Jeff envisioned it, a fat sticky lump of Mexican heroin. Enough to keep him, Ricky, and Crystal high for days.

"What if the door is locked?"

"I have the goddamn key to the front door. I made a copy last week when he sent me out to the store for cigarettes. Fucking asshole, making me fetch him shit like some kind of gopher. Serves him right."

"I mean, what if there's a dead bolt or chain or something on the door?"

"So what? Then we walk away. He's not gonna wake up, that's for sure. That prick sleeps like he's dead."

"What if he's not alone?"

"He's alone. Who the fuck in their right mind would sleep with that arrogant piece of shit?"

"I dunno, man. Sounds risky."

"Risky? Ricky, are you kidding me? Fuck this asshole. He takes our goddamn money every day, makes us wait forever, treats us like children. Do you wanna get well or not? I got Crystal waiting for me at home, and she's gonna wake up sick, and I'm not coming back to my baby empty-handed."

"Yeah." Ricky's tone was sheepish.

"All right then."

The two junkies walked up the marble steps and studied the intercom bank for a button to push.

"Pick one on the third floor."

"What if they walk down to check?"

"Just fuckin' pick one and stop being such a chicken-shit."

Ricky hit a random button on the third floor. No response. He hit another. Same. Jeff reached past him and, using all four fingers, hit four at once. The front door buzzed. They were in. They walked down the first-floor hallway, light on their feet. They could hear sounds of life from the other apartments: TV, dishes clamoring, a small dog yelping. The apartment they wanted was toward the back of the building.

They came to the door. Jeff turned toward Ricky and whispered, "I work too hard hustling all day to keep giving this prick my money for those tiny slivers of dope. He might as well just factor my goddamn dignity into the price." From his pocket he pulled out a single bronze key. He slid the key into the lock and turned the knob. They were met with stale cigarette smoke, body odor, and darkness.

With a plastic disposable lighter for a torch, they entered the dealer's apartment. Jeff knew right where the dope was stashed, beside the computer monitor in a pale-green plastic box. He put away the lighter and picked up the box. He opened it up, felt inside for the lump of dope, and found it. Ecstatic, his heart skipped a beat. The lid to the box fell loudly onto the keyboard in front of the monitor. The blank screen flashed on brightly, illuminating their horrified faces.

"Shit," mouthed Ricky.

"Hello?" They heard a voice say. A female voice. "Hello, is there anyone there?"

The two junkies froze. The bare lightbulb above their heads flared, and they stood looking at a woman with a small silver handgun pointed toward them. She was in one of the dealer's ugly paisley dress shirts, unbuttoned, no bra, no panties.

"Jeff?"

"Crystal?" said Jeff. It was his girlfriend, fiancée in fact, the love of his miserable life. It wasn't registering. His mind raced to find a reason for her to be there. Maybe she was doing what he was doing—working hard to bring home some dope so the both of them could have wake-ups tomorrow. Working hard—with no panties.

"What the fuck?"

She said nothing.

The two junkies knew at once they weren't going to be shot. But it didn't matter. Jeff looked like he'd already been shot.

"C'mon!" said Ricky. The two fiends ran out the front door of the apartment, down the hallway, and out into the cool night air. It was blocks before they slowed down to a walk. Ricky finally said it.

"You're right, Jeff, dignity is factored into the price."

—◆—

THIS STORY WAS FIRST PUBLISHED IN *THE FLASH FICTION OFFENSIVE*.

Tom Pitts received his education on the streets of San Francisco. He remains there, working, writing, and trying to survive. His novella, Piggyback, *is published by Snubnose Press. Find links to more of his work at Tom-Pitts.blogspot.com.*

DEATH BUYS A BURGER

Stephen D. Rogers

"That will be a few minutes, sir."

"I've got six bullets and a trigger finger that say it will be sooner."

The young girl shrugged and looked past me. "Can I help the next person in line?" Either the green dye in her hair affected her hearing or I'd lost my touch while I was in the stir.

I hoped it was the dye.

Standing there like some kind of idiot, I watched the pimply kids behind the counter bump into each other while buzzers buzzed and beepers beeped. Only one guy seemed old enough to drink, and he looked like he'd been hitting the bottle since breakfast. He also had a ring in his nose.

So this was the fast-food revolution I'd heard so much about.

There used to be a diner here, the Silver Room. Steak and eggs for four bits served by a waitress named Mabel who didn't take shit from nobody. I once saw her chase a guy out into the parking lot with a meat cleaver, and all he'd done was stiff her on a fifty-cent check. She never did like cops.

"You're all set, sir." Miss Green Hair pushed a tray toward me: burger in paper, fries in cardboard, and soda in plastic.

"This is my meal?"

"Napkins are over there."

I skipped the napkins and grabbed the booth that had the best view of the office building where Terrance worked.

The diner where we planned the robbery was long gone, but Terrance had a job right next door.

A kid toddled up to my table, handed me a ketchup packet.

"Thanks. Now make like a witness and disappear."

His mother scooped him up, glared at me. I tried to smile, but I must have been out of practice because she beat a hasty retreat. Fuck her.

Pushing the tray to the other side of the table, I thought again about Mabel. What I wouldn't pay to see her approach with my slab of rare steak, black coffee with a shot of Jack, some wisecrack fresh from the gutter.

The bank job had gone smooth as silk until someone tripped an alarm and the cops descended like flies on a corpse. By the time the newspapers tallied up the score, I was behind bars, Walters was dead, and an unidentified third man was wanted by the FBI.

Through a prison guard, I slipped Terrance a single note: "Save my share."

He should have done like I asked.

The front doors of the office building opened, and a steady stream of suits and dresses came pouring out onto the sidewalk.

Terrance hadn't aged a day.

Tracking Terrance through the windows, I was out of the booth and heading for the exit. I crossed the parking lot, quickly closing the distance.

Even if Terrance did manage to slip out of my sight, I knew I wouldn't lose him. Twenty years of long gray days and longer dark nights I'd thought of little else but meeting up with my ex-partner.

Terrance stepped around a bum holding up a can, took a left into a parking garage.

I followed.

The stairwell smelled like prison without the bleach.

I caught up with him on the third level.

There was no one else within sight, not that it would have made any difference. "Terrance."

He paled as soon as it clicked who I was. "You got out." His eyes dropped to the gun in my hand.

"I thought it was time to take advantage of this Internet thing, use my share from the bank job to seed an e-commerce business."

"Look, I'm going to pay you back. I just need to get all my ducks in a row." Terrance stepped to the side so he'd have the option to bolt.

I countered the move, keeping him trapped between me and the car. "Speaking of waterfowl, how does the phrase 'dead duck' grab you?"

"I swear I'll make it up to you."

"And how do you figure to do that?"

"I could deal you in." He glanced around. We were still alone. "After the bank job, I went straight."

"So did I. Straight to jail."

"I took some classes, learned the business. I might have started at the bottom, but I have my own office now." Terrance stopped as if waiting for congratulations.

"I process appraisal forms for a large insurance agency. I know everything that's worth stealing in this town. I even know what kind of security the owners have installed on the premises."

I had to admit the situation had potential. "So what?"

He lowered his voice. "I keep a list of the best places to hit, sort of an insurance policy. It's sweet."

"Keep talking."

"The list is in my desk back at the office. I can take you there right now. I've just been waiting to put together a team. We knock

304 — STEPHEN D. ROGERS

them over one at a time. Bang, bang, bang. Then we split. It would be like old times."

"For some of us, old times weren't that good."

Terrance licked his lips. "Look, nothing I could have done would have made any difference, but I'm sorry you were caught."

"I'm sorry you spent my share. I asked you nicely not to."

His eyes were skipping around, looking for a way out. "A lot can happen in twenty years."

"Tell me about it."

"The past is the past." Terrance didn't realize that he was adding salt to the wound. He was talking fast now, trying to sell me. "This is better than a bank job. It's a sweet deal."

"Not as sweet as this." The first bullet flung Terrance back against his car, the second two pinned him there long enough that I was ten feet away before I heard him hit the ground.

I should have asked him first if he knew where I could get something decent to eat. I hated to break and enter on an empty stomach.

❧

Stephen D. Rogers is the author of Shot to Death, Three-Minute Mysteries, *and more than seven hundred shorter works. His other mysteries of under a thousand words have appeared in the anthologies* Blood Moon, Border Noir, Dime, Discount Noir, Hardboiled, KnitLit (Too), Quarry, Seasmoke, Short Attention Span Mysteries, Small Crimes, Windchill, *and* Year of the Thief. *His website, StephenDRogers.com, includes new and upcoming titles as well as other information.*

HAIL, TIGER!

Cindy Rosmus

"Come on, baby!" Tony said. "You can't mean that."

Giulietta just smiled.

"Torn up by a tiger." Tony shuddered. He appealed to Lou, the bartender. "No girl would let her man die like that."

"'S only a story," Lou said wearily, "in my kid's eighth-grade reader."

"But it's timeless," Giulietta said. "'The Lady or the Tiger?' is all about human nature. Obsessive love, and…"

The back door buzzed open, and two giggly blondes came in. One short, one tall. The tall one caught Tony's eye.

"…*Jealousy.*" Giulietta dug her nails in his arm.

Bitch, Tony thought.

The blondes sat far enough away not to look suspicious. Maybe too far away.

Here at Royal Flush, Giulietta called the shots. It was the classiest bar her family owned: shiny hardwood floors, top-shelf booze. Swarming with cougars and wiseguys. And the occasional model-svelte blonde.

If you knew, he thought smugly, *who I fucked last night.*

"She loved him to death," Giulietta said. "Literally."

"It's the old man's fault," Lou said, after he'd served the blondes. "The fuckin' king's. He made her choose."

"He made *him* choose," Giulietta said. "Lowlife scum. Daddy was pissed he loved his daughter." With a side look at Tony, she said, "Can you blame him?"

"No," he said, wearily.

Like that king, Giulietta's dad would kill Tony if he knew they were fucking. "Nino the Ice" was a tiny mobster whose pinky ring boasted a diamond twice his size. You could see your face in it.

But "the Ice" didn't stop there.

Tony shivered. Nino was the coldest fuck out there. He'd order a hit with his morning coffee, want it done by the last bite of breakfast.

Nino's *look* could freeze you to death. Even if he liked you. And *I don't like you, shithead*, Nino told Tony more than once. God knows why Nino kept him on.

'Cos I shut up good, Tony thought. Like about fucking his daughter. Besides fucking every…

Again he eyed the tall blonde, who pretended not to notice.

"Can you blame *her*?" Giulietta asked Tony.

"Huh?"

"For choosing the tiger." Her smile unnerved him. "She'd rather see him get torn apart than be happy…with some *blonde*."

Tony's chest felt tight.

"Wait a minute!" Lou swung around from the register. "It don't say that." On his stubby fingers, he began counting. "Number one, shithead loves princess. Number two, king finds out. Surprise, surprise!"

Tony wiped his sweaty forehead.

Lou kept going. He ignored customers waving for drinks. By the time he got to "One of the fairest damsels in the king's fuckin' court," Tony wished he were on a plane to fucking Cancun.

"In other words," Lou said, finally, "the story don't say nothin' about her bein' a *blonde*."

An uncomfortable silence followed.

"You're right." Giulietta had the Ice's chilly blue eyes. "It *don't*."

Shit, Tony thought. She knows.

He forced a smile. "It's a dumb story," he said. "No girl who loves her man, like…" He slid his arm around her stool. "Like you love *me*, would hurt him. Not on purpose."

She smiled up at him. "No?"

"If I were a chick," Lou said, "I couldn't do it."

Giulietta didn't see Tony wink at Lou. "She didn't do shit," she said stubbornly. "It was the tiger." Bracelets jangling, she held up her hands. "*Her* hands were clean."

The moment Tony saw the blonde texting, his cell vibrated. *Oh, yeah!* he thought, in the midst of all this. Pictured those luscious pink lips around his cock. His pants felt unbearably tight.

"Louie," Giulietta said. "Buy the house."

As Lou set up free drinks for everybody, Tony peeked at his cell. His heart leapt: CUM OUTSIDE 4 A BIG SURPRISE! the text read.

He slid off his stool, flashed a Marlboro. "Smoke," he told Giulietta.

Usually, her icy stare would've sat him back down. But tonight his cock was doing the thinking.

"No jacket?" she said. "It's cold out there."

He turned, suddenly, to Giulietta's strange smile. Her bracelets jingled as she stroked his leather jacket on his stool. It was butter-soft leather, a Christmas gift from the Ice himself.

As Tony passed her on his way out, the tall blonde didn't look at him. Again she was texting.

Now what? he thought.

But it wasn't for him.

Outside the back door, the Ice's boys were waiting.

"Shii—" Tony said. Before he found the *t*, he was down. Never felt the next shot.

THIS STORY WAS FIRST PUBLISHED IN *YELLOW MAMA*.

Cindy's a Jersey girl who talks like Anybodys from West Side Story. *She works out five or six days a week, loves peanut butter, rare meat, and Jack Daniel's. She's been published in the usual places, such as* Hardboiled, A Twist of Noir, Beat to a Pulp, Pulp Metal Magazine, Shotgun Honey, *and* Powder Burn Flash. *She is the editor of the e-zine* Yellow Mama. *She's also a Gemini and a Christian.*

FALL GUY

Jim Spry

The bloated gypsy stamped around like a hippo with a hard-on. Twenty-four stone of cheap booze and fast-food, he pumped his fists like a TV wrestler, hacked a ball of phlegm onto the concrete floor. His cocaine gaze bored into me like maggots in dead flesh. He dragged a thumb across his tattooed throat.

"I'll rip yer foken head off," he screamed, shoving a fist in the air like he already had me beat.

The Chinese, pikeys, and assorted violence junkies outside the circle brayed their delight at the fat man's showboating. Bookies took bank notes like fry cooks taking orders. Donny Yip, arms crossed and face impassive, stared at me with Arctic cool.

Malone made his move a second before the bell. Dropped his lard arse into fifth. Trampled the distance between us. Looked to knock me flat with a shoulder barge.

Smooth as a matador, I stepped to the right. Hammered his liver as he barreled past. Tried not to sneer as he dropped to the deck. Ignored the booing jeers of the crowd around me.

"You'll pay for that," he bellowed, both hands on his knee as he struggled to stand.

He came in again. Fists tight to his chin. Elbows tucked to his shit-sack body. Shoulders hunched like a wiseguy in the wrong part of town. Sweat leaking from his bald head thirty seconds into the fight.

For the joy of the crowd I made my move. Ducked and weaved around his death-slow haymakers. Tested his guard to the rhythm of jab-jab-hook. Rapped on his skull with a Witness's insistence. Shit bricks when a cross took him square on the jaw.

My hands dropped with my chin. I watched him stagger. Saw every ripple in his bulky gut. Watched his bat-wing triceps flap in the breeze of his windmilling arms. Watched his eyes roll back to white. Felt my guts clench around pig iron.

"Don't." A one-word prayer to whatever power would listen.

I threw a look to Donny Yip, saw his glacial cool replaced with a question. Knew the answer and turned back to the game.

Malone brushed off his second. Came at me like an elephant trying on a salsa dance. Swung low like a chariot. Swung high like an idiot. Tried to focus with KO eyes.

I ducked back in. Choked on his body odor. Drummed a limp-wristed tattoo against his arms and stomach. Wound up for a big right. Telegraphed it to my ma back home in New Zealand.

The smart fucker read it.

My world turned red as Malone slammed his forehead into my face. Blood and snot filled my mouth with bitter copper. I hit the deck like an insane DJ. Felt my ribs buckle under Malone's stamping kicks. Heard the crowd roar before it all went black.

I could have taken him. Could have sent him home to his caravan with one less eye and an important lesson. But Donny Yip asked me a favor. And when Donny asks, the kids ain't safe till you say yes.

◆

THIS STORY WAS FIRST PUBLISHED IN *SHOTGUN HONEY*.

Jim Spry lives in Europe's most densely populated city. He writes about what he sees on a daily basis, but tones things down so no one gets upset. He's currently putting together a collection of his own works, tentatively titled Dirty Words.

DEATH BY SOBRIETY

J.M. Vogel

Darius jumped up on a table and began leading a chorus of an old Irish drinking tune. I looked at Bill, who just shrugged. The normally demure twentysomething appeared to be giving it his all. The crowd seemed to enjoy the performance and joined in with gusto. When he sloshed down his pint in between verses, the crowd roared with delight. We, however, were not quite as amused.

"So this is what one beer does to him?" Bill asked. Bill had suggested the beer when Darius's nerves about our upcoming encounter appeared to be getting the best of him. It was clear he now thought better of the idea. "Well, he'll never go undercover as a singer of any kind. And we also need to work on his tolerance. One drink and the enemy will know any secret we have." I rolled my eyes. Bill didn't really like our new colleague, and Darius wasn't doing much to ingratiate himself. "Go up there and get him," he said, nudging me with his elbow. "We're trying to keep a low profile here."

Although he was right, I didn't want to even attempt plucking him from the grips of his adoring public. It was kind of nice to see this side of the nervous newbie. "I'm not his keeper," I said, returning the nudge with a little too much vigor. Bill glared but continued watching Darius's one-man show. He didn't want to go up there either.

"If our contact shows up here and he's in midperformance, we've not only lost our jobs, we've quite possibly lost our lives," Bill said as Darius began singing "My Wild Irish Rose."

I sighed. It was still early, but he was right. Being a spy was all about discretion. "Fine." I wormed my way through the crowd to Darius's makeshift stage. I pushed between two girls at the foot of the table and tugged on his pant leg.

"Get down here!" I yelled, my voice barely audible over the din of the crowd.

He smiled and started the crowd singing "Danny Boy." He reached in his pocket, pulled out a note, and let it float to the floor. To anyone else, the action would have looked accidental. I bent down, picked it up, and unfolded it hastily.

Cover blown. Contact not coming. Best to be somewhere public until help can arrive. Shan't be terribly long.—A.F.

I searched the pub until I recognized someone vaguely familiar ducking out the door. Albert Filmore, our messenger. I looked up at Darius, who winked and extended a hand to help me up on the table. I grabbed his hand, stumbled slightly to hint at inebriation, and giggled as he pulled me up beside him. I grabbed his beer, took a swig, and joined in the chorus.

My heart started racing as I surveyed the crowd to see who our assassin might be. If he were there, I couldn't pick him out. He was playing his part as well as we were playing ours. Despite my trepidation, I kept on singing, as sloppily and off tune as possible. I knew that public drunkenness might just save my life that night, so I tried my best to be convincing. Over the heads of our fans I noticed Bill, his hands raised in confusion.

"Come on up, Bill!" I slurred, motioning wildly. Darius laughed and did the same before convincing the crowd to chant his name. Bill shook his head and crossed his arms in defiance. He just wasn't getting it.

I began a rousing chorus of "When Irish Eyes Are Smiling," and started to jump down to retrieve Bill when Darius's hand restrained me. I looked up and saw him give a very subtle shake of his head. I stood back up, continued singing and swaying, and looked out over the crowd again in search of Bill. It took a few minutes before I finally found him, slumped over the bar. To a patron or bartender, he appeared to be passed out. Darius and I knew, however, that Bill was dead.

I hoped that Darius's knowledge of Irish drinking tunes was more extensive than mine because I was about out and we were going to be here awhile.

THIS STORY WAS FIRST PUBLISHED IN EVERY DAY FICTION.

J.M. Vogel lives in a suburb of Columbus, Ohio. She is setting out to show the world that a degree in English does not predestine one to life in the unemployment line. Keep up with J.M. Vogel by following her blog at JMVogel.blogspot.com.

A RUSSIAN STORM

Andrew Waters

The day started at four a.m. Waking up in the humid July heat, I was on the road to Raleigh even before the fast-food restaurants opened. During the drive he thought about the day she gave him the painting. Senile, angry about something—not him, thank God—but raging nonetheless. It was Mother's Day and he was in the neighborhood, thought he'd drop by, ask about the painting.

"Mortimer," she said, calling him by his father's name. "What are you doing here?"

"Came to see you, Noni. I just thought I'd stop by. You know I like to admire the painting."

"Yes, the painting," she agreed. She led him to it. A storm-tossed sea, a boat in the distance struggling against the waves, a trim sailing sloop with yachting flags. Sunlight just breaking in the foreground, off the canvas. But, oh, what light, golden and pink, illuminating the storm and the sea with unearthly magnitude.

"I wish you'd just take the thing. You're the only one who truly loves it," she said. Was this insanity or was this real? He searched her face for the answer. She nodded competently.

"You boys will just fight over it when I'm gone anyway." She walked to the wall, stared at it one last time. "Its ghosts are gone now."

That was the last time he saw her. Dead from a stroke two months later. Anthony was furious when he found out, of course, but it was a year later and his older brother had not yet launched his retaliation.

And now he was to have it appraised on *Antiques Roadshow*. He'd done his homework: the signature on the painting belonged to a Russian émigré, French trained, who lived in Brighton Beach and painted on Long Island in the 1900s, known for his depictions of yachts. One of the artist's pieces had sold at Sotheby's for $25,000 several years before, but that was the only auction sale he could find on the Internet. His grandmother's family were Russian émigrés in Coney Island about this same period, could easily have known the artist. Nothing but scoundrels and thieves, Noni always called her family, which she'd escaped after a mysterious incident she would not discuss; but he always considered it possible the painting was traded for some good or service rendered long ago in the slums of Brooklyn.

He waited for hours until he finally got to the table for American Impressionism, less grand than he'd imagined, in the far back corner of the coliseum. But the appraiser was Lesley St. Clair, one of his favorites, a lively, intelligent brunette with a Brahmin accent. Not as renowned as Nigel Higginbotham, the Scottish appraiser from Christie's, famous for his accent, but feistier, more thorough in her research.

"What have we got here?" St. Clair said with a clipped smile. "Mhhmmmm." She took the piece from him carefully and placed it on an easel for examination. "Interesting," she said, studying the signature. "You're familiar with the artist?"

"I believe the signature is Vladimir Roikoff," he responded. "I think he was an associate of my great-grandfather."

She smiled knowingly. "I believe you're right. Certainly in his style, and the signature looks good. I think I recognize the flag. New York Yacht Club, I believe."

She asked him a few more questions about his relationship to the piece, how he came to acquire it, then excused herself to consult the computer. He tried to contain himself while she was gone. This was as good as he could have possibly imagined. Better. He could finally pay off his credit card and get Donna that surgery she wanted.

But St. Clair was huddled over her computer, typing furiously. Then she made a call on her cell phone. Something was wrong; maybe the painting was a fake. Impossible to believe, really, the way the gold washed over the angry waves, the luminosity of the lightning on the far horizon. But these things happened all the time, and deep down, he always wondered how his grandmother had come to possess such a fantastic piece of art.

St. Clair put down her phone and came back to the easel, her smile more clipped now. "Well, I know you have a long history with this piece, with the connection to your grandmother," she said in what now seemed like a television persona. "The good news is that the painting is absolutely authentic, a fine example of Roikoff's work. One of his most famous pieces, in fact. Its value is estimated at more than two hundred thousand dollars."

He forced himself to smile. His mind was a blur. The news was fantastic, a miracle, yet this created new complications. He would have to cut Anthony in now, no question about that, and maybe he and Donna should separate for a while, see how things go after he gets the money. But despite his rehearsed response, despite watching others a million times before, he expressed only the most obvious. "Are you kidding me?"

She nodded enthusiastically, happy to be sharing with him in this moment of revelation. Expensive art was thrilling. Everyone knew that, Lesley St. Clair most of all. But her demeanor saddened as she took him by the arm. "Unfortunately, I'm sorry to tell you this painting was stolen from the New York Yacht Club in 1916. Under US and international law, the piece must be returned to them. There are some gentlemen from the FBI on their way here to see you. I'm sure there won't be a problem."

Security men in blue blazers approached him from behind. He thought about his grandmother's last words. The ghosts! Russian ghosts, scoundrels and thieves. His grandmother had escaped them somehow with the painting. In that moment, he glimpsed the untold story of her life, something dark and mysterious at the heart of it. He turned toward the men, resisting the impulse to snatch the painting and run. His grandmother's haunting may be over, he realized, but his had just begun.

Andrew Waters works for a nonprofit land trust in Salisbury, North Carolina. His short fiction has been published in The Bad Version, Pembroke Magazine, *and* The North Carolina Literary Review. *His flash fiction has appeared online at* Every Day Fiction, Grift Magazine, Yellow Mama, Flash Jab Fiction, Black Heart Magazine, *and others.*

HELL'S BELLE

Jim Wilsky

Luke comes roaring down the dark lane like Dale Earnhardt Jr. after a quick pit at Daytona. He bangs through and over an old cow gate without even thinking about the brakes. Sneaking a look in the rearview mirror, he sees nothing but swirling dust.

The high weeds are lit up by the bouncing headlights and they blur by. A tilted mailbox up ahead signals a blacktop country road coming up fast. Downshifting now, cranking hard to the right, he fishtails onto the main road. Loses it to the left, gets it back, and then flirts with the ditch on the right.

Winding out second gear, he grinds it into third and stands on the gas pedal. The dark road ahead is arrow straight. The land is flat as grandma's pancakes, lit only by a crescent moon in a cloudless sky. Spider's truck is shivering and shaking, but he coaxes it up around sixty.

He's beat all to shit. Bruised bad from being clubbed. Bleeding from all the cuts she did, and the deep gash at the hairline is the worst. Flowing blood keeps getting in his eyes. Swiping at it with his forearm, he shouts out in pain. He's got to have some busted ribs. His breathing is ragged, wet. The only thing he's wearing is jeans, and those are soaked in blood.

His Katy is gone. They'd messed with him plenty but made sure he stayed conscious to see what they were doing to her. He wasn't sure how long this shit had been going on, his head wasn't right, time was screwed up. Could have been two days down in that dank-ass storm cellar. Maybe three. They tried to make it last. Make her last.

Spider had been bad enough, but Alex, his crazy-bitch girlfriend, was the one he feared most. She looked like a homecoming queen and had a smile that would melt you, but the girl was the devil's own. The things she'd done. The chants and language he couldn't understand. Her dancing eyes. He could still hear the echo of her deep, husky laugh.

He looks in the rearview again. Nothing but darkness and the single pole light at the old farmhouse. Spider has to be dead. He'd caved his head in with a spade, took his keys, and split. Alex though, he didn't know where she was.

The engine coughs, pauses, coughs again, and finally roars on. He's still doing fifty, but his eyes click over to the temp gauge. He's blown a hose or some fucking thing. Ten seconds later and the old Silverado sputters out for good. It rolls to a smoking stop only about a mile and a half away from hell.

Luke falls out of the truck as much as he steps out and doubles over after a lightning bolt in his ribs. He stands bent over, weaving in the middle of the road.

It's around ten miles to town. He'll never make it, but hey. He starts down the road with a painful shuffle, as fast he can go without falling down or passing out. Clearing the fading arc of headlights, he just keeps gimping along in the dark.

Then he hears it. Way off. Not a scream, more like a whoop.

There it is again.

Like a goddamn war cry.

He veers like a drunk over to the shallow ditch and goes down to a knee, looking back toward the truck. He'll go into the corn rows if he has to.

Time stops.

Then the truck taillights light her up in red. An Olympic track star. At least that's what Alex looks like as she comes busting ass down that blacktop. Really pickin' 'em up and puttin' 'em down.

Slowing to a trot at the truck, she stops dead just past it. Short-short cutoffs, tennis shoes, and an old ZZ Top T-shirt. She has that large butcher knife, and it reflects a quick sliver of light. She doesn't move.

The crickets and night bugs drone on.

Finally in the dying headlights, her head swivels slowly up the road. She looks right at where he's hunkered down. He swears he sees that gleaming homecoming smile.

He struggles toward the corn with clenched teeth.

<hr/>

THIS STORY WAS FIRST PUBLISHED IN *SHOTGUN HONEY*.

Jim Wilsky was born and raised in the Midwest. His debut novel, a crime fiction work titled Blood on Blood, *was released in August 2012; it is the first of a three-book series. He has also had short stories featured in some of the most highly respected online magazines such as* Beat to a Pulp, Yellow Mama, Shotgun Honey, Rose & Thorn Journal, All Due Respect, Pulp Metal, *and* Mysterical-E.

ABOUT THE EDITOR

Otto Penzler is a renowned mystery author, editor, publisher, columnist, and bookstore owner. His love for mystery stories inspired him to establish the Mysterious Press, which published only crime and mystery, and eventually led him to found the Mysterious Bookshop in New York City. Today, the Mysterious Bookshop is known as the oldest and largest bookstores solely dedicated to mystery novels.

Penzler's award-winning career includes fourteen years of service on the board of directors for the Mystery Writers of America, and he is the recipient of two Edgar Allen Poe Awards, an Ellery Queen Award, and a Raven Award, among others. To date, he has edited more than fifty crime-fiction anthologies. He currently alternates between living in New York City and in Connecticut with his wife.